John Lennon's Glasses

John Lennon's Glasses

JIM OCEAN
with KATHY OCEAN

This book contains mentions of suicide and suicidal ideation.

If you or a loved one is at risk of suicide, call 988 to reach the National Suicide Prevention Lifeline.

First U.S. Edition, 2025

Print ISBN: 979-8-9920782-0-6

Ebook ISBN: 979-8-9920782-1-3

Printed in the U.S.A.

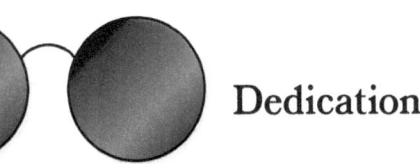

Dedication

This book is dedicated to all the victims of gun violence in America and around the world. During my formative years, there were four murders/assassinations that stole the innocence of my generation: JFK, his brother Robert Kennedy, Martin Luther King, and John Lennon.

According to a post from Yoko Ono on the thirty-ninth anniversary of Lennon's death, "Over 1,400,000 people have been killed by guns in the U.S.A. since John Lennon was shot and killed on December 8, 1980."

Ono added, "The death of a loved one is a hollowing experience. After thirty-nine years, Sean, Julian and I still miss him. Imagine all the people living life in peace." Let us work for that day.

Contents

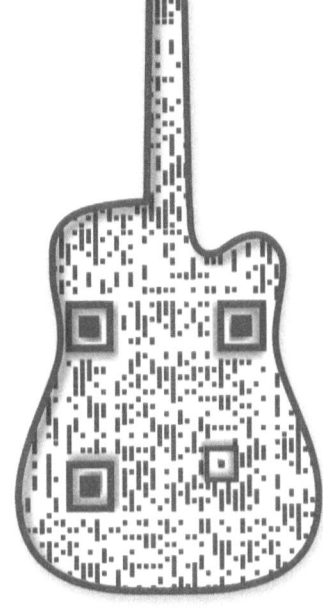

John Lennon's Glasses includes an accompanying collection of original music. All original songs referenced in this book are notated with an asterisk and can be found at JohnLennonsGlasses.net. A full list of these songs appears at the back of this book.

Preface

The spirit of John Lennon entered my life during the final mixing process for an album called *Pop Tunes for Mystics* that I recorded several years ago at my good friend Brian Whistler's studio. As a songwriter, I can't just stand by while producers and techie engineers micro-inspect every frequency and arrangement while I do my best to feel like the whole project is not a waste of time.

To soothe myself during the mixing process, I often hold an acoustic guitar in my hands like a pacifier. On this occasion, I started playing a chord progression in the absent manner guitarists do when distracted by something else. As my head caught up with what my hands were playing, I noticed the riff was reminiscent of something John Lennon might play. So, I committed it to memory and for the next several days imagined that Lennon was looking over my shoulder while I labored under his exacting eyes to write a song about universal love.

It's no easy task writing for the man who wrote "All You Need Is Love" and "Give Peace a Chance." Nevertheless, I persevered and wrote "The Lennon Song" as an homage to the man who had influenced me and so many other songwriters around the world. The song made it just under the limbo line and became the unexpected caboose on a collection of personal tales from my life. Since the time *Pop Tunes for Mystics* was recorded, mixed, and mastered, the project mostly gathered virtual dust as I went about my busy thirty-plus-year career as a concert promoter producing concerts for cities, colleges, and nonprofits.

But not only did the vague feeling of Lennon "looking over my shoulder" not leave me; it intensified and eventually morphed into this book. That and a few other coincidences related to this project have left me feeling a bit haunted by him. But then, if you're a fan, you might feel the same way. Forty years later, many of us have still not quite come to grips with his death.

If John Lennon is indeed haunting me, it is in the spirit of peace that he's doing it, and I am grateful for my time with him.

PART ONE

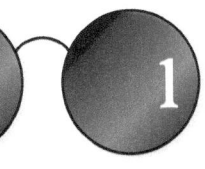 # 1 The Jolly Rancher Incident

Hard candy is so good, to taste it is a treat. Hard candy is the sweetest thing you'll prob'ly ever eat. Hard candy is delicious, I'm sure you will agree. But hard candy's the one thing that really rots your teeth.
—DAVID JONES, "HARD CANDY"

Every happy ending needs to have a start.
—JUSTIN HAYWARD, "YOU CAN NEVER GO HOME"

"All you need is love." What a bunch of crap! John Lennon sure caught a lot of fish when he released that song in 1967. And I was one of them.

A whole generation of guppies flopping in the net of a song that promised human salvation through universal love. I believed it the first time I heard it. I swallowed it hook, line, and sinker; and the hook set itself into my heart. I'd go around singing it, hoping for a better world. I'd hum it in high school for girls to hear. (In those days it was cool to be sensitive.)

When I started writing songs in my mid-teens, I argued for it; and by age twenty, I had dedicated my life to it.

Sure, Lennon. All you need is love when you're rich and famous and adored by millions of fans. The truth is . . . love distracts you. It sends you down blind paths. It gives you a mission, then leaves you stranded on a beach with unrealized dreams and a broken heart. The truth is, Lennon . . . love can get you shot! You certainly learned *that* the hard way. All I needed . . . was rent.

I wasn't mad at Lennon, personally, just angry for leading me to believe that the world would be a more peaceful place by now. I mean, songs like that have good intentions, but do they really change the world? Or do they mislead us into some kind of liberal naivete? I don't know about you, but looking around the world today, I don't see the sun coming up in the Age of Aquarius.

My pissy mood, steeping for years, was now boiling over. I'd flown to L.A. for a soul-crushing meeting with Platinum Music Publishing in hopes of finding placement for my songs. Two hours earlier, I'd been in a meeting with their assistant director of marketing, Mark Westhrope. He told me that my songs were dated and too intellectual for an American audience. But for another $1,500, they would shop my stuff to the international market. Westhrope, twenty-five years my junior, said that songs about universal love went out in the '60s and that I'd be better off singing about romantic love . . . sex, trucks, beer, guns, or just about *anything* else.

"You know, Mr. Drake . . . can I call you Jimmy?" Without stopping to get my consent, he continued: "*You* know, Jimmy.

The *chase*, the mating game, the dating game, boy meets girl, boy meets boy, girl meets girl, whatever. The conquests, the heartaches, the STDs—ha-ha, just kidding. Universal love is *boring*, dude." He rolled his eyes and glanced at his cell phone.

"But I'm not into the chase. I'm focusing on my music right now." That was a lie. I had a painful crush on a woman who worked at my local coffee bar. But I wasn't chasing her; I was just buying my mochas, leaving extra tips, and waiting for the universe to make it happen. I believe that if you stand in the path of Cupid long enough, you'll take an arrow.

Westhrope wasn't buying it. "Well . . . *fake* some heartbreak, dude. That shouldn't be too hard for you. I mean, *look* at you, man. You *reek* heartbreak!" He checked an incoming text, snickered, and, smiling, considered me again. "Go to some clubs, Jimmy. Get on Match. You're too old for Tinder or Bumble. Buy some new clothes, dude. *Get a life!*"

"But I don't go to clubs. I don't do internet dating. I run a concert series for the Daly City Parks and Rec, and all they want are cover bands. With any time left over, I write and record music." This was true.

He studied me for a moment, bored but sympathetic, then stretched and said, "Okay, boomer. Here's an idea. Imagine you're married and your wife is dumping you for a younger man. That's the shit these days."

Young Mr. Westhrope sniggered at yet another text interruption, giving me the distinct impression he was sleeping with an older married woman right now.

"Okay, dude. Let's say you're married to a stone-cold fox, fortyish, a real MILF who has a thing for younger guys. Oh yeah! Wait a minute . . . wait a minute . . . I'm getting a title. 'Mama Wants a Baby Boy.' Yeah . . . that's it!"

He started tapping a hip-hop beat on the edge of his desk and singing, "*Mama wants a baby boy. Uh-huh. Uh-huh. Uh-huh . . . Mama wants a baby boy. Uh-huh. Uh-huh. Uh-huh . . .* That's it! A modern twist on the old incest taboo. 'Mama Wants a Baby Boy.' *Take* it, dude. I give it to you *free*. People will love it. Especially the cougars. It's the best advice I can give you." Another text came in, and he went back to his phone.

"But that isn't who I am. Shouldn't music try to take the human species to a higher level? Shouldn't songs offer hope for the future?" I pleaded.

"Don't confuse music with politics or therapy, dude. You're a songwriter, not a politician or a therapist. Here's the deal. I know it's hard to take, but y*our* generation is dying off. And *my* generation is taking over. We just wanna have some fun before the world ends. We want songs to get us *off*, not turn us *on*. Don't you watch *The Walking Dead*? Might as well have a little roll in the hay before doomsday, dude!"

His eyes grew wide, and he exulted, "There's *another* one for you Jimmy. 'A Roll in the Hay Before Doomsday'! What a title! A real 'Apocalypso'! Go ahead, take it, dude. Run with it! Maybe you can sell it to Netflix. *Shit*, man. Your neediness is inspiring me!"

I had heard of L.A. jadedness, but this was ridiculous! "So, what you're saying is that as far as the human race goes, every-one's screwed, and sex and violence is all we have left?"

"Right! Sex, drugs, and rock 'n' roll! Your generation *invented* that, Jimmy. We were just listening. Look . . . I see guys like you all the time. Older musicians influenced by the Beatles, the Stones, the Eagles, Pink Floyd, whatever. All looking for a way to stay relevant in the business. I'm telling you, man, that if John Lennon were alive today, he'd be writing different tunes altogether."

"Like what?" I asked, deflated.

Westhrope paused for a moment, pinched his nose and wailed in a fairly convincing Lennon, "*All you need is* lust." Enamored with himself, he snorted a laugh as if it was the funniest thing he'd ever heard. "Oh, sorry, dude!" he said, seeing me wipe his snot off my shirt. Tears of mirth were pouring from his eyes. "Oh my God. That's *so* funny. 'All You Need Is Lust.'"

"Are you serious?" I asked.

He pinched his nose again and sang more of the parody with the same fake British accent, "*There's nothing you can lay that can't be laid.*" He snorted again. More snot. "Oh my God, that's so funny! Go ahead, dude. I'll give it to you free!" He wiped tears of self-adulation on his sleeve, shaking his head at how funny he was.

His heretical parody literally stopped my breathing. I sat there frozen, like I'd been turned to stone. Blasphemy! Desecration! He wasn't just putting down John Lennon; he was putting down the core values of my whole generation! And for him to defile the one song that summed up my musical worldview was more than I could take. I wanted to jump over his desk and strangle the motherfucker mid-text!

Meanwhile, in my paralyzed state, the Jolly Rancher I had picked up at the front desk and was nervously sucking on slid backward on my tongue and lodged itself in the back of my throat, threatening to go down my windpipe.

For a moment I had the twisted fear that this A&R guy would not only kill my desire to write music, but in an ironic twist of fate would get to save my life with the Heimlich maneuver. I'd rather die; so, I coughed as hard as I could to clear my throat and sat there wondering where the hell the Jolly Rancher went. It had miraculously disappeared. I practiced breathing and swallowing. It didn't seem to have gone down either my windpipe or my esophagus. I scanned the room, thinking maybe I had coughed it onto the carpet, when I was struck by a mighty allergic reaction. Something acidic trickled down the back of my throat.

"Hey, dude. Are you all right?" For the first time Westhrope stopped fiddling with his phone. "Oh my God. There's blood coming out of your nose!"

I poked at my nose and saw blood on my fingers. Horrified, I stood up, knocking the chair backward, and ran down the hall to the bathroom.

Westhrope called after me, "Dude! Are we done here then?"

Looking in the bathroom mirror, I saw a copious quantity of red goop pouring from my nose. *Stroke! Aneurysm! Cancer!* No. Wait a minute. *Shit!* I had coughed the Jolly Rancher into my nasal passage! A mighty sneeze erupted. Bloodred strawberry goop shot from my nose, splattering the sink along with the Rancher remnant, which landed with a forceful *clink.*

I grabbed a towel and turned on the water, dabbing at the ruby-colored syrup on my upper lip. I watched as a whirlpool of scarlet goo swirled around and down the drain. I picked the Jolly Rancher from the sink and scrutinized it. It was splintered, deeply grooved, and flattened out. Not much was left. Like me, I thought. There wasn't much of *me* left.

I studied myself in the mirror and shook my head at the haggard reflection. "I'm *through*. I'm *done*!" I muttered. I flicked the not-so-Jolly Rancher into the garbage.

2 Three Kinds of Heaven

Paradise is exactly like where you are right now, only much, much better.
—LAURIE ANDERSON, "LANGUAGE IS A VIRUS"

"As your friend and sponsor, John, I'm reminding you there are no shortcuts in Near Heaven, Nearer Heaven, or Heaven itself. So, stop resisting! Please. Just do the work or you'll *never* get out of here!"

John Lennon listened to his old bandmate George Harrison with a mixture of irritation and resignation. They had left Earth somewhat estranged. The tragic surprise of Lennon's murder didn't give them enough time to resolve their differences. And without their mutual rival, Paul McCartney, to bind them in the afterlife, it had taken them a while to reconnect.

The two old bandmates were conversing in the first-level lucid dream space that John inhabited. In this realm known as Near Heaven, departed beings can linger and communicate holographically. For different reasons, neither Beatle had reincarnated, allowing them to continue their relationship beyond the grave. Dreaming on Earth is only a taste of what can be dreamed after death. It takes years for our sleeping selves to catch up to who we really are. Being newly dead, at least in the face of eternity, Lennon and Harrison still preferred to visit each other in the form of their last incarnations. Rock stars don't surrender their mortal forms as easily as others.

Sprawled out on white couches, they faced each other strumming big, beautiful blond acoustic guitars with shell inlays. The yawning expanse of Near Heaven, a beige-on-beige opaqueness, stretched on forever in all directions. Everything was serene and beautiful, but as pale and faded as a photograph left in the sun too long.

"You can't stay here forever, John. This dull nirvana will drive you mad. God is merciful, but she created this place to motivate souls like you to move upwards. You need more spiritual bandwidth, anyways."

"I know, I know. I've been here longer than I thought I'd be." Lennon tuned his E string a little flat on purpose. He had begun doing that in his recording days with the Beatles so he could hear himself in the mixes. John strummed a G chord and surveyed the scene, nodding his assent. "You're right. Yoko would hate this place, that's for sure! Better Hell than mediocrity, she'd say."

"Yes. Yoko would hate it. And she'd be extremely disappointed with you for staying here so long."

It's true, John thought. The bardo of Near Heaven reminded him of those landscaped American shopping malls where everything was immaculate but sterile. Different shades of taupe, sand, and beige as if color were a crime and contrast a felony.

Lennon had been spiritually stuck in Near Heaven ever since that crazy assassin Mark David Chapman put a bullet in his back. George was right. He really would go mad in what he dubbed the "Outskirts of Heaven" or the "Brigitte Bardo," tongue-in-cheek references to, respectively, the afterlife bardos from *The Tibetan Book of the Dead* and the French movie star whom the band had had childhood crushes on.

For a soul as daring and intrepid as Lennon's, Near Heaven was a kind of hell, and his first instinct was to get out of there as soon as possible. Most of the other souls around him couldn't make up their minds whether to wean themselves from Earth or to reincarnate and go back for another ride. "You're all a bunch of bloody fence-sitters," he had blurted out at a workshop on transcendence that George made him attend. John knew he had to do the work. He knew he had to get out of there. He knew all of this. But he was holding himself back on purpose . . .

Lennon had a secret; one he didn't share with Harrison or any other souls waifing around Near Heaven. He had a veiled gamble and strategy. John was waiting for Yoko to pass.

Lennon figured that in the unlikely event Yoko decided to reincarnate, he would too. In Near Heaven, souls could still decide to do that. John was so confident of his and Yoko's immortal connection that he was sure they would meet again in the next life. But considering the hell she had been through during her childhood with the firebombing and nuking of her home country in World War II, plus the purgatory of fame he'd put her through with the Beatles, John guessed Yoko had had enough of the pleasures and frenzied, bipolar dualities of Earth. It was more likely that she would jump right over his head and fly straight into Heaven to stare into the feral eyes of God herself.

In this event, he would do exactly what George wanted of him. He would climb the stairway to Heaven to be with her for eternity. If, however, she chose to reincarnate, he would follow. For now, he feigned diligence and dog-paddled his way through the spiritual lessons, tasks, and missions that Harrison gave him, biding his time.

Harrison interrupted his reverie about Yoko. "Listen, John. Jimmy Page was right. There really *is* a stairway to Heaven and *you* should start climbing it. At least get one step closer and join me in Nearer Heaven. From there we can play music on a much deeper level and decide together whether to relinquish our stories and move on to new ones with greater purposes."

Lennon strummed the chords to "Dear Prudence" and gazed off into the anemic blue sky. "Didn't we pay our dues while we were on Earth? I mean for Christ's sake, I toured me ass off, worked for peace, wrote the best songs I could, and got shot for all me efforts."

He strummed a big E minor chord and let it ring in frustration.

Harrison closed his eyes and fingerpicked a high solo run that chased after Lennon's chord, then circled around it, changing the E minor to an uplifting E major. The combined sounds shimmered, then dispersed into the elegant but wan-looking trees of Near Heaven.

Harrison opened his eyes and smiled kindly at his old high school friend. "You and I took what the world had to offer. We took the money, we took the fame, we took the girls. And now we've got to give something back. Our work influenced many people, and influence has karmic consequences. You know that."

"Yeah, yeah, so you keep saying. I guess I just need more motivation. A reason to move up. Tell me again what it's like where you are in Nearer Heaven. Do you *really* get to hobnob with the angels?"

"Nearer Heaven is way better than here. Color is back in shades you've never seen before, colors you can play music with as well as see. And everything harmonizes. It's like living inside a song. And it's blissful, John. Remember, bliss moves up. Bliss *always* moves up."

"To be honest, I don't know if I can take that much bliss. I'm too intense for bliss. Bliss is for cows, man. Chewing their cud all day long under a cerulean sky. It's not for me."

"Bliss isn't a neutral state where a mind turns to mush. It's an expansive state where a mind spreads out and gains strength and momentum for doing good in the universe. True bliss widens the beam and intensifies illumination to take in more truth."

"Did your guardian angel teach you that?"

"Well, yeah, he introduced me to the idea."

"And who might that angel be, Georgie boy?" Lennon had asked this before, to no avail. Cajoling Harrison for the answer had become an afterlife preoccupation and a way to keep Harrison distracted from Lennon's real intentions.

Harrison wanted to reveal the identity of his angel mentor, but he flashed Lennon a shrewd smile and offered a bargain instead. "John, if you succeed with your next client. I'll tell you who my guardian angel is."

"Now, that's motivation for you! A spiritual game show for Ol' Johnny Boy." Lennon improvised the melody line from the game show *Jeopardy* on his big blond guitar. The tune, a perfect theme song for all Near Heaven, sailed across the bucolic land.

Harrison rolled his eyes. "I love you, John, but this isn't a game. I swear if I still had an ass, you'd be a pain in it."

"Now, that's funny, George! People always underestimated your sense of humor. They all thought of you as the *spiritual* one, the *serious* Beatle, but you were as funny and sarcastic as the rest of us." It's amazing, Lennon thought, how humor and other earthly things like friendship could exist beyond the grave. As long as the storylines stay intact, so do the jokes and camaraderie.

"That's true, I was deemed the spiritual one, but your sarcasm and wit revealed a lot of truth. You were a scrappy songwriter, and willing to tell it like it was. Nevertheless, you tended to minimize the depth of your own inspirations." Harrison pushed a bit into Lennon's sensitive areas. "False modesty perhaps?"

"I know, I know. And my bloody muse wasn't happy about that, was she?" Lennon strummed a rockabilly chord and sang, "*Oh, I've been used and abused by the muse, and if I ever get to Heaven, she'll get a piece of my mind!*"

"She's already got a piece of your mind, John. She took you on as a young songwriter and worked hard to inspire you in spite of your life challenges, sarcasm, and dismissals. It was her recommendation to God that you do service here in the Outskirts of Heaven until you stop resisting your gifts. Will you do the work, then?" Harrison put his guitar down and gave Lennon the look that musicians give each other in the recording studio when they dig their heels in to get their way.

Lennon could tell his old friend was tired of joking around. "All right, George, I'll do the bloody work. Who's my next client? What's his trip?"

"The usual. A veteran singer-songwriter influenced mostly by you about to do himself in."

"Has he tried to kill himself yet?"

"No, not yet, but soon."

"Then how did he get on Heaven's radar?"

"After receiving soul-destroying advice about his songs, he almost choked to death on a Jolly Rancher."

"A jolly what?"

"It's an American hard candy, John."

"Bloody hell! Well, he picked a funny way to almost die. Is the rest of his story as funny as this? I could use a good laugh!"

"It's not about your amusement, John; it's about being a muse. The poor fellow has real talent. He was just born a bit too late. The world has turned away from songs like ours and his. You need to keep him going. Keep him alive. Keep him writing. God likes his stuff and has a plan for him."

"Well, sure, God's old-fashioned and seems to be a bit of a rock 'n' roll groupie. But even with the big woman on his side, he's too old to be a rock star, George."

"Look, John, you're criticizing a man so influenced by you that at the stroke of midnight each New Year's Eve he takes out his guitar and sings 'Imagine' to start the new fucking year."

Lennon's face dropped for a second. "Sometimes I wish I hadn't written that bloody song!"

"Are you still tripping on that, John? I thought we went over that last visit."

Lennon shook his head in embarrassment. "Well, it's still in heavy rotation on Earth and it's spreading a false cosmology. How could Yoko and I have been so bloody wrong about the afterlife?"

"Part of the reason you're here is to not be so hard on yourself. How could you have known that there's not only one but three kinds of Heaven?"

"Well, reality does leave a lot to the imagination." Lennon smirked, then strummed the opening chords of "Imagine." "*Imagine there's three Heavens,*" he sang. "*It's easy if you try.*"

They considered each other for a moment, then laughed as hard as beings without lungs can laugh.

3 Earworm Attack

After I saw Annie, *I had to hit myself on the head with a small hammer to get that stupid "Tomorrow" song out of my head.*

—IAN SHOALES

I mopped up the goopy red remains of the Jolly Rancher still dribbling from my nose and stared at myself in the bathroom mirror. My laugh lines were slack, creating canyons of despair on my face. Who was I kidding? A fiftysomething man trying to run in a young man's race. In my forties I had given up being a rock star—it was already a ridiculous idea—but I thought maybe my songs could live on as I got older. I would lurk in the background. A mysterious figure collecting royalties from my bell tower of songwriting. I'd be the Quasimodo of rock 'n' roll, ringing my bell for all to hear but remaining in the shadows, with my hump of old age hidden from view.

I smiled briefly at the image of myself as the Hunchback. My laugh lines filled in for a second, revealing a happier, albeit older-looking, face. A face that really was only good for smiling. A face many people said resembled Mick Jagger's. That had always been a blessing and a curse. Looking like Jagger isn't so great when you don't have the fame, the money, or the band to back up the ugly-sexy thing.

The smile disappeared and my lines came back. I turned away from the mirror, dabbed the final bits of Jolly Rancher from my nose, and went back to face young Mr. Westhrope for a final soul execution. *Let the slaughter begin.*

Westhrope looked up from his cell phone as I entered the room. "Oh my God! You're back! You're alive! Dude. You gotta stop doing so much coke." He laughed and turned a thumbnail to his nose in a well-practiced mimic of a snort.

I licked my upper lip and tasted the sickly-sweet strawberry blood of the Jolly Rancher still seeping down from my nose. "I've never done coke," I said, dabbing my nose with a Kleenex. Well, only once, with a floozy from Bakersfield, but it was so long ago it hardly seemed to matter.

Besides, I hated how cocaine made me feel. Plus, it killed the hippie music scene of my youth. Before cocaine, people smoked weed, brought out their guitars, and sang together all night. When cocaine arrived, the guitars stayed in their cases and disco started pumping from the speakers as people paired off into rooms for sex. I held cocaine responsible for that and never tried it again.

I told Westhrope about the Jolly Rancher incident.

"OMG, that's too funny. Hey, dude, you should use that! A song about a girl who's like hard candy! Seriously dude. You should *really* use that! Okay, okay. Wait a minute, I'm getting another title! I swear, I find depressing people like you—inspiring."

He started tapping a beat on his desk again, turned his cap backward, and white-boy rapped, "'*She's stuck in my heart like hard candy! Um uh-huh uh-huh. Stuck in my heart like hard candy!*' Dude, that's such a good hook! I give it to you free. Run with it! It'll be a hit! No wonder I work here!" He smiled and winked at his reflection in the eighth-floor window. "So, dude, I've given you three songs to work on." His face glazed over, and he stifled a yawn. "Are we done here, then?"

I was feeling nauseous, shot to shit, deflated. "Sure, dude . . ." An image flashed of myself in an army of rock 'n' roll zombies, guitars strapped to our backs, outstretched hands holding our latest irrelevant CDs. "I'll send you the demo."

"Cool, yeah, send me the demo. Take your time. There's no rush." He stood up and offered me his left hand to shake; with the right, he checked an incoming text. Never taking his eyes off the screen, he said, "Keep on writing, Jimmy, just write different songs. Yeah! Incest and hard candy. Get it on, dawg! Um, bye!" He abruptly let go of my hand, sat back down, and leered at his phone's screen, his thumbs pumping madly, breathing like an elk in rut.

Walking down the hallway to the elevator, I heard a death train start up in my head. It chugged, *End of the line, end of the line, end of the line.* Reflecting on my songs, I imagined my creative life lying down on the tracks as the train rolled over my tunes, splattering my dreams and inspirations, mowing down everything I believed in. From down the hall, I could hear Westhrope tapping his desk, still singing, "*Stuck in my heart like hard candy. Uh-huh, uh-huh, oh yeah!* Damn, that's so sick! I shouldn't have given it to the old geezer."

The elevator doors closed mercifully on Westhrope's singing, but it was too late. "*Stuck in my heart like hard candy*" was now stuck in my head. Meanwhile, the death train kept rolling over the tracks—*end of the line, end of the line*—thumping annihilation, picking up speed. Going down the elevator, the two earworms merged in my mind. They started eating my brain one neuron at a time, a zombie rap song chewing away, getting hungrier by the second.

In a daze, I stumbled from the elevator into the bright, electric sun of L.A. and started walking down Wilshire Boulevard. The soulless street stretched endlessly before me as the earworms kept crunching away, getting louder and louder in my head. I shouted toward the low-rise buildings on my left, "Shut up, shut up!" trying my best to silence the two songs in my head. Covering my ears with my hands, I continued shouting, "Shut up! Shut up! Shut up!"

"Gawd! Meth freaks, schizophrenics! Where do they all come from?" remarked a gaggle of millennials, pointing their phones at me as they emerged from a Jamba Juice. A thin young woman in black tights sized me up. She folded her arms and said to her friends, her voice sizzling with vocal fry, "Haven't you heard? They're the new zombie underclass!" They all laughed. But a young man with a thick red hipster beard right out of the Civil War came to my defense. "My history professor said it's all Reagan's fault because when he was governor, he took the state money to help mentally ill people like this guy and spent it on the war on drugs to kill pot." That seemed to do the trick; even the girl in black tights softened a bit. "Aw, it's not his fault," she said, and they ambled down the street.

I started running, feeling a panic attack coming on. An imaginary pop-up window flashed in my head: *Twenty-five hundred people have died of earworm attacks. Click here to learn more.*

I was losing it. I felt dizzy, hot, and lightheaded. Right about the time I thought I'd be kissing the pavement, a friendly female voice called to me from the street corner. "Hey, good-lookin'! Where you runnin' to?"

4 Sexy Sadie

If you're a really mean person you're going to come back as a fly and eat poop.

—KURT COBAIN

The sun was setting on another peaceful day in Near Heaven. Billowy ivory clouds turned the palest hint of peach. The sun itself was pale yellow, and you could stare at it all day without squinting or going blind. Sunrises in Near Heaven were nearly identical to sunsets, so neither got much notice. When God painted Near Heaven, she used watercolors, diluted on purpose to get souls like John Lennon to move on.

Lennon sat on his plush white couch and strummed the chords to "Sexy Sadie" on his guitar. "George," he said, "look at that bloody sunset!" He stopped playing for a moment and pointed at the pale-peach clouds. "God must be laughing! I mean, day after day of this. I swear they're the same bloody clouds. It's a bit of a joke, isn't it?"

He continued strumming and humming "Sexy Sadie," a song he had scratched on a piece of wood in Rishikesh, India, about the Beatles' former guru, the Maharishi Mahesh Yogi. The Maharishi, born Mahesh Prasad Varma, graduated college with a degree in physics before becoming a devotee of Guru Dev and developing Transcendental Meditation. The relationship soured when the Maharishi, a self-proclaimed celibate, purportedly hit on actress Mia Farrow during a TM retreat in 1968 attended by the Beatles. Nonetheless, the Beatles returned from Rishikesh with forty new songs, including the bulk of those on the *White Album*.

George Harrison chimed in from his own comfortable couch. "No, John, the sunsets here are no joke. They're a reminder that there are more beautiful sunsets waiting for you in Nearer Heaven. By the way, I know why you're playing 'Sexy Sadie.' Come on, be fair. The Maharishi was a good man. He just couldn't do the whole celibacy thing. People expected him to be celibate. Just because you're getting laid doesn't mean your ideas aren't sound. We were no angels ourselves. So don't be so hypocritical."

"You've got me there! Anyways, it all seems a bit funny from *this* distance, doesn't it?" Lennon sang, "*Oh, Sexy Sadie, what have you done?*" He stopped playing and turned to Harrison. "Sorry, man. I know you loved him. Where do you think the Maharishi is now? Have you seen him in Nearer Heaven?"

"Angelic rumor has it that when the Maharishi died in 2008 his soul reincarnated back on Earth as a female teenage Bollywood pop star named Lata Chitra."

Lennon laughed. "To paraphrase Voltaire, that proves 'God is a comedienne playing to an audience too afraid to laugh!' Have you ever wondered why there's so little humor in religion?"

"I guess when people consider God, they're not looking for humor, they're looking for meaning."

"I know, but look at the Bible, the Koran, the Old Testament. They're all bloody painful tales that promise peace and redemption, but only in the afterlife. Well, here I am, *in* the bloody afterlife, and I'm still paying my dues!"

"Well then, that's spiritual humor for you, John. Here's some more. Before death, chop wood, carry water. After death, chop holographic wood, carry holographic water."

"There you go with that Zen paradox stuff again. It's about the work. I know, I get it. It all comes back to the work. I totally get it." Lennon tried his best to sound sincere, but in his heart, he was still holding on to his secret plan to catch up with Yoko after her death. Until then, he'd go where Harrison sent him and would put up with whatever mediocrity Near Heaven had to dish out. He found the occasional field trip to Earth kept him sane while waiting for Yoko to show up.

After dealing with Lennon's antics for decades, Harrison could read Lennon well. He saw that he'd pushed John as far as he could with this visit. He knew Lennon's half-hearted efforts to change his karma were rooted in something deeply personal and private, so he didn't question him further. But he had his suspicions that Lennon was up to no good. He stood to leave and gave Lennon a hug, which appeared more like two streams of warm water running into each other than arms embracing. "Thanks for the jam; it's always great seeing you. I've got to get going."

"What, so soon? Rushing off to your guardian angel, are you? The one you'll eventually pawn me off to? It's Ravi

Shankar, isn't it?" Lennon hazarded a guess, since it was Shankar who had showed Harrison how to play the sitar and later became his music mentor.

"No. Ravi hasn't been seen. Some say he chose to reincarnate, that the strength of his connection to his daughter Norah pulled him back to Earth. Listen, if you can keep your next client alive and inspired, many truths will open for you. Weren't you the one who sang, '*Gimme some truth, all I want is the truth*'?"

"Fair enough. I did say that. All right then, what's my new client's name?"

"His name is James Drake, or in the business, Jimmy Drake."

"Seriously? Isn't he the guy who tried to make 'John Lennon Day' an International Day of Peace after I passed?"

"One and the same, John."

"Bloody hell, this is getting serious, isn't it? The guy's in it bloody deep, isn't he?"

"We're all in it bloody deep, John. That's why there's not much humor in religion." George put his guitar on the couch and stood. "Are you ready to go?"

Lennon stood up and threw his guitar in the air. It hovered for a second, then disappeared in a puff of white smoke before it had a chance to hit the ground. "All right, I'm ready. Bring on Mr. Jimmy Drake! I've read the notes. It'll be cool to see San Francisco again. Let's dissolve, man!"

"Okay, John. You know the ropes. Heaven has issued you a temporary soul exit visa to help you save the life and creativity of James Drake. And no funny business. Stop asking your clients for favors. Oh, and yes, I do believe you'll get an excellent view of the Golden Gate Bridge. Let's dissolve!"

Lennon and Harrison began to glow as their human images burned away. Mini-suns appeared in their chests, growing larger and larger, swirling with brilliant blue-white tendrils. They drifted toward each other, pulsing with energy, growing brighter with each orbit, faster and faster, until they were brighter than the sun in Near Heaven. One final brilliant pulse, and they shot off, comet-like, in opposite directions. Harrison, for a cryptic meeting with his guardian angel in Nearer Heaven, and Lennon to his beleaguered ex-planet Earth to bring a weary, desiccated soul a little water.

5   Wilshire Annie

"Oh, you can't help that," said the Cat: "We're all mad here. I'm mad. You're mad."

"How do you know I'm mad?" said Alice.

"You must be," said the Cat, "or you wouldn't have come here."

—LEWIS CARROLL, "PIG AND PEPPER,"

ALICE IN WONDERLAND

My panic attack cresting, the sidewalk seemed to be spinning toward me. The earworms were going in for the kill. Just when I thought I'd do a face-plant on the cement, a beautiful Black woman about my age with waist-length dreadlocks wearing the most colorful tie-dye outfit I'd ever seen appeared in front of me. "I said where you runnin', honey?" she said, then enthusiastically waved me over to her ragtag display of jewelry, glass pipes, paintings, and garage sale items spread out on an old Persian carpet.

I hesitated, momentarily astonished because the earworms that had been eating my brain a moment before had suddenly, miraculously disappeared. No more hard candy. No more end-of-the-line death train. "Oh, sweet relief!" I said out loud.

"Sweet relief from what, honey?" She smiled, her warm brown eyes mirthful behind pink and blue sunglasses.

"Oh, nothing." I averted my eyes, trying to hide my anxiety. "I was just out getting a bit of exercise."

"You shinin' me on, ain't you? *Nothin'?* I swear your face is a land of woe, handsome. Come on now, what's *really* goin' on?"

I didn't want to share my crises of the soul with anyone, especially someone I didn't know. I had learned over the years how to hide my panic attacks. They'd plagued my family on my German mother's side for centuries, ingrained by years of war, famine, and alcohol abuse. I had inherited the syndrome and was in good company. David Bowie, Robert Plant, even people seemingly as strong as Oprah Winfrey have admitted to and learned how to deal with these leftover Stone Age reactions to stress. When your amygdala goes rogue and throws gasoline on your imagination, creativity doesn't seem so glamorous anymore.

"Seriously. I'm just a little bit out of breath. I'll be okay," I lied. I was definitely *not* okay.

"Uh-huh." She regarded me skeptically and continued, "I know L.A.'s a tough place. What is it? Can't find a job? Blow an audition? Screenplay get trashed? I see it all the time from this street corner. Uh-huh. Every day, honey." She leaned forward as if to tell me a secret. "Here's the thing. La La Land's full and always ready to show you the door. Am I right?"

"Something like that," I said. Her ability to read me was uncanny. She had a quality that naturally inspired trust, so I took a risk and blurted, "Okay, so I've just been told by the new master of the fucking music business that my songs are irrelevant, I'm too old, and that I should just hang it up."

"Ah, a *song*writer. I should have known. Anybody ever tell you you look like Mick Jagger? A more handsome version of him for sure." She gave me a wink and said, "Still, you're feelin' *so* sorry for yourself, ain't you?"

"Yeah, I guess I am. I've been going down this road a long time and it's apparently the wrong road. Songs about universal love are dead on arrival. And that's what I sing about. Or at least that's what I *used* to sing about." I couldn't believe I was telling her all this.

She furrowed her brow sympathetically, squinted her eyes, leaned forward, and said, "Who told you that? Was it Mark Westhrope?"

I was thunderstruck by her guess. "Goddamn. Yes. It was him! How'd you know?"

"I saw you comin' out of the Platinum Music building. I put two and two together. Well, the great Mr. Westhrope don't know shit about real music. He only got that job cuz his uncle's the owner. For Heaven's sake, don't give up on music cuz of *him*. He's a sex addict! That's all he cares about."

"That's the truth! Say, how do you know all this?"

"I never divulge my sources, honey," she said playfully. Abruptly changing the subject, she said, "Hey, check out my stuff. How about a nice tie-dye T-shirt to raise your spirits?"

"No, I don't wear tie-dye anymore," I lied. I owned several tie-dye shirts that I liked to sleep in. She was starting to blow what was left of my mind.

"What's the matter?" She eyed me up and down. "You got somethin' against color? I see you wear a lot of black. Black jeans, black shirt, black shoes, black attitude. You tryin' to be a Goth or somethin'? Plenty of time for that when you're dead. Okay, how about a beautiful, custom-made glass pipe? Real deep artist shit on sale today."

I deflected her offer. "I'm sorry. I only use compostable pipes. I make them out of apples, cucumbers, and especially zucchinis. They're the best. It cools the smoke, then when I'm done, I just throw it in a stir-fry to hide the evidence."

She laughed. "Hey, man, cool! That's real old-school dope-smokin' shit. Hmm." She steepled her fingertips looking me up and down, clicking her tongue and noting how I slumped. She started slowly nodding her head, looking me square in the eyes. She smiled and said, "I know, I know. How about a nice pair of genuine John Lennon glasses? You into Lennon?"

That threw me for a loop. Who *was* this person, some kind of psychic? I tried to hide my surprise and said, "Well, I *used* to be into Lennon, but now I'm not so sure." That was the truth.

"Why not?" She put her hands on her tie-dye hips, swaying as she said, "He wrote some of the greatest songs of our generation. You got a problem with that?"

I felt guilty saying it, but replied, "Yeah. But did he really believe what he was singing about? Or was he just stringing words together and parroting the values of the hippies to be cool and sell records?"

"You're questionin' reality and that's good, but I think you're overthinkin' it. Lennon wrote about the world as he saw it. And it touched you, honey. Ain't nothin' wrong with that, gettin' touched." Before I could reply, she motioned downward and asked, "How about these?"

From under a yellow silk scarf, she picked up a pair of clear John Lennon glasses with silver wire rims. Lying in her mahogany hands, they glinted in the sun. I couldn't take my eyes off them. They looked authentic.

Every Lennonhead knows John Lennon's glasses were really military-issue English safety glasses. He got them in 1967, for the movie *How I Won the War*, and adopted them as a part of his style thereafter. Plus, he was blind as a bat without them. I had studied nearly everything ever written about the Beatles, but I had never owned a pair of Lennon glasses.

The woman could tell I was fascinated. "I'm gettin' a feeling you should buy these. They're just for looks, no prescription, just clear lenses. Try 'em on, honey, here's a mirror." From inside the folds of her colorful dress she produced a silver hand mirror with an abalone inlay handle.

She held out the glasses to me, then held up the mirror. Obediently, I put the glasses on, blown away by her ability to distract and guide me.

I considered my reflection in the mirror. It was like seeing Mick Jagger wearing John Lennon glasses. Or vice versa depending on who's your favorite rock star. A strange mix for sure, but the glasses suited me somehow. The frames hid the bags under my eyes. My vanity approved. *You could grow old with these*, I said to myself.

She turned the mirror and a flood of sunlight hit me square in the eyes. I said, "Whoa! Ow! Hey! That's blinding me!" I shielded my eyes with my hands, but it was too late. Even with my eyes closed, a brilliant afterimage lingered. It appeared as a sun with Tesla-coil energy threads rotating and swimming toward me. Time slowed. The threads began resolving into the outline of a face. A familiar face, but in the flood of light, it was too bright to place. My irises squeezed tight to reduce the stream of sunlight. I could feel my pupils retreating into my head. The face was mouthing something, but there was no sound. All I could hear was my own breathing as I tried to make sense of the situation.

"Oh, sorry." The woman turned the mirror away from the sun and back to my reflection, smiling mischievously. My eyeballs were still smarting. The afterimage slowly disappeared as my eyes recovered, and my weird Lennon–Jagger reflection returned.

"Well, what do you think? I think you're real handsome in those. Gives you an older-rock-star kinda look. Like Lou Reed meets Bowie or somethin'. What do you say? Come on, I haven't sold anything all day," she pleaded.

"How much?" I asked in a daze, still recovering.

"For havin' sympathy on how my city treated you, not to mention how that don't-know-shit deviant troll Westhrope traumatized you, fifteen dollars."

"Fifteen dollars? Well, *that's* certainly reasonable."

Even the cheapest pair of Lennon glasses with quality silver frames and clear lenses went for about a hundred dollars on the web. "Okay, you got a sale." I whipped out a twenty-dollar bill and said, "Keep the change." I knew she had undercharged me, plus I was a petty socialist at heart.

"Well, ain't you generous! You just made a great choice." She smiled lovingly and hummed "Let It Be" while she wrapped the glasses in the 1970 *Rolling Stone* issue with John and Yoko holding white doves of peace on the cover. She tied the package with a red ribbon, handed it to me solemnly, and said, "May you see clearly again, my friend. Namaste!"

"Thank you. Namaste. Hey, what's your name?" I asked.

"Folks on the street call me Wilshire Annie, but just call me Annie." She smiled coyly and made a little bow.

"Well, Annie, you're the one good thing that's happened to me in L.A." I tucked the package into my black day pack and said, "Have a great life. I've got to catch a plane."

"All right. But we'll see each other again."

"I don't think so, Annie. I'm never coming back to this city ever again."

"Oh, don't be too sure of that. Never's an angry word, James. Unlearn your anger and let love come in the door."

"Hey, how'd you know my name?"

"I told you, I never reveal my sources." She smiled that beguiling smile again and abruptly turned away to help a young Latina looking over the children's tie-dye tank tops. "*¡Hola! ¿Tu hijo le gusta azul?*" she said in perfect Spanish. "He likes blue swirls, right, *¿Estoy en lo cierto?*" The woman nodded in amazement.

I continued walking down the street, my head spinning. I turned to get one last look at Annie. She waved a final goodbye, a brilliant rose in a desert of dreariness. Blowing me a kiss, she shouted, "I'll see you again, sweetie!"

With that, I wandered down the street and went into a TOGO's. I had no appetite; I just wanted to do something that felt normal. I ordered a number three without consulting the menu. It doesn't matter, they all taste the same. I fumbled around for my Visa card. "Sorry," I said to the hipster cashier, who waited patiently. She looked as if she'd stepped out of a punk version of *Game of Thrones*, her long gray-white hair tied back in a ponytail and silver rings on each finger. "Sorry," I said again. "This has been the strangest day of my life."

With the enigmatic, self-assured gaze of dragonmaster Daenerys Targaryen, she handed me the sandwich and said, "Don't worry, strange is good."

6 The Black Chord

In an infinite multiverse there is no such thing as fiction.
— SCOTT ADSIT

George Harrison sat with his legs crossed playing a sitar on the luminous grass of Nearer Heaven. Sitting next to him, his guardian angel blissfully smoked a jay, eyes closed, listening. Harrison was playing music in color now, strumming the spectrum as if inside a prism. The grass literally sang green, while a ridge of snowcapped mountains in the distance sang blue. The green grass, blue mountains, and a paisley-bloused Harrison all jammed together.

It had taken a while for Harrison to acclimate to the incredible spiritual bandwidth of Nearer Heaven, but he was deep into it now. With his guardian angel's help, he was exploring a new level of musical creativity: playing colors. Harrison's raga picked up speed, and a host of other rainbow colors came swirling out of his sitar and blended with the green of the grass, the blue of the mountains, and a bolt of purple from Harrison's heart. Swirling sound and color reached a crescendo and crashed into the brilliant white snow of the mountains. Deep booming sounds reverberated from the cliffs and echoed off the mountains, creating an avalanche of snow that thundered down the canyon, shaking the landscape, then breaking apart and tinkling away like an orchestra of tiny bells.

It was Harrison's improvisation down to the finest detail. The colors, the landscape, all reminiscent of his time in the Himalayas spent with the Maharishi.

"Bravo! Cool, man, cool!" said Harrison's guardian angel, clapping his long, ring-bejeweled hands, nodding his majestic lionlike head, and smiling with his hooded Haitian–Cherokee eyes still closed. "George, you are nailin' it here in Nearer Heaven. That was gorgeous. I swear God must have made this place just for you!" He opened his eyes and gave Harrison a skewering look that seemed to say, *I've got your number, don't I!*

Harrison knew this was not only a compliment but also a test. Could he ever let go of such a place? He wondered himself. He knew attachment wasn't good, but in Nearer Heaven you could still assume Earthly states, and that pleased him. He also liked playing music on familiar instruments. Earthly trappings still held their sway in Nearer Heaven, a realm where souls made the final decision to move on from old stories and material reality into the purely energetic space of Heaven itself.

"You've got me there, Richie. But why would I want to leave this place? It's not perfect, but it's pretty damned close." He shook his head and said wistfully, "Maybe I was just a younger soul than everyone thought." He set his sitar on the grass and accepted a hit on the joint. Then he lay back and blew the smoke up into the crystalline aqua sky of Nearer Heaven. "Ah,

Richie. I like it here. Heaven can wait. Besides, I've got eternity, don't I?" Harrison's guardian angel closed his eyes again and fell silent.

Richard Pierce Havens. The angel known on Earth as folk-rock legend Richie Havens offered Harrison another puff with his eyes still closed. Whether playing Woodstock or a coffeehouse, or just listening to a friend in the afterlife, Richie Havens saw most clearly with his eyes closed.

Richie Havens was thrown on the main stage at Woodstock when the scheduled headliner got stuck in traffic. The shock of playing to four hundred thousand love-drenched, acid-melted hippies for nearly three hours had permanently cracked him open spiritually. He spent the rest of his life playing songs of freedom and starting organizations such as the Natural Guard, turning low-income kids on to caring for the earth. When he died in 2013, his ashes were spread across the Woodstock site and his soul ascended straight to Heaven like a feather in an updraft of love.

"George," he said patiently, "Heaven is the source of all meaning, the source of all creativity in our universe. Everything that has ever inspired you got its start in Heaven. Aren't you curious to see what's up that river?"

"You mean like finding the source of the Nile?" Harrison sat up, curiosity aroused.

"Exactly! Where's your spirit of adventure? You should grab an oar and go up that river. We can go together."

"But, Richie, can't I just rest here for a millennium or so? I mean, my life on Earth was like being in a bloody hurricane. I got famous at an early age and was mobbed by fans. Then my band broke up, I got taken to the cleaners by the taxman, got cancer, and was stabbed by a raving madman. I need some rest. This place suits me. I need peace. I want to stay here a while."

"Hey, that's cool! Nearer Heaven is your reward for all the good work you did on Earth. But like our mutual friend Mr. Lennon said, 'Life is what happens while you're busy making other plans.' The same applies in the afterlife. I have something to show you, George. Watch this."

Havens took a big last puff on the joint, then tossed it in the air, where it tumbled for a second before dematerializing. He blew the smoke toward Harrison, and it grew wide and formed a rotating mass that transformed from white to gray to black and began emitting a metallic sound that seemed to suck the green right out of the grass, turning it a dismal gray.

Harrison felt a strange foreboding, a sensation he hadn't felt in a long time. Only the near-fatal stabbing he experienced on Earth in the year 1999 came close to what he now felt looking at this thing Havens had conjured. "What the bloody hell is that, Richie?"

"*That*, my friend, is the Black Chord, an anti-sound from another universe. And it's coming our way. In fact, part of it is already here."

"The Black Chord?"

"It's the negative experience of music, the opposite of music. The Black Chord is coming to suck music, art, and light from our universe. Every melody line, every chorus, every lyric, every solo ever written. Although it's not visible to mortal eyes, we are under attack. A rift has opened near Alpha Centauri, 4.3 light-years from Earth, and we are its next target."

"Who or what in the bloody hell would want to do that?" Harrison knew his sessions with Havens would test his limits, but *this* was unprecedented.

"See, George, as you know, we live in an emotional universe full of stars and light with a God that likes to create and enjoy herself. She paints, she dances, she lives through us. She loves rock 'n' roll, having a good time, impregnating virgins, making crazy animals like bonobos. Hell, she even likes death and destruction, the full arc of experience, learning and choice. You name it. Our God is considered dangerous in some cosmic circles. They fear her power, creativity, and exuberance. And these are her enemies. The Black Chord is coming to change all that, and Earth, as one of the universe's most musical planets, is ground zero."

"Where's it coming from, Richie?"

"From a vastly older universe where all the stars have burned through their fuel and only wormholes are left. A dark universe where music ended eons ago. The first subspace waves of the Black Chord are washing through Earth even now, spreading dissonance and violence. ISIS, the Taliban, the rise of autocratic leaders, misogynistic rap, death metal, insipid pop, and mediocrity. Haven't you ever wondered why so many musicians have died in small planes? Or why you and Lennon were both violently attacked? It's all related to the Black Chord, George."

Harrison put his hands over his ears. He couldn't take the sound of the Black Chord any longer. He pleaded, "Please, Richie! Turn that bloody thing off!"

Havens blinked his warm brown eyes twice, and the Black Chord disappeared. Beneath their feet, the grass slowly greened. "George, God is calling the souls of all musicians who've recently passed to join her in Heaven to create an epic masterwork that will heal the rupture. A work of love so powerful it will not only save music but also penetrate the rift and pave the way for a second wave of star creation in that bleak other universe, giving it a new beginning. I know you like it here in Nearer Heaven, but you and I, and John, Janis, and even Kurt have got to grow up *now*. We're the shock troops in God's defense of her universe."

"Kurt Cobain! Janis Joplin!" Harrison was surprised to hear their names and learn of their divine purpose considering what a hell they lived on Earth.

"Yes, Janis and Kurt, David Bowie, Prince, Nina Simone, Mama Cass, Freddie Mercury, Michael Jackson, a battalion of rockers to fight the darkness! We all benefited from a time when the milk of the muse flowed like cream. Where do you suppose all those great songs came from? Now she's calling in her troops. This is the great flushing of the bardos. We're all being fast-tracked to the front. This is our epic chance to give something back. We're all going upriver to make rock 'n' roll history in Heaven."

7 Death Wish

*Suicide is man's way of telling God, "You can't fire me.
I quit!"*

—BILL MAHER

I was going home to a different life for sure. A life devoid of all that had kept me going for years. I wasn't sure it would be a life worth living. Sure, Lennon. "All you need is love." That, and a fricking reason to get up in the morning. A long life is meaningful only when there's a reason to live it.

The Bay Area appeared through the clouds as my plane began descending to the runway at SFO. The man across the aisle from me was breathing hard, nervous sweat breaking out on his forehead. He's never landed in the Bay Area before, I thought. There's at least one on every plane.

I leaned across the aisle. "Don't worry. It just *looks* like we're gonna crash in the bay, but where the water leaves off the runway begins."

"Thanks!" he said. "I've never landed here before."

I guess he didn't believe me, though, because he kept white-knuckling the chair arms, pulling up on them as if he were landing the plane himself. The jet landed with a deep thud. He let out a "Whoa Nelly!" but once we were rolling on terra asphalta again, he released the chair arms and said with a thick Southern accent, "Lawdy! That's quite a landin'!"

"Welcome to the Left Coast," I said to annoy him, stereotyping him as a Southern right-wing conservative nut. "See. We're all still alive." I can be such an asshole sometimes, I swear. It comes from living too close to Berkeley. Liberals care more for starving people in other countries than for the troubles of the person right next to them.

"Thank you, sir! I'm here to help build houses for Habitat for Humanity. Jimmy Carter's a neighbor of mine in Georgia. So far, I've helped him build over fifty houses. Homes for poor people. Hey! I didn't know you had any of them left out here. I thought you were all millionaires. Heh-heh!" He slapped me on the back good-naturedly as we waited to exit the plane.

Sure enough, he was wearing Birkenstocks. A Southern liberal! Shit! An oxymoron in the flesh! I felt guilty and foolish for judging him.

I mused silently, *I really am a liberal asshole, and I don't deserve to live!* The throwaway thought stuck in my head. It reverberated in my brain, growing deeper, darker, and more threatening. *You don't deserve to live.* It kept repeating, linking itself to my recent debacle at Platinum Music Publishing. Taking on a heavy New Jersey accent, the voice accused, *You don't deserve to live.*

Like most Americans, I've watched way too much TV and seen way too many movies. So when the voice of Tony Soprano sounded from the back of my head trying to take charge of the situation, I really wasn't surprised. He shook his head with gangster pragmatism. "It's true. You don't deserve to live. Nothing personal, but me and the guys are gonna have to do you in, and it's all your fault. It's the only way outta this mess. See what you're making us do!" He shrugged his shoulders.

Where were these thoughts coming from? Was Tony Soprano my death wish speaking? I walked down the passageway feeling oddly high and a bit dizzy, like I was on acid or something. The passageway seemed to narrow and grow longer the further I walked down it. For the first time in my life, I started thinking about suicide. This was new. Even during my worst panic attacks, band breakups, or romantic heartbreaks, I had never felt suicidal. This was different. And for some reason, it didn't scare me as much as I thought it would. Whoa. That was different too. I kinda liked feeling less scared. And so did Tony Soprano, who said, "Now go get your bags. Me and the boys will meet you outside."

I surveyed the baggage claim area. As if their bags were long-lost relatives, people were scurrying around, jostling for position, trying to be the first to see their luggage emerge. I studied the baggage carriers with their faraway eyes, lost in daydreams while they did their jobs. I felt a strange but loving detachment from them all. Thoughts of leaving Earth released me from the constant pressure I felt trying to stay driven and creative.

Tony Soprano returned, trying to comfort me. "See, Jimmy, this is your last luggage carousel, your last tour. Appreciate it! Now it's over." I imagined his gangster arm over my shoulder in a kind of *Goodfellas* goodbye.

I stood with my back against the far wall and let the luggage divers have their way. To my disassociated mind, they seemed more seagull than human with their eyes frozen on the carousel, ravenously pecking at the bags as they came within reach. I felt sad for our species. So brilliant, but so aggressive and out of touch in many ways. I pondered a personal Brexit from it all.

From my dark reverie, Tony Soprano's voice returned one last time, bearing good news and support for my coming demise. "Hey, Jimmy! Turn around. You gotta see this."

I turned and saw a large framed picture of the Golden Gate Bridge with its bold caption, Welcome to San Francisco, city of love, city of dreams. I scanned the photo from the top of the bridge to the water below several times and wondered what it would be like to jump from one of the world's most iconic landmarks. I sat in a blue plastic terminal chair, took out my laptop, and googled "Suicide Golden Gate Bridge."

An estimated 1,700 people have taken the leap since the bridge was finished in 1937. Forty-six people took the plunge in 2013 alone. Only twenty-six survived the 245-foot jump, giving it a 98 percent kill rate. Good odds, I thought darkly. Water turns as hard as sheet metal with such an impact. I remembered *that* from science class.

In medieval times, life was so hard that people routinely killed themselves just to get out of living. Well, life was feeling pretty medieval to me lately. A personal dark age seemed to be settling in. I felt that by killing myself, I would at least get to cheat the chronic pain of a shipwrecked life.

I closed my laptop and examined the photo again. Welcome to San Francisco, city of love, city of dreams, it boasted. How can you live in a city of love and dreams if you don't have any? Something clicked. I needed out of this crazy world. I decided to jump off the bridge that very afternoon, on my way home, before I could change my mind. *Thank you, Tony!* I said silently, but he didn't answer. Other people to kill, I suspected. Death wishes have busy schedules.

8 Vertigo

*Here I was born, and there I died. It was only a moment
for you; you took no notice.*
— MADELEINE ELSTER (KIM NOVAK), *VERTIGO*

I hailed a Lyft and got in the car. The driver, an eager young
man with surfer-blond hair who looked like he had just got his
license, welcomed me. "Howzit!" he said. "Thanks for choos-
ing Lyft. I'm Kekoa. Where can I take you?"

"Take me to Fort Point, please."

"Fort Point, Fort Point. Hmm. Sorry, man. You got an
address? I just moved here from Hawaii."

"It's at the foot of the Golden Gate Bridge. Catch 280 North
and I'll direct you from there."

"That's okay. I just found it on my GPS."

"So, Kekoa, are you Hawaiian?"

"Nah. I'm from New Jersey. But I lived on the Big Island for
a year before my—accident." He smiled broadly, his young
face begging to be asked.

"Accident? What happened?" I inquired absently while taking in my last views of this weird rocky planet.

"Yeah, man. I got bit by a tiger shark while learning to surf. Ha-ha-haaa!" He emitted three short, high laughs. More a trill, really. "Wanna see my scar? One hundred twenty-five stitches. Just a nibble." He genuinely thought it was funny to be attacked by a shark. Guys like that should go into the music business.

"No thanks! I'm squeamish about that stuff." I shuddered. I imagined my body getting eaten by sharks after I jumped off the bridge. "So, you left Hawaii because of the sharks?"

"No, sharks are *way* cool, man. I was out in *his* territory. That tiger shark thought I was a sea turtle. It tasted me for a second, then spit me out. Guess I don't taste much like sea turtle. Ha-ha-haaa!" The youthful trill again. "No, I left Hawaii because of the vog."

"The what?" Everything sounded far away. I kept thinking this might be my last conversation on Earth. "The vog?" I asked vacantly.

"Yeah, the vog. The volcanic emissions from Kilauea. A mixture of ash, dust, sulfur dioxide, carbon monoxide—real nasty stuff. I coughed myself to sleep every night, mon." He broke into a passable reggae song, "*Pele never stops, mon. 24–7. The bad breath of the planet, mon.*"

I brightened a bit. "Hey, did you just improvise that? That's pretty good. Too bad about the vog, though. I remember it now. Some slack key guitar guys told me about it at a festival a few years back. They said it's like living in L.A. on a bad day. Hey, is Kekoa your real name?"

"Nah." He dropped the reggae and went back to his New Jersey native tongue. "I took the name in honor of my shark attack. It means 'courageous spirit' in Hawaiian. I figured after the tiger shark bite, I deserved it. Besides, girls love it! My real name is Devin."

"Well, Kekoa-Devin, why didn't you move to Kauai? The volcanoes are extinct there."

"Yeah, I thought about that, but while I was healing from the shark bite, I met a girl from SF at a yoga retreat in Hilo. One thing led to another, and as of last week, I'm living in the city of love with the girl of my dreams, driving for Lyft. Like the ancient Hawaiians said, 'If can, can. If no can, no can.' The ancient Hawaiians were so wise!"

"Kekoa, the ancient Hawaiians were cannibals with death taboos for everything. They would have said something more like, 'Hey, Kekoa, pass me that thigh bone,' or 'Hey, Kekoa, let's kill a few slaves and have a luau!'"

"Hey, man! You're a funny guy! You should do stand-up!"

I was impressed I had any humor left considering where I was headed. I felt reckless and light. Knowing I would be dead soon relieved me of all Earthly concerns. I was a black feather drifting down to the rocks. I stared out the window as old memories came flooding in.

"Well, satirical comedy was my specialty. When I was your age, I was in a social satire band called the Nebulous They. We played the college circuit and did sarcastic songs with long titles such as 'Love as Real Estate, You're My Fixer-Upper' and 'High on Stress.'"*

* Listen to "Love as Real Estate, You're My Fixer-Upper" and "High on Stress" at JohnLennonsGlasses.net.

"LOL, man! That's *too* funny! What happened to the band?"

"Kekoa, bands are like snowflakes falling on hot Camaros. Most don't survive, and I made the cardinal mistake all young male musicians make."

"What's that?"

"I slept with the female singer. That killed it. The Nebulous They became the Nebulous Nobodies."

"Aw, sorry, man. Yeah, it happened to a friend of mine in Jersey. He was in a band called the Promosexuals. The minute he dropped his pants for the woman drummer, the band dropped them both."

We approached the bridge. "So, Fort Point, right under the bridge, huh?" He caught my reflection in the rearview mirror and noticed my strange dark smile. "Hey, man!" he teased. "Are you gonna jump off the bridge? Ha-ha-haaa!"

His trill and precocious leap of association chilled my spine. There must be a metaspace, a psychic connection between us all, I thought. I let out my own fake laugh that was more of an "Ah-ha, you got me" than a laugh.

"No, Kekoa, I'm uh, uh . . . I'm a Hitchcock fan. I want to see the place where Jimmy Stewart rescued Kim Novak from drowning in *Vertigo*." He smiled. I'd thrown him off the scent. I was always able to lie on the fly convincingly. It was one of my worst characteristics, but it came in handy at times.

"Oh, sick! My parents are Hitchcock fans! They let me watch *Vertigo* on my fourteenth birthday! We even went down to San Juan Bautista on vacation once. Did you know there's no suicide tower there? Hitchcock put that in. It's a fake. I guess that's why people use the Golden Gate Bridge. Ha-ha-haaa!" He watched me curiously in the rearview mirror, sniffing around the edges of my weird energy. I avoided his eyes and pointed at the exit.

"We get off here, Kekoa."

As we left the freeway for the Presidio and Lincoln Boulevard, I could feel my last minutes on Earth ticking away. I directed Kekoa to the small parking lot at the end of Marina Drive, below the base of the bridge. We both got out and took a good look at the dark, choppy water.

"There it is, Kekoa. That's the spot. That's where Jimmy Stewart saved Kim Novak in *Vertigo.*" I pointed at the water breaking against the pilings of the bridge.

"Sick! This is where she faked suicide!" He whipped out his phone and took a selfie next to the water. "My parents will love this!"

I really had no idea if this was the exact spot or not. My storytelling friends say there's the truth, and then there's the "better truth." This was definitely the latter. While the truth can kill, a better truth inspires.

I opened the Lyft app and gave Kekoa a hefty tip as I'd soon have no need for money. He said, "You know, you really are a funny guy. Before you jump off the bridge—just kidding—you should do some stand-up. You'd be a real hit. Ha-ha-haaa! Thanks for using Lyft!" As he drove off, he flashed the "hang loose" sign.

His final laugh released a gaggle of goose bumps that traveled up my neck and spread over my scalp. He had the insight and naivete of youth, hitting on truth, but not yet trusting his own perceptions. I liked the exuberant millennial, but now I just wanted to get on with dying.

Once his car was out of sight, I ordered my feet to start hiking up the trail toward the bridge. It towered over me like the Balrog in *The Lord of the Rings*. A flaming orange giant in the setting sun, ready to pick me up and swallow me down.

9 Jumpin' Jack Flash

Jumpin' flapjacks give you gas, gas, gas!
— MONDEGREEN OF ROLLING STONES LYRICS,
"JUMPIN' JACK FLASH, IT'S A GAS GAS GAS!"

*Fame means millions of people have the wrong idea of who
you are.*

— ERICA JONG

I walked onto the bridge and breathed in the briny scent of the blue Pacific with its whitecaps and fog framed by the rolling green hills of Marin. *Such a beautiful sight*, I thought. It was magic hour. The sun was falling west into the sea. The scene was bathed in the glow of the setting sun. *Maybe I'll see the green flash as I'm falling.* What a weird time to be thinking about the green flash. Once you've untied the knot to stay among the living, you find you're not as attached to life as you think you are. I ruminated further. *My life was like the green flash, combusting red in the late '60s and flashing out green in just a few seconds.*

Crowds of people from all over the world were holding up their phones taking selfies to shine up their Instagram profiles. I guess postcards don't cut it anymore. That's the way the world works now. Everything's so instant, you don't have time to miss anybody. As my old friend Dan Hicks sang: *"How can I miss you when you won't go away?"*

It would be hard to find a moment when people weren't watching, so I kept walking until I was about halfway across. Finally, I was alone. I closed my eyes and got ready to climb over the railing for my final act when—

"Watashi no kamisama! Oh my God! It's Mick!" A heavily accented Japanese voice said, "It's Mick Jagger! Mr. Jagger. Jagger-san, Jagger-san! Please, sign autograph *kudasai?"*

I looked up to see five young Japanese women grinning ear to ear, coming my way. "Mr. Jagger-san. We can't believe it! Please sign autograph, *kudasai."* Bowing the whole time, they held out their Golden Gate National Recreation Area brochures for signing.

Oh shit! This has happened to me before—more when I was younger, and especially with people from Asia, for some reason. I don't know why. Several times I've walked into a Thai or Japanese restaurant and the maître d' announced for all to hear, "Oh! Mick Jagger. No charge, no charge!" Now why on Earth would Mick Jagger need a free lunch? He's filthy rich. Nevertheless, I must admit that on occasion I have taken advantage of the offers. My biggest score was a fantastic full teppanyaki dinner comped at Benihana. Another time a Thai waitress literally fainted taking my order, and I got the pad Thai for free. It was that bad or good, depending on your point of view. I figured the universe owed me payola for my problematic face.

I decided to go along with the ruse. I don't know why, except that if these were truly my last few moments on Earth, why not give these girls a thrill.

I put on my shades, feigned boredom, and said in my best British accent, "Oh, ladies, I do believe you caught me. I was just out for a walk. I didn't think anyone would notice me. All right, I'll sign. But please, ladies, I don't have much time. I've got a party to go to."

The young Japanese women bubbled over with excitement, saying stuff like, "Oh, Mr. Jagger, you look so much better than your pictures."

"It's the light, the fresh air, and, of course, your company, ladies." They squealed, holding their hands to their mouths and giggling in disbelief as I signed each brochure.

I signed, "Yours for a song, Sir M. Jagger," with lots of X's and O's, which sent them reeling. The one in a dayglow orange i heart sf T-shirt started crying at being in the presence of one the world's last great rock stars. I endured a few group photos and sent them on their way. They kept looking over their shoulders at me. I could see they were tearing up now. *What a bizarre thing fame is. Just another reason to leave this crazy world behind,* I thought.

I closed my eyes, trying to clear my mental palate of the tourist encounter. I offered a prayer to God, covering my bases in case there was one. I said I was sorry for extinguishing myself. And because I was a science nerd at heart, I apologized to the 37.2 trillion cells in my body all going about their business unaware that my brain and my heart had given up on them.

I opened my eyes and gaped at the clouds whipping over the peak of the bridge towers. I wondered if they might be the ghosts of the people who had stood here before they jumped. Tears came to my eyes as I prepared to climb over the rail.

I heard a commotion coming from the direction of the Japanese tourists. Apparently, they had tweeted that they met Mick Jagger on the bridge. Dozens of people started running toward me trying to get a glimpse of the legendary rock star.

"Oh no, oh *shit*!" I said aloud to a passing seagull. Panic-stricken, I held out my thumb to escape, and miraculously a car stopped to pick me up. Shaken and cold, I settled into the seat and thanked the driver just as the mob appeared, pointing at me through the glass and saying, "Look, everybody. There goes Mick Jagger!"

The driver flashed a wide smile, ecstatic to have rescued the rock star. He reminded me of Newt Gingrich as a hippie, a pouty red face with long gray hair. But instantly his pouty face turned sour, and he said accusingly, "Hey, wait a minute! *You're* not Mick Jagger!"

"No, I'm not," I confessed. "It's just a case of mistaken identity. Can you please take me back to the city? I promise I'll be no bother." I was so rattled and confused by what had just happened, I'd forgotten to turn off my English accent!

"Listen, man! You shouldn't pose as someone you're not. It's not cool!" He gave me a once-over. "Besides, Mick's way better-looking. Okay, *Miiick*," he said, his voice dripping sarcasm, "I'll take you over the bridge, but from there you're on your own." He turned away and slouched down in his seat, grumbling.

He drove on in disgust, crestfallen at not having met the real rock star. He dumped me off on Nineteenth Avenue and sped away in his neon green Honda, giving me the finger out the sunroof. I had no idea killing myself would be this hard.

10   Chairman Meow

There are two means of refuge from the misery of life—
music and cats.

—ALBERT SCHWEITZER

I caught a bus to my flat off Oak Street in the Haight-Ashbury district. I'd been living there the past five years. The heyday of the Haight was over, but I'd moved to the legendary district in 2012 to immerse myself in the mythos and history of hippie culture, or what was left of it. I was content to live in the event horizon of the Summer of Love, if only for its residual effects.

The dismal trip to L.A., plus the failed suicide attempt, had worn me out. It seemed I'd been gone for years. The climb up the stairs to my third-floor apartment might as well have been a hike to the tree line. I hardly had the energy to make the ascent. The musty smell of my apartment building, like most in the Haight, filled my lungs with a mixture of famil-iarity and dread.

I had no way to kill myself at home. No guns, no pills, no gas, no razor blades, no rope, just an old, serrated knife that could barely cut bread. Besides, there was no way I was going to kill myself indoors. Especially not in my drafty old apartment. Urban flats have a way of holding on to spirits. I didn't want to be the ghost of apartment 315 wandering through the walls in my underwear, looking for my rhyming dictionary for all eternity. As I turned the key in the lock, I resolved to return to the bridge tomorrow, but this time with a hoodie and sunglasses, in case other misguided tourists mistook me for Jagger.

When I opened the door, my cat, Chairman Meow, greeted me loudly with his feline litany of woe after being left alone for a couple of days. "*MmmNeeYooYoww! MmmNeeYoww!*" he yowled, which meant, "Other cats would have peed on the carpet, but I always used the box. Other cats would have shredded the curtains, but I used my scratching post. You don't deserve me, you inconsiderate primate shit!"

Poor Chairman Meow. What would happen to him after I was gone? I inspected my cluttered apartment. And what about all my stuff? Who would deal with all my shit? I swear. For the consciously evolved, suicide is a tricky business. For the first time since the bridge fiasco, I was thankful I'd botched it. At least now I had time to tie off a few loose ends. And maybe a "polite" suicide would buy me a point or two on the other side—if there was one.

I gave Chairman Meow a bowl of half-and-half from the fridge. It was his reward for my frequent absences. He lapped it up, purring loudly. Cats are the perfect companion for songwriters. They know when the muse is in the room and stay quiet and out of the way. Dogs, on the other hand, are jealous of inspiration and often interrupt the creative flow.

A wave of guilt swept through me as I thought of abandoning the Chairman. I had always felt bad leaving him alone for hours and days; but leaving him forever was another level altogether.

I had stolen Chairman Meow from my ex-girlfriend, Marcy, as an act of revenge after she dumped me for the dreaded drummer Gustavo. Like many other white girls, she had a thing for Latin guys. I called it her LGD, or Latin Guy Disease. A Hungarian friend of mine named Lucien with a thick Eastern European accent couldn't get a girlfriend, so he asked my advice. I sarcastically suggested he tell women he was from Brazil. "With your accent, they'll never know the difference," I'd said. It was meant as a joke, but Lucien took me seriously and adopted a whole fake Latin mystique to get dates. Soon he had more women than he knew how to deal with. So, as a final curse on Gustavo and all Latin lotharios, even fake ones, I decided to give the cat back. It would relieve my feelings of guilt for having taken him in the first place, and be a double curse to Gustavo, who I knew was horribly allergic to cats. *Take that, fucker!*

I had written a note and taped it to the cat food bag: "Dear Marcy, I apologize for having taken your cat. I was just so heartbroken at the time. I will never understand how you could leave a songwriter for a drummer. Anyway, if Gustavo truly loves you, he'll accept your cat even if it makes his nose run." I finished by scrawling a cat emoticon next to my signature.

Chairman Meow was licking the last bits of half-and-half from his paws. He gazed at me with feline bliss, his eyes mere furry slits that said, "All is good again. My god is back to open cans, clean my box, and give me half-and-half."

His god was back. That's true. But he was coming unraveled. I gave the Chairman more half-and-half. He held his fluffy orange and white tail high in the air, a signal that he had forgiven me once again.

I wondered if I could forgive myself.

11 Call Me Ishmael

If his chest was a cannon, he would have shot his heart upon the whale.

— JEAN-LUC PICARD, *STAR TREK: FIRST CONTACT*

Music is spiritual. The music business is not.

—VAN MORRISON

I went into my bedroom. My bed pillows appeared as the beautiful sirens from *The Odyssey*, beckoning me to crash on their shores. "*Lay down*," they sang. "*Lay your body down and sleep.*" After all I'd been through, I needed no convincing. I grabbed the DVD remote and started a documentary I often fell asleep to. David Attenborough's voice washed over me: "What humans do over the next fifty years will determine the fate of all life on the planet. I have no doubt that the fundamental problem the planet faces is the enormous increase in human population . . ." And I was out.

I dream I am in one of six whaleboats rising slowly up and down on the swells of a deep black ocean. The sounds of crashing waves, wind, and screaming seagulls fill my ears. Many of my old musician friends and bandmates are in the boats, holding spears, looking cold and fearful while waiting for something to surface.

There's Steve Saginaw, my buddy from high school, who taught me my first chords. He was the best guitar player I'd met up to that time. Later, he sold his guitars, got married, had three kids and went into real estate, selling mansions to millionaires in the South Bay. In another boat there's Randy Buplinger, the drummer from my first band, who gave up the sticks to pursue a corporate law career. And then there's Tobias. I never knew his last name; he kept it secret. He was the deepest artist I'd met in my youth. He wrote stories, danced, did theater, and played flute and percussion. Tobias never joined a band but sat in with many. A fanatical improviser, he never played the same song twice except the note-for-note flute part on Traffic's "The Low Spark of High-Heeled Boys," which always blew our young minds. He was our peer group's mystic, or at least he acted the part. In those days, young people tried on many disguises. Dreamy and relentlessly creative, Tobias later changed his sex. He dropped the *a* from his name, becoming Tobis, and formed a spiritual group called the Transcendental Transsexuals, who sought enlightenment through gender reassignment.

Even self-assured Tobias sits in the boat, cowed like all the others, waiting with the same expression of fear and dread for something monstrous to come out of the depths.

Seagulls wheel overhead, shrieking for scraps of meat. Maybe our own. A commanding voice sounds from the bow: "Be ready for him, boys!" It's Jimi Hendrix in full rock costume, leather vest and pants, holding a fearsome-looking, double-necked guitar that ends in jagged, lethal spears. He begins strumming the power chords of "All Along the Watchtower" as something huge ascends from the depths. Holding the guitar-spear high over his head, Hendrix shouts, "He rises, boys! He rises! *Strike!*"

A monster breaks through the water, but it's no whale. It's the ten-story Platinum Music building in L.A., rising like a monolith out of the sea. It looms higher and higher, towering over our heads. We throw our spears, but they bounce harmlessly off its sides. The dirty-white colossus careens forward and hits our boats with a tremendous splash, scattering us into the sea. We can see Hendrix lashed to the building with his guitar amp power cords. In a final act of rock fury, he hurls his guitar-spear through an open window as the building sinks into the black sea. One by one all the other musicians are sucked under by its wake. Tobias and I lock eyes, knowing that we are next. He looks at me with profound love and says, "Open your eyes, James. Open your eyes!"

I woke with a start, feeling dizzy and nauseous, the bed rising and falling in a swell between this world and that. I lay on my back, a shipwrecked sailor rolling on a plank somewhere between the nightmare of my dreams and the uncertainties of my waking life.

Slowly the bed settled down and I came fully awake. The dusky light of early dawn filtered through the shades. Chairman Meow purred at my feet. He seemed unaware of my still-reverberating nightmare. *So much for pet intuition*, I thought. I sat up and scratched his favorite spot behind his ears. He started drooling and we both went into the kitchen.

I prepared his favored chicken with carrots Friskies, stirred with a little water and nutritional yeast, and made myself French toast with scrambled eggs. I savored my last meal and cup of coffee. Every condemned man gets a last smoke, at least according to the old Westerns. So I made a pipe from an old zucchini, found a jar of organic Blue Dream that I got during a recent trip to the Russian River, and enjoyed the last smoke of my life.

PART TWO

12 The Visitation

*As far as I'm concerned, there won't be a Beatles reunion
as long as John Lennon remains dead.*
—GEORGE HARRISON

*Ghosts don't haunt us. That's not how it works. They're
present among us because we won't let them go.*
—SUE GRAFTON

I looked outside my window to see the Haight just waking up. The night residents were going back to their hidden hovels to sleep off the day. Lights were switching on in the coffee shops. In a few hours, the locals would put on their whimsical costumes for another freaky day of working in the Haight.

I sat on my couch and decided to write a suicide note to my brother and friends. It ran five pages long, full of metaphors and poetic attempts to lighten the load of my decision. I read it through a couple of times and found it rambling, incoherent, and insincere. "Shit! I'm too high. I shouldn't have gotten high!" I said out loud.

"Fuck!" The Chairman yawned. He'd seen me like this before.

Irritated at myself, I tore a new page from my notebook, grabbed a Sharpie, and after a songwriter's life swollen with words, wrote the shortest suicide note ever. "Dear Friends and Family, Like Stephen Stills said, 'Everybody, I love you!'" I walked across the room and taped it to the inside of the front door.

I wrote other notes willing items of value to various people. The Post-its appeared as little flags of surrender hanging limply around my apartment.

I scanned the rooms, noting they were dirty and in disarray. Feeling a pang of guilt, I grabbed the Johnny brush and got to work. I figured the least I could do was to not leave a mess. It's one thing to cheat God, but quite another to leave your friends to clean up after you.

After hours of sativa-fueled cleaning, I opened the case of my big Guild F-50 sunburst guitar and fished around for my lucky Richie Havens pick. He gave it to me after a gig one time, saying, "Jimmy, never write a set list. Just know your first and last songs, close your eyes, and feel the rest. The audience will tell you."

I held the pick in my hand. It was bowed from ferocious strumming and felt warm to the touch, as if he'd just been playing with it. He was the coolest, most spiritual person I'd ever met in the music business. I would hold the pick on my plunge from the bridge as an homage to his amazing energy and rhythmic brilliance. "I'll see you in Heaven, Richie," I said as I put the pick in my pocket.

I decided to will my guitars to Guitars Not Guns, a charity that gives guitars to low-income kids. That would piss off my brother. He wanted them, but not being a guitar player, he'd just hang the guitars on hooks and never play them. Guitars are wormholes to other universes—not wall hangings, for Hendrix's sake!

I sat in my easy chair, noted the time, and was startled to see I'd frittered the whole damn day away. *Too stoned*, I thought. The setting sun cast a kaleidoscope of rosy colors through the window. It was time. No more delays, no more distractions, no more housecleaning, no more overthinking it. No more weed, no more cat feedings, it was time to go.

I grabbed my black day pack. It was only then that I remembered the John Lennon glasses. I unzipped the pack, felt around, and found the package Wilshire Annie had made for me. There was the *Rolling Stone* wrapping paper with John and Yoko on the cover just as she'd left it. I lifted the Scotch tape, pulled out the silver-rimmed glasses, and held them in my hand. They, too, felt warm to the touch and seemed to vibrate a bit.

My eyes moistened as I held the glasses. I was no longer angry with Lennon. Annie was right. He was doing what he did best—write songs. I just followed along. I decided to wear the glasses when I jumped off the bridge as a final tribute to the songwriter who had so influenced me. Besides, they would be part of my final disguise before I exited my body.

I unfolded the glasses and carefully, lovingly put them on . . .

On my sofa directly in front of me sat a cocky boy of about fifteen, his penny-loafer-clad feet on the couch, hands behind his head. He wore a red checkered shirt, sleeves rolled up, and sported a lanky, greasy replica of an Elvis pompadour.

He eyed me teasingly and in a youthful English accent said, "That was quite a dream you had last night. Very phallic the way that building came out of the sea." Seeing the shock on my face, he held up his hand and said, "Wait! James! Please don't take the glasses—"

Before he could finish speaking, I stood, thunderstruck, and shook my head violently. The glasses flew off and skidded across the floor, hitting Chairman Meow, who hightailed it under the bed.

I looked back at the couch, but it was empty. Warily, I approached the glasses, muttering, "This is crazy, this is so crazy . . ." Still, that kid, he seemed so familiar. I got down on my hands and knees and nudged the glasses with my index finger, half expecting them to shock me, but nothing happened. I picked them up. They felt even warmer now.

"Spooky!" I whispered to myself. I leaned back in my big easy chair, putting the glasses on my lap. The room was still and empty, just the low rumble of five o'clock city traffic seeping through the windows. Chairman Meow returned, glancing this way and that to see if the scene had cleared. I blurted out, "Curiosity killed the cat!" In terror and anticipation, I put the glasses back on and felt the hair on my neck stand at attention.

This time with his face inches from mine and looking *seriously* annoyed was the same kid, a few years older now, with faux-Elvis hair and sideburns and wearing black jeans and a short-sleeved white shirt with a skinny black tie. He leaned into my face, nose to nose, and said, "You can't hide from me forever, James. Please leave the bloody glasses *on*."

I couldn't take it. I ripped off the glasses, once again in shock. I could hear him saying, "No! Shite!" as he disappeared. Again, I paced around the room, holding the glasses at my side. "Oh my God. Oh *shit*! That was John fucking Lennon!" I exclaimed to the cat. "A young John Lennon, for sure. But it was him, and the other kid too—like how he looked in his first band the Quarrymen." The Chairman blinked at me sympathetically. He didn't really believe me, all he wanted was a little more half-and-half.

I had the sinking feeling that my suicidal ruminations had pushed me over the edge into insanity. Instead of flying off the bridge in an epic death plunge, I would spend the rest of my days in an institution hallucinating John Lennon. I remembered *A Beautiful Mind*, the movie about John Nash, the Nobel Prize–winning economist and schizophrenic who dealt with his apparitions by ignoring them. I steeled myself to do the same, and slowly put the glasses back on.

I glanced around the room. John Lennon was back on the couch. This time looking very much a young man, smoking a cigarette and wearing a gray Nehru suit with his gleaming black Beatles boots propped on my coffee table. "You know, James"—he took a puff and exhaled—"I have eternity, but your life here on Earth is bloody short, so would you please leave the fucking glasses *on*? We have bloody work to do."

"Work to do?" I asked, trying to stay calm, but teetering on the edge of hysteria.

"That's right. You need to keep it together and leave the bloody glasses on. Haven't you noticed I get older every time you remove them? And in case you forgot, I didn't live that long."

"Only forty years . . . ," I said, squinting my eyes, expecting him to disappear at any moment.

"That's right, only forty years, practically a child, really. Please remember, each time you take the glasses off, the sooner we say goodbye. So, listen to me! First thing, *relax*. You're not crazy."

"I'm not crazy?" I repeated, not believing him.

"Heavens no! Look. You survived the bloody music business for all these years without going crazy. So, you're not crazy now. This situation is what we in the spiritual trade call a visitation." He smiled broadly and searched the room for an ashtray.

I handed him an old abalone shell I'd found at Point Reyes. "A visitation?" *Wow!* I thought, *I just handed the apparition of John Lennon an ashtray!* He flicked his ashes into the shell, where they settled for a moment, then vanished.

"That's right, James. A visitation. You're a lucky man! I've been sent on a mission to revive and inspire you!"

"Inspire me?"

He leaned forward and regarded me intently. "Yeah! To *inspire* you. You've got to stay the course. This killing yourself shit has got to end. You're overthinking your life, man. Your bloody ego has turned on you."

"My ego has turned on me?" How convoluted! I was getting psychological advice from a ghost!

"Yes. Your ego has turned on you because it didn't get what it wanted, and egos eat what they can't have, James." Lennon scowled at me, suddenly seeming much older.

"What did it want, John?"

"Oh, come on, man! You *know* what it wanted. It wanted you to be a famous rock star. Like me!"

For a crazy apparition, he had excellent insight.

"You!" He pointed at me accusingly. "*You*, my friend, cannot take the easy way out. Unlike me, a short exit from this world is not in the cards for you." Another lit cigarette appeared between his fingers. He took a drag and blew the smoke toward me, but I couldn't smell it.

"All right, supposing I'm not crazy, what are we going to do?"

"We're gonna write some songs. That's what we're going to do. We're going to write some bloody songs together. But first we're going to get high." He flashed a mischievous smile.

"I'm already high. Can ghosts get high?"

"I'm not a ghost, James. Ghosts are boring. I've seen 'em; they're just as deluded as people. Now me, I'm a cosmic emissary, a phantom on a mission. And no, I'm not talking about getting high on dope. I'm talking about going high up on the Golden Gate Bridge. You know, to where you almost threw it all away yesterday. We have to start there."

"The Golden Gate Bridge? You know about that?" Cold fear raced down my back. I'd been so distracted by the apparition of Lennon that I'd completely forgotten about jumping off the bridge. The thought of it now turned my stomach. "The bridge?" I asked again, feeling nauseous.

"That's right, James. You've been falling for years. Anyways, it's no wonder you've been thinking this way. I can hear the air rushing out of you even now." Lennon pointed at my chest and said, "Close your eyes and listen!"

I closed my eyes and heard a small rushing of air, like a pin-prick in an inner tube, coming from my heart. I covered my heart with my hands, and now I could feel it rushing through my fingers. Panicked, I turned to Lennon for an answer.

"Don't worry." He blinked his eyes and the leak stopped. "I just wanted to show you what's happening. You're bleeding out. All the conviction and hope you felt as a young songwriter is blowing out of your heart. I'm here to patch you up and get you rolling again. Old tires *can* still roll, James."

He put a sympathetic hand on my shoulder, which I couldn't feel, and gestured toward the door. "Come on now, it's time to go." He reached inside his Nehru jacket, pulled out a harmonica, and blew a run reminiscent of the beginning of "Apple Scruffs" from George Harrison's *All Things Must Pass*. I followed him out the door and down the stairs into the colorful chaos of the Haight. He blew enthusiastically on the harmonica, a rock 'n' roll pied piper. He walked straight into traffic, jamming away as the passing cars cruised right through him.

13 Falling

Don't fall for someone who's not willing to catch you.
—ANONYMOUS

It was tough. I wanted to believe him. I wanted to believe this cocky young man in a Nehru suit with the boyish smile clomping down Haight Street in his Beatle boots. Was he truly an emissary from the afterlife coming to save me from myself? As crazy as it seemed, a small hope winked to life inside me, a pilot light sparking in an old gas stove.

I fixed my eyes on Lennon, who was delighted to be back in San Francisco. I asked him in a whisper, "Are you sure it's okay to walk and talk with you in public?"

"Sure, nobody else can see me, and with all the local crazies walking about these days, people will just think you're mental like everybody else. Or you could put in your—what do you people call it?—your blue teeth and pretend to be on the phone."

"You mean my Bluetooth?"

"Yeah, yeah. Whatever it is you people put in your ears these days."

We walked down Haight Street to catch a bus to the bridge. People were oblivious to John's presence whenever he poked his head right through a door or brick wall to have a look around.

"Fascinating!" he quipped. "Tie-dye lives! I smell the incense, the crazy clothes, but where's the love? Everyone's acting so cool and aloof, and they're all lost in their phones. Where did all the flower children go?"

"I guess you haven't been in these parts for a while," I replied, trying to appear as if I were talking on my Bluetooth.

"No. It's been a while and not since I've been dead. I remember George had a terrible time here during the flower power days. All he found was a bunch of drugged-out hippies looking to grope or rob him."

"That's right. I felt so let down by them when I read that. What do you think of the Haight now, John?"

"Well. It's bloody commercial and full of vanity as far as I can see, but it's a damn sight better than where I've been lately."

"Where was that, John?"

"For some reason, most of you 'John Lennon was wrong, woe is me, I'm gonna kill myself' types live in backwater places. I've been to Bakersfield—bloody hot there; Fargo—bloody cold there; Winnipeg—too many mosquitoes. The Haight is at least—shall we say—interesting. I'll give it that."

We both gawked at a young woman walking past us wearing what appeared to be a tuxedo top and a poofy red tutu. As she passed, we saw she was totally naked from behind. "A bit out of the box around here, isn't it," I commented.

"Yes, James, but when everybody's trying to be out of the box, that's a bit of a box too, isn't it?"

"Fair enough," I assented. As usual, Lennon could see all the way around the subject. We couldn't help but gape as she sauntered past. The young woman gave me a stern look that clearly said to mind my own business, completely unaware of Lennon. I cast my gaze to the sidewalk, embarrassed, while Lennon laughed, saying, "Now, there's an outfit you won't see in Omaha. How do her clothes stay on, anyways?"

We both laughed. The banter with Lennon was starting to normalize. I began losing myself in it. I liked it. Insanity is seductive. It pulls you in a bit at a time.

"So, John," I asked casually, as if I'd hung out with him all my life—which in a way I had—"do you ever get back to New York, London, or Liverpool?"

"No. Sadly, I can only go where the client I've been assigned to goes. I've never been back." His young eyes turned downward for a moment. "I'd love to go to New York again, but I've had no assignments there."

"You mean you have to stay with me?"

"Oh yes, as long as you're wearing the bloody glasses, I have to stay close. We in the afterlife refer to souls like yours as magnets. You are the magnet that holds me here. I just follow you around like a bloody paper clip. I go where you go." I could see the frustration in his face. Lennon was *not* fond of rules.

"Well, unfortunately, it's gonna be a boring ride with me, too, 'cause I'm goin' nowhere." It felt good to air my misgivings and pessimism with him. Given his cynical nature, I thought he would understand.

"But you *are* on your way somewhere, Jimmy boy." He gave me a wink and yet another lit cigarette appeared between his fingers.

"Where do you keep getting those cigarettes?"

"It's a reward for promoting world peace while I was on Earth."

"God gives you cigarettes for promoting world peace?"

"Yeah, that's right, and many other perks. But don't worry, James, a great thing about being dead is you can't get cancer or any other Earthly disease anymore."

I laughed and realized Lennon's company and his natural sarcasm had sidetracked me from my original suicide mission. All I wanted to do now was to keep talking with him. I wanted to talk music and life as we watched the sun go down from a beach. I wanted a bromance! How ironic that my waxing insanity would strive to keep me living, while just a day before I was ready to throw it all away.

I winced and said, "So, you think we should still go to the bridge?" I was hoping he'd say no. I was enjoying his company, even if it was all in my head. I had no desire to end the delusion prematurely.

"Yes, James, it's essential. You've got to go back to the point where you almost ended it. But don't worry, we'll get something bloody special out of it. I promise!"

The 22 Fillmore squealed to a halt, and we got on the bus. Lennon took the window seat and studied the San Francisco hipster scene. "Blimey! Look at all the young people. They're everywhere."

"It's the millennial generation, John. Bigger than the boomers. Nearly ninety million of them in America alone."

"So, who's their Beatles?"

"They haven't got one."

"Why not? Many of them look like we did in the late '60s."

"They have total access to every song ever made and every group, alive or dead. With so many radio stations, podcasts, and YouTube videos, not to mention social media platforms—Facebook, Twitter, Instagram—their whole cultural universe is fragmented, shallow and constantly changing."

"Podcasts? Whose tube? Insta-what?" interrupted Lennon, perplexed.

"YouTube, John, it's all related to the internet. Some people call it the World Wide Web."

"The inter what? The World Wide Web? Sounds like a bunch of bloody spiders having sex. Sounds overwhelming."

"It is. Especially if you say the wrong thing and end up at the bottom of a virtual dogpile. Young people spend a huge amount of time curating their image and comparing themselves to their peers."

He looked perplexed, as if I were speaking a foreign language. I had no desire to talk tech with John Lennon, but he was intrigued. "Look, John, the world has changed, and the music business is way different from when you were alive. A mass audience like yours was created by a few big radio and television networks that every kid listened to. That's all gone now. Music is free for the most part and dispersed over thousands of sources. I doubt a supergroup like yours will ever surface again."

Lennon knitted his brow and looked down at his boots. "Kinda sad, don't you think? I mean, people can really come together over a band."

We fell silent as Nineteenth Avenue rolled by. What a different world it must seem to someone who died in 1980. So much more fractious. Maybe a new Beatles *will* arise someday, and a latter-day Lennon will emerge writing songs that galvanize a future generation. But right now, in the year 2019, it wasn't happening.

I pulled the bus cable and Lennon shot out the door, setting a brisk pace. He took a deep breath. "Ah! I forgot about the smell of eucalyptus around here! It reminds me of being back in bloody Australia. Oh God! That bloody Pacific tour." He shuddered. "Now, *that* was the fucking tour from hell, I tell you! We stopped touring after that, you know."

"I know, John. It's all on the internet."

"I'd like to see this internet thing sometime. Sounds bloody fascinating!"

"It is, John, it is. You're all over it."

Lennon was like a kid on his way to an amusement park. He bounded up the walkway toward the bridge. I hallucinated that we were both in a scene from the movie *Help!* I struggled to keep up.

"Whoa! It's chilly up here!" I said, shivering and hunching my shoulders against the wind. Lennon was unfazed by the cold Pacific fog that whipped about and cut through my shirt.

"Hang in there, James. Adrenaline will soon keep you warm." He nudged my elbow playfully.

Adrenaline? I thought. *Why'd he say* that?

About a third of the way across the bridge, he asked, "Where's the spot you almost jumped? The spot where those Japanese tourists interrupted you?"

"Hey, how'd you know about that?"

"It's a bit complicated, but there are forces on the other side that created that distraction, giving me extra time to contact you. I was in transit. You remember? You saw me coming the first time you put the glasses on."

"You mean it was you who blinded me in Annie's mirror? You were in that ball of light?"

"Yeah! I look pretty cool that way, don't you think?"

"That scared the shit out of me, John! So, you know Wilshire Annie?"

"Oh yeah. She's a spiritual operative, dispersing talismans—in this case, the glasses—so that 'Great Balls of Fire' like me can do our stuff."

So. Annie's a part of this. I should have known. I was really losing myself to this insane story. With all its friendly intrigue and camaraderie, it was fun, but it felt too strange to be comfortable. I only gave myself a fifty-fifty chance I would survive this trip on the bridge. Beneath all the Lennon distraction, I could still sense my death wish sharpening its teeth.

We approached the midpoint of the span, exactly where the Japanese tourists had accosted me the day before. This time there was no one in sight. The sun was going down. The sky was suffused in a golden amber light. Lennon peered out at the Pacific Ocean, breathing in the sea air, a young rock star in his prime, the world his oyster. You could almost hear teenage girls screaming "*John!*" in the distance.

"It's gorgeous up here. Fantastic view. Even better than in Near Heaven."

"Near Heaven?" I asked, feeling a growing sense of vertigo with each step.

"The place I'm from, Jimmy boy. The Outskirts of Heaven, a kind of spiritual suburbia, I call it the Brigitte Bardo."

"A counterculture guy like you existing in a spiritual suburbia? That doesn't seem right, John."

With flushed cheeks that betrayed his cool demeaner, he replied, "That's right. I'm stuck at the mall, trying to buy me way up the escalator, and you're going to help me."

"You're speaking in metaphors now, right?"

"Right! Isn't that what we songwriters do best? Look. There's a way down." He pointed at a place between two metal beams. "Let's climb down there."

Lennon started climbing over the barricade, motioning for me to do the same. I followed him with a growing sense of dread at each step.

We got to a level spot on a metal walkway, and I surveyed the sea. The view was absolutely staggering. It hit me hard in the gut. I closed my eyes and my knees started knocking.

Lennon laughed and began cajoling me to open my eyes. He sang a line from "I've Just Seen a Face" on the album *Rubber Soul* to try to cheer me up. "*Fallin', yes, I am fallin', and she keeps callin' me back again,*" he crooned. "Normally I don't sing bloody Paul McCartney songs, but this one seems appropriate, doesn't it?" He tried again. "You know, if Paul wants to, he can think. This line was really good." He sang, "*The love you take is equal to the love you make.*" His attempt to lighten me up had the opposite effect. "Come on, James. Open your eyes!" he yelled.

Reluctantly, I complied. Lennon playfully jabbed me in the shoulder with his elbow, though I felt nothing. Wisps of fog raced under my feet. The whitecaps were far below, sharpened teeth ready to tear me apart. I struggled to tame my bladder, but fear had turned it feral. I had to admit, though, that the warm pee felt good flowing over the goose bumps on my legs.

"Don't be embarrassed," Lennon said, noticing my damp pant leg. "I've pissed me pants many times. Now, come on. Don't be afraid. Look down, James." I glimpsed downward and instantly threw up, horrified at the distance from the catwalk to the sea. The cold breeze blew droplets of vomit onto my shirt while the rest descended and disappeared.

Lennon continued, unfazed, "Done that too. No worries, man. Okay. You can close your eyes for a moment. I have something to tell you."

I gratefully closed my eyes, not wanting to stare down any longer, feeling nauseous and unsteady. He leaned in, so I could hear him over the wind, and sang a lovely line of verse into my numb ears.

"*There are times in life when the road is clear, when you've found your passion, and love is near, like a river knows how to find the sea, you flow with purpose so easily.*"

I opened my eyes. Teeth chattering, I asked, "Is that a new song, John?"

The wind whipped his Beatle bangs around his smiling face. "No, James. That's *your* new song! You just haven't written it yet. You'll have to give me cowriting credit, though." He paused, then pointed at a seagull flying by. "Look! It's a sign!

You're a bird, not a bloody turtle. You're meant to fly, not hide inside your shell!"

I watched the bird soaring skyward. Lennon stepped close and apologized. "Sorry, mate, but this must be done." He grabbed me, and for the first time I could feel his fingers— cold, steely appendages sinking into the flesh of my shoulders and reaching into my soul. Then, effortlessly, he threw me off the bridge, shouting, "*Goo goo g'joob*," as I flew over the edge. I screamed and began falling the 245 feet to the blue Pacific.

14 The Happy Rishikesh Song

All you need to do is say this little word, I know it sounds absurd but it's true, the magic's in the mantra, will give you all the answers, just swallow this, that's all you gotta do.

—JOHN LENNON, "THE HAPPY RISHIKESH SONG"

John Lennon and George Harrison—unshaven, shaggy, and serene—had conjured comfortable warm, flat stones in Near Heaven on which to sit beside a holographic river that reminded them of the Ganges. They were playing guitars and singing campfire songs like they had in 1968 when they journeyed with Donovan, Mia and Prudence Farrow, Mike Love of the Beach Boys, and others to Rishikesh, India—the Gateway to the Himalayas, the Place of the Sages—to learn Transcendental Meditation from the Maharishi Mahesh Yogi.

It had been a hip trip suggested by Pattie Boyd, George's first wife, who later married Eric Clapton. She inspired such great songs as Clapton's "Layla" and "You Look Wonderful Tonight," as well as Harrison's "Something" from the *Abbey*

Road album. They sang a medley of "Camptown Races" and "She'll Be Comin' Round the Mountain," with "Jingle Bells" thrown in for fun. They finished with "The Happy Rishikesh Song," a satirical little ditty Lennon wrote about Transcendental Meditation, describing it as a pill you take in the morning to solve all your problems and make life beautiful. Lennon had explored many philosophies but remained militantly iconoclastic and was perennially skeptical of dogma.

The faux Ganges flowed peacefully on its way to the dreamtime conjured city of Rishikesh. In the muted views of Near Heaven, the Himalayan foothills behind the city were washed-out facsimiles of the real thing. Cute monkeys worked the shoreline and tropical birds sang in the trees.

Lennon's and Harrison's Beatle cuts were grown out now as they, and a whole generation of young people, abandoned haircuts and shaving altogether in the late '60s. India had embraced them, beards and all, and so did Near Heaven.

Harrison shook his shaggy head, smiled, and then winced. "So, John, did you really throw Jimmy Drake off the Golden Gate Bridge?"

"Well, only his astral body of course. You know. To crack him open."

"He certainly needed that, but you do realize the shock of astral projection, especially at his age, could have stopped his heart."

"It was a risk I was prepared to take, George. An old songwriter like Jimmy has a shell on him thicker than a Tory. It was a real nutcracker, but we got it off!" Lennon seemed quite pleased with himself.

"Did he return to his body intact?"

"No problem. Pissed his pants, threw up on himself, but no worse for wear. A moment after he hit the water, he shot right back into his body. He was in and out of consciousness like everybody else on Haight Street that time of night. But I guided him home."

"He's asleep now?"

"Yes. And loaded with experiences to write about. He'll need a bath when he wakes up, that's for sure. I felt sorry for the people on the bus ride home! He reeked!" The lack of a smile on Harrison's face deflated Lennon's enthusiasm. "Hey, Georgie, you don't seem too inspired by me efforts."

Harrison's face went dark, and he furrowed his black eyebrows. "Oh, sorry, John. No, it's not that. You've done an excellent job so far. I'm a bit distracted, that's all."

"Distracted by what? What's the matter, George? Are you getting bored slumming around with us postmortals in Near Heaven?" Lennon smirked at his own joke.

"No, I like spending time with you even in these mediocre environs," George quipped back. "No, it's something else. I have news that's going to blow your postmortal mind."

"Oh. A ghost story, is it?"

"Worse. It's about physics and universal rupture."

He told Lennon about the Black Chord and its nefarious intention to delete music from this universe. He told him how God was calling an army of musicians to stop its progress. He told him about the masterwork they must compose collectively to heal the rupture. He told him that his guardian angel had specifically said, "We need Lennon at the front!"

"That's the craziest thing I've ever heard, George, either in or out of the body!"

"I know it sounds crazy, but just look at Earth. You can see something bloody weird is going on down there. Look how we both died. You by a bullet, me by cancer and a madman's knife while I was recovering. We did what we could to write songs about universal love to encourage a peaceful planet, but the aggression goes on and on and keeps getting worse. To really stop this thing, we've got to go to its source and take it on there."

Lennon stood up and skipped a flat stone across the river. It hopped to the opposite bank, turned around, then hopped back to his hand. "Tell me more, George." He skipped the stone again.

Harrison told Lennon all he knew of the Black Chord. About how its universe contained only wormholes of darkness and how it feasted on the stars, music, and light of other universes like our own. He told him that Earth was its first planetary target, and an easy target at that. He explained that the cacophony created by all manner of human sound—both pleasant and not—spills into space forming a sonic beacon. For being such an aggressive, know-it-all species, human beings are cosmically naive.

Harrison regarded Lennon as they both listened to the simulated Ganges flowing softly by. After a few moments of silent contemplation, he spoke. "Earth is a canary in an extremely dark galactic coal mine and it's about to stop singing."

Lennon, ever the feisty one, took this as a call to action. "Well, come on then! There's no time to waste. I'll strap on me Rickenbacker and off we go!"

"I've always admired your bravery, John, but you still have to finish your deal with Jimmy Drake. He's a part of this too."

"The whole bloody universe is at stake, and you're sending me back to Earth to help an old songwriter?"

"That's right, John."

"But he's never even had a hit. He has no influence and probably never will."

"God works in mysterious ways. Heaven needs you badly, but you've got to work out your karma with James Drake first. He's the main Earthly connection in the coming struggle with the Black Chord. He's at the far end of the chain between the living and the dead, pulling you in at a time of great personal and cosmic crises through the love of *your* music. Renew him, John, and a great healing can begin for you both."

"How's that, George?"

"God has chosen you and James Drake because you're both holding back *love*." Lennon shifted uncomfortably and skipped the stone again.

Harrison continued. "*Love* that could be used to help the universe. Anaïs Nin was right when she said, 'the only abnormality is the incapacity to love.' You're both caught in the surf of your own resistance. You each have the gift of channeling light but stay wrapped in a cloak of fear. You each find comfort in a cave of cynicism when you have the power to break free and fly. *If* you can save each other, that reservoir of love you are both repressing will be released. James Drake will lead a revival in songs about universal love that will inspire hope and faith and spark movements to heal the human psyche, reshape cultures, and heal Earth. But *only* if you can get through to him. If you can't . . . well . . . all is lost."

Lennon stopped skipping the stone and gazed at the faded Himalayas in the distance. With no hint of sarcasm, he said, "*Fucking hell!*"

 **15** Four Seconds, 245 Feet, 75 MPH

I have no fear of falling. But I hate hitting the ground.
—THE BADLEES, "FEAR OF FALLING"

You don't drown by falling in the water. You drown by staying there.
—EDWIN LOUIS COLE

I *can't* believe it! John Lennon just threw me off the fucking Golden Gate Bridge!

Time turned elastic. In the first second of my fall, all I noticed were the physical effects of hurtling through the air at seventy-five miles per hour. My cheeks, nostrils, and eyelids puffed out like mini parasails, all doing their best to slow me down. My shirt and pants flapped wildly in the wind. Looking down through a blur of tears, I saw the whitecaps coming closer.

In the next second, I flipped out of my body and saw the back of my own head from fifty feet away. I saw myself splayed out, poised to do a mortal belly flop onto the gray-blue asphalt of the Pacific Ocean.

During the third second of my fall, I glanced right, and *there*, flying next to me and smiling, was John Lennon in his gray Nehru suit. Shouting to be heard over the wind he said, "James, remember *this*. A good song is a good song. You can jazz it up all you like, or not. If the song is solid, it'll stand!"

I thought, *I'm about to die and he's giving me songwriting tips!*

The final second, we both hit the water, thunderclapping into the sea. Underwater, I rushed back into my body, amazed to be conscious. And there was Lennon floating next to me, still smiling.

"James, like I told Bowie, say what you mean, make it rhyme, and put a backbeat to it!"

I'm about to drown and he's name-dropping? I was furious! I wanted out of this crazy delusion more than I wanted to live. I opened my mouth and shouted, "Fuck you, Lennon! You misled me! You killed me!" But only muffled air came out. I watched my last precious breath rise in big silver bubbles to the surface.

Lennon smiled and pointed at the bubbles, saying, "Look! There goes your last breath. Now you can start over." He held my shoulders and locked eyes with me. "Now listen carefully. This is *very* important. Write a couple of songs before contacting me again. Not before. *Remember!*" He reached out as I floated downward, into the depths, and snatched the glasses from my face. He disappeared mouthing, "Remember!"

I watched the light from above dimming quickly. I felt a stabbing coldness as my crumpled body sank the 377 feet to the ocean floor. The murky outlines of the wreckage of the SS *City of Rio de Janeiro* dubbed the "*Titanic* of the Golden Gate" came into view. I had read about the 19th-century iron-hulled steamer that sank in 1901 within ten minutes of hitting submerged rocks in dense fog, killing 128 of the 210 souls aboard, mostly Chinese and Japanese emigrants. With horror, I drifted toward the outstretched skeletal arms of the long-dead passengers. Then . . . everything went dark.

16 Catching Clouds

You'll never meet a greater adversary than your own potential.

—FROM SEASON THREE, EPISODE ONE ("EVOLUTION"), OF *STAR TREK: THE NEXT GENERATION*

I dream I am in the International Space Station floating in the command module with astronaut Sally Ride. She looks like a friendly Medusa, her hair sprouting wildly in all directions. She points out the window and says, "Jimmy, everything in the universe is falling toward everything else. We're not circling Earth. We're falling toward it, just as Earth falls toward the sun. Gravity is love, and everything, *every*thing, Jimmy, falls in love—even you." She motions toward another brilliant sunrise, one every ninety minutes, emerging over the cerulean Caribbean Sea. "Here comes the sun . . . again, Jimmy!"

I woke to the morning sunlight streaming through my bedroom window. I felt groggy. "Here Comes the Sun" played
on my clock alarm just as it had each day for as long as I can
remember. I ached all over. At the foot of my bed, Chairman
Meow squinted at me sideways, nose twitching, probably
wishing I would take a bath.

Feeling fuzzy and disoriented, I sat up slowly. A moment
later, memories of the previous day came flooding back. The
glasses, the appearance of John Lennon, Lennon throwing me
off the bridge, the sea in my lungs. It all came rushing back.
But how did I get home? How did I even survive? I wondered.

The glasses! Where are the glasses? I rummaged around the
bed. "They're gone!" I said out loud as a post-nightmare chill
spread down my spine. "The whole goddamn experience was
a dream! A crazy, exhausting, wet-the-bed kinda dream!" I
studied my cat. "That explains it, Chairman Meow. It was all a
fucking dream!" The Chairman stood and arched his back, his
sign for me to scratch his ears. And there, folded neatly under
his belly, were the glasses.

I picked them up. They were warm to the touch. I held them
for a long slow minute as creepy-crawlies slithered down my
spine. But not being one for suspense—and expecting the
worst—I put the glasses back on.

I braced myself to see the rock star, the guy who inspired
me, the guy who threw me off the bridge. But John Lennon did
not appear. I peered toward the sofa where the young Lennon
had previously materialized. I combed my apartment, but it
was empty. I removed the glasses, cleaned the lenses, then put
them on and took them off a couple more times. Nothing!

"A dream," I muttered, "just a dream." A protective delusion. Some crazy psychological construct. I took the glasses off and placed them on the coffee table. As I stared at them, my eyes filled with tears. I *missed* the crazy construct. I *missed* Lennon. I guess I'd rather live in my own delusional, wacked-out world than deal with the real world anymore.

Right then, as if to rescue me from my own thoughts, my nose took charge. I reeked. I headed to the bathroom to clean up from the misadventures of the night before.

Removing my clothes, I decided I must have had a psychotic break on the bridge and soiled myself and then somehow made it back to the Haight. I was glad not to be in jail or a psych ward. It felt good to be home.

I ran a hot bath and slid down the tub's sloped English backside. *The Brits really know how to make great tubs*, I thought as I submerged my head.

I enjoyed a second or two of blissful silence, but then remembered the sensation of being underwater, choking and drowning. I felt the opening salvos of a panic attack. Just as I was about to bolt from the tub, I heard a faint harmonica melody, like the one Lennon had played as we walked on Haight Street the day before. The sound grew louder, distracting me from my panic. It was a joyful melody. I felt a pain in my chest and realized I was running out of air. So I sat up and the harmonica tune instantly vanished. *No!* I took a deep breath and slid under the water again. The melody returned and grew in volume. I heard a bright and lively guitar part reminiscent of George Harrison's rhythm guitar work. The lyrics Lennon had sung in my ear while on the bridge flashed through my head. And as simple as that, a new song erupted in my heart.

I sat up abruptly, sending a mini tsunami wave splashing to the floor. I jumped from the tub, hastily toweled off, and found my lucky Richie Havens pick in the pocket of my soiled jeans. I grabbed my guitar and sat naked at the kitchen table— just as I did in my early twenties—while a songwriting fever took hold.

Catching a song is akin to catching a cloud with a butterfly net. It requires stealth. You must sneak up on it and coax the ether into your net. A song formed about losing gravity, becoming lost, falling. It sang of the perils of failure and missed opportunities. But like fledgling birds, we fall before we fly. We need to open our wings, trust the air to buoy us, and keep at it.

The song skewered me. It shone a light on me, revealing my resistance and loss of hope. It exposed my fear of failure. In my avoidance of sinking, I'd lived my whole life in shallow water, a timid fish hiding among the coral. From now on, I would come out of my hole. I would swim. More than that, I would fly!

All these thoughts spun through my mind as I played the song again and again. Like Jackson Browne, who tormented his roommates by playing new songs over and over, I played my new song all afternoon, probably driving my neighbors nuts. Once I've written a song, I play it until it's in my DNA. By evening the song was part of me, as if it had always been there. I called the song "Falling."*

---

* Listen to "Falling" at JohnLennonsGlasses.net.

As the sun went down and the songwriting fever passed, I returned to my body. The room felt chilly, and I was painfully hungry. It was only then I realized I was still naked. Something soft and furry brushed my leg. It was Chairman Meow, offering congratulations on my new song. The first one in over a year. He remembered that new songs meant a happy and generous human. Together, we walked to the kitchen for food and half-and-half. I saw the note willing Chairman Meow to Marcy and Gustavo taped to the bag of cat food. I tore it off, crumpled it up, and threw it in the recycling bin. I wasn't going anywhere. I was back!

17 Is It Too Late for Hippies?

If you're not barefoot, you're overdressed.

—HIPPIE PROVERB

Richie Havens sat on an old wooden stool in Nearer Heaven holding his holographic Guild D-50 guitar as if it were a lover. His right hand was a blaze of rhythm. He barred a quick succession of chords with his long left thumb singing, "*Sometimes I feel like a motherless child! A long way from home, a long way from home.*" A nearby field of tall blond wheat listened intently. Havens was in a deep trance playing impossible counter-rhythms. Opening his eyes for a second, he nodded to his accompanist to take it away.

George Harrison leaped onboard with a masterful slide guitar solo as the wheat pulsed to each note. For miles in all directions, the golden wheat swirled and rushed to the soulful rhythm of the song.

His ivory tunic soaked with sweat, Havens nailed the song's climax, singing passionately, "*Freedom, freedom, freedom!*" his right hand a blur of a blur. Harrison joined in a final rush as the wheat rejoiced, bounding out of the ground, roots twirling in the open air for a moment before returning to the soil.

Laughing, Havens and Harrison both hit a big open E chord and finished on a seventh, giving the folk power tune a lounge feel. They bowed to the wheat, which was drooping a bit sadly now that the song was over. Havens rose to his feet, his six-foot-six frame slightly stooped from years of playing guitar. He contemplated the resplendent vista, holding his long-fingered hands together in a prayerful gesture of appreciation. "Thank you, thank you, my golden friends. We're going to take a break now. But we'll be back, so stay rooted!" The glowing grain stood upright in happy anticipation.

"Ah, thank you, George. It's so good to play that song again. I haven't done it in a while."

"Great song, Richie! When you played it at Woodstock, I think it scared the hell out of Nixon and the conservatives."

"Yeah, well, I'm afraid when we were younger, we thought it was cool to scare the squares. But fear always creates a backlash, doesn't it? We should have been more inclusive. We had a chance to turn the conservatives on to our vision. Maybe if we hadn't been so arrogant and impatient, they would have feared us less. Who knows, maybe we could've sent in the hippie goddesses of our time and gotten them high! Instead, we saw them as the enemy. We had our noses up our tie-dye asses." Havens shook his head at the lost opportunity and rolled a joint with his elegant fingers.

Harrison nodded. "I guess we were just young and full of ourselves. From what I see, humanity hasn't figured out whether it's a competitive or collaborative species."

"True enough. But in spite of all the divisions and constant squabbles, there is compassion and kindness at the core of humanity. Did you know that Max Yasgur, a conservative, rented his dairy farm as a venue when the town officials of Wallkill, New York, got cold feet and pulled out of the deal with Howard Mills Industrial Park a month before the festival? And when the festival ran out of food, people from the Republican towns of Bethel, White Lake, and Smallwood—who were opposed to the festival—came to the rescue by raiding their own pantries. Those communities made and delivered sandwiches to the hippies, who were too young, stoned, and unprepared to live in a cow field for three days."

Harrison sat up straight. "I'd forgotten about that."

"It'll take centuries, George. But here's the deal: the dominant force in our universe is dark energy. It's an expanding liberal universe, not a shrinking conservative one. That's why conservatives are so afraid of change. They know on an instinctive level that the dynamic of the universe is set against them. They're cosmically outvoted. But every once in a while, dark matter, the more conservative force, has its day, slowing things down, letting things coalesce. Otherwise, this expanding progressive universe would pop as easily as a soap bubble. There'd be no planets, no solar systems, no galaxies, no life—only relentless expansion. That's the consequence of too much progress too fast."

"But isn't the balloon *already* popping, Richie? What's happening with that rupture, the Black Chord?"

"It continues to expand through subspace faster than the angels predicted. It has discovered Earth's hum and is emitting a dissonant anti-E-minor harmony that will amplify discord on the planet. People are feeling an impending sense of doom and hopelessness. There is growing anxiety as societal systems deteriorate. In the meantime, dystopia flourishes in movies, literature, and the media. We're running out of time, George. But the troops are massing. Has there been any progress with John?"

"The initial news is good, though John's radical methods leave the outcome a bit inconclusive."

"His radical methods?"

"Apparently, in an attempt to crack open Jimmy Drake's cynical shell, John threw Drake's astral body off the Golden Gate Bridge."

"He ripped away his astral body? With *no* warning?"

"John thought the element of surprise was needed in this case."

Haven's eyes grew wide. "Terrifying, man. But in a way, refreshing and original. That's John for you. So, how's Jimmy doing? He's not a young man anymore, you know."

"Well, his body's no worse for the wear. John's convinced that the near-death experience will get him writing again. That's all I know."

"Well, George"—Havens smiled, puffed on a joint, and blew the smoke toward the wheat fields, and the heavenly grain sucked it up for a contact high—"maybe John's radical methods are what we need right now. We don't have time for half measures."

"I guess we'll have to trust that John knows what he's doing. Hey, Richie, do you think it's too late for hippies like us?"*

* Listen to "Just a Hippie Thought" at JohnLennonsGlasses.net.

"You mean on Earth?"

"Well, yeah, but anywhere really. I mean, we grew our hair long, preached nonviolence, and marched for peace. But it eluded us on Earth and now there's trouble here in the afterlife. Will things ever settle down? Can true peace ever exist?"

"The universe will never settle down. At least not this one. God's too restless, too creative. Sometimes I think she's got a case of cosmic ADD, but you gotta love her. She's a spirited deity. Peace is relative. And like everything else, it appears from time to time, then moves on as the structures of reality tumble."

"The Beatles had the ears and hearts of an entire generation. We preached peace. Do you think we were naive believing we could bring peace to Earth?"

"No way, man! You were warriors! My old jazz buddy Joe Gallivan used to say, 'Old hippies don't die. They just lie low until the laughter stops, and their time comes round again.' No, George, it's not too late for hippies. In fact, like that old song by one of my favorite San Francisco bands Those Darn Accordions said, 'Them hippies was right!'"

18 A Bathtub of Dreams

Songwriting's a weird game.

—KEITH RICHARDS

Cold and starving from hours of composing and playing guitar, I got dressed and made myself a peanut butter and jelly sandwich. From the kitchen, I could see the Lennon glasses where I had left them on the coffee table. Chairman Meow was sitting right next to them, seemingly aware they were special. In my songwriting fever I had completely forgotten them. Holding my breath, I put the glasses on. Lennon did not appear. All in all, I tried them on at least three times to no effect.

It was then I had another memory—something Lennon said to me underwater during my last breath after he threw me off the bridge. He said, "Write a couple of songs before contacting me again. Not before." The memory slapped me upside the head. Maybe he wouldn't appear until I wrote a second song. I had to write a *second* song to find out if the glasses were real. It would confirm or deny if I was dreaming, delusional, or if, fantastically, I was being haunted by and badgered into songwriting by a dead rock star.

I was shivering and needed to warm up after sitting naked for so many hours writing "Falling." So I ran another bath and put on my old vinyl Beatles *Revolver* album. I sat in the hot water feeling quite pleased with myself. The glow of a new song was flooding me with serotonin. All songwriters feel this rush. It's the best drug there is, humming your own song.

I sang along with Paul McCartney on "Got to Get You into My Life" while I waited for my favorite song, "Tomorrow Never Knows," the last track on side two of the time-honored album, to begin. Lennon wrote the song on LSD after reading *The Psychedelic Experience: A Manual Based on the Tibetan Book of the Dead* by the three kings of psychedelia in the late '60s: Timothy Leary, Richard Alpert, and Ralph Metzner.

The song's use of electronic effects and backward looping was innovative then and still sounds fresh today. I listened to the vinyl popping between the tracks and anticipated the opening sounds of the psychedelic masterpiece with its crazy-sounding crows and Indian harmonium. Just as the crows started cawing and Lennon sang, *"Turn off your mind, relax, and float downstream,"* I slid deeper into the water and submerged my head.

Underwater, I could still hear the bass thrumming through the tub and Lennon singing, *"This is not dying. This is not dying."* In an instant, more memories of my last breath under the bridge returned. I began to choke as a suffocating panic attack welled from the blackest depths of my subconscious. I thought about Elvis, Lenny Bruce, Jim Morrison, and, hell, even the popcorn king, Orville Redenbacher. They all died in the bathroom. Maybe I was next. I sat up and almost leaped out of the tub, but heard Lennon singing from the turntable, "*Lay down all thoughts. Surrender to the void.*" So I did.

I remembered a hard-won insight from my lifetime struggle with panic attacks. The body's fight-or-flight hormones conspire to create a feeling of dying. Panic attacks are little rehearsals for the ultimate act of leaving the body permanently. I shouted out loud to darkness, "Fuck it! Let's die!" and slid back under the water.

It was then, as "Tomorrow Never Knows" was ending and Lennon was singing, "*Play the game existence to the end . . . of the beginning . . . of the beginning,*" that I felt the song pulling something out of me. Maybe it was just oxygen deprivation, but the song reached inside me and another new song materialized.

I could hear a trippy intro in a suspended A key. I felt as if I'd entered a river of cascading images and emotions that spoke of the vastness of existence as it squared itself against the minuteness of our tiny lives. I wanted to stay underwater longer to listen to the song, but I was running out of air. I sat up to take a breath and the song disappeared. *Fuck this holding my breath shit!* I bolted from the tub, leaving wet footprints down the hallway to my bedroom closet. I dug around until I found my old snorkel. I returned to the tub and stuck the yellow snorkel in my mouth, splashing water everywhere as I hastily submerged myself again. Immediately the song returned! I remained underwater, listening to the song unfold, until the water was lukewarm and my skin was wrinkled and pruned.

I sat up and removed the snorkel from my mouth. In the living room, I could hear the needle of my old turntable scratching the label on the record. *Shht. Shht. Shht.* The arm had lost its return function years ago, but because of its sentimental value, I never replaced it.

I got up, toweled off, put the turntable cartridge back in place, and shut the unit off. This time I remembered to put clothes on, then deliberately walked to the kitchen table, where all my songwriting stuff was still scattered. I sat down and in less than twenty minutes another song spilled out of me. The panic attack had morphed into a blaze of creativity. I was in a state of bliss as I finished the last verse. Once again, I was rewarded with the dopamine rush that follows from pushing through a panic-induced near-death experience. Every terror has its silver lining if you stick with it.

I called the song "Deep Blue Sea" even though I knew both Jimmy Dean and Pete Seeger had written songs with the same title.* My song explored a number of mysterious states inspired by a lifetime of dealing with existential anxiety and by my near-drowning experience with John Lennon. I played the song all evening, working out the guitar parts until, at midnight, my neighbors pounded on the wall for me to stop. Being musically inspired can be quite irritating to others. I made a note to do something nice for them.

My fingers were sore and my voice was ragged, but I felt great. I hadn't felt this good in years. I knew it was crazy, but the whole time I was writing, I sensed Lennon was watching me from some quantum place. With two new songs under my

* Listen to "Deep Blue Sea" at JohnLennonsGlasses.net.

belt, I vowed to put the glasses back on in the morning. Though, considering what happened the last time he visited, the thought of contacting him again gave me the heebie-jeebies.

Chairman Meow smiled from the couch, jumped down, and executed several enthusiastic figure eights around my legs with his furry orange Maine coon body. He knew I'd finished another song and was rewarding me for my efforts. He also knew completing a song was his cue to be fed.

He was the perfect cat for a songwriter. Waiting patiently for his Friskies and half-and-half until my creativity ebbed. I vowed never to give him back to my ex-girlfriend Marcy and her asshole boyfriend Gustavo. That Latin Casanova may have the sticks, but I had the stones—my songs. And I was ready to throw them out into the world again.

I fed Chairman Meow, scratching him between his ears as he chowed down. Hearing him purr calmed me enough to realize I was exhausted. I made a cup of Sleepytime tea and swallowed a few sips, then fell asleep on the couch watching the Netflix documentary *Life on Our Planet*. David Attenborough's voice lulled me to sleep as it had many times before.

PART THREE

19 Proxima Centauri

The cosmos is also within us. We are made of starstuff. We are a way for the cosmos to know itself.
—CARL SAGAN, *COSMOS: A PERSONAL VOYAGE*

The little red star Proxima Centauri was preparing to host more entities than it ever had in its four and a half billion years of existence in the Milky Way. It was ripening like an ovum. The multitudes that would soon gather in its ruby-red plasma were mostly the souls of passed musicians—which was a bit odd.

Red dwarfs, the most common stars in the universe, are low heat and relatively small. Immortal and stable by stellar standards, they last far longer than stars such as our own capricious yellow sun. Though hard to see from a distance, red dwarfs are where most of the spiritual action is going on in the universe. Only 4.3 light-years from Earth, Proxima Centauri was an ordinary red dwarf, but something strange was going on.

As part of a trinary star system with Alpha Centauri A and Alpha Centauri B, Proxima Centauri had long ago learned how to sing with its two larger siblings. The three had been harmonizing together for eons and their songs attracted soul travelers to this isolated part of the galaxy where stellar music was less dense. An interplanetary way station as vital as a gas station in the middle of a desert, the three Centauris supplied spiritual sustenance for infinitudes of souls.

Lately, however, something was interfering with the way the three stars "sang." Something was making the stars tone-deaf. Like Crosby, Stills and Nash at Woodstock with a bad monitor mix or almost any show by the Grateful Dead during their drug years, the three stars' harmonies started sounding off—almost atonal.

Unfortunately for Proxima Centauri and her brother and sister, they were in the immediate path of the Black Chord where the rift between the universes had been breached. It allowed the Black Chord to regurgitate vast amounts of dark matter from its own universe to neutralize the voices of the three stars. These particles of dark matter are known to scientists by the acronyms WIMPs and MACHOs, meaning "weakly interactive massive particles" and "massive compound halo objects," respectively. They were bombarding the trinary star system relentlessly, annihilating harmony and paving the way toward the primary target—hypermusical Earth and its big blond sun.

The spiritual horde that would soon infiltrate Proxima Centauri was currently gathering in the center of the star known as Sol, or more commonly known as the sun. Although he hadn't been in Heaven long, Havens had adapted to a pure plasma reality faster than most souls. He was there, in the middle of the sun, to fast-track the recent arrivals. Aretha Franklin and Dr. John were in shock at being dead and having been placed so suddenly in the middle of a crisis. It was a lot for a soul to take in, and Havens was there to blunt the blow and orient them.

Many joyous introductions and reunions took place as souls intertwined and danced in the sun's undulating yellow-orange plasma. Havens's favorite was with David Bowie, who seemed genuinely delighted and well-suited for a life without a body. "We will be holographic heroes!" Bowie quipped.

Meanwhile, in Nearer Heaven, away from the action, George Harrison began to tire of playing ragas with colors and tawny fields of wheat. Many of his old friends had already left. Even his recently arrived friend, Tom Petty, had taken the Spiritual Express to the growing assemblage at the center of the sun. Harrison had been hoping to hang out with Tom and share a few Traveling Wilburys stories, but after learning about the Black Chord, Petty was convinced it was linked to an arsonist's setting fire to his house in 1987. Harrison knew his friend would "not back down."

Petty was all business. "Bad vibes, man. Comin' after musicians. Gotta go fight 'em." And off he went.

Harrison felt helplessly stymied by the karmic drama going on between Lennon and Jimmy Drake. As Lennon's guardian angel, he was tied to the relationship. He couldn't go anywhere until it was resolved.

He raised his arms to a sky so lovely any average Earthman would buckle at the knees at the sight of it, and offered a prayer, "Please, Lord; please, Vishnu. Help John Lennon and Jimmy Drake achieve success in whatever form that might take."

He felt a rising irritation at his old bandmate, like in the old days on the road when they were cranky and exhausted, just kids really, running from gig to gig. "Why has John been such a laggard in moving on?" he pleaded to the sky.

Irritation has no tether in Nearer Heaven. It doesn't last. A distant clap of thunder sounded the answer. "Yoko!" it boomed. The name echoed down the canyon, growing dimmer as it trailed away. *Oh!* Harrison thought. *That makes sense. I should have known! He's waiting for Yoko.*

20 The Mother of All Dreams

Remember you are half water. If you can't go through an
obstacle, go around it. Water does.

—MARGARET ATWOOD

"Anyone who believes in indefinite growth on a finite planet is
either mad or an economist. We need to kick the carbon habit
and stop making our energy from burning things." David
Attenborough's urgent but gentle voice droned on from my
television, but I was already fast asleep on my couch. My system of "documentary sedative therapy" had worked again.
Star Trek reruns were also quite effective at helping me fall
asleep, but nothing worked better than David Attenborough,
the alpha sandman of sending me to dreamland.

I sit cross-legged on the banks of a mountain stream as it cas-
cades white and frothy down a mountainside. It is morning
and clouds of mist rise from a deep green forest of alders and

pines. Beautiful crystal dewdrops hang everywhere. I look up and see one drop hanging from a leaf ten feet over my head. It glistens in the sun and falls off the leaf toward me. Time slows as I watch it glide downward, a tiny prism of water, swirling and glowing with all the colors of the rainbow. With a splash, it lands between my eyes. A diamond coldness penetrates my mind and engulfs my consciousness. I fuse with the drop and roll with it off the end of my nose and into the stream below.

I forget everything except the sensation of movement and light. I rush forward, laughing and playing. I am in the moment with no awareness of who I am, what I am, or where I am going. I don't care. I am young. I delight at being alive.

The mountain stream empties into a larger stream with deep pools. For a moment I slow down, hover above a trout, then rush on, relishing the speed of the stream. I merge into a succession of larger and deeper streams and feel the current slow.

Thoughts return. *What the hell is going on? Where's my fucking body?* I realize I am dreaming. I remember being told if you can find your hands in a dream, you can control it. I search for my hands. All I see is water. I try to open my eyes. My eyelids feel glued together. Feeling that I'm drowning, I panic and moan.

I hear a voice with an English accent say, "For Christ's sake, James. You're just having a lucid dream. *Go* with it, man!" I relax.

I enter a powerful river and feel a deep sense of purpose. I am a river in my prime, a surging force to be reckoned with, carving continents. I am strong and free.

Now I taste salt and notice a change in buoyancy. With an epic rush, I meld with the sea. The current stops and I sense myself expanding. I feel ancient, boundless, and wise as all the streams and rivers of Earth return and become one with me. I perceive the moon pulling on me from outer space and intuit that I cling to the planet like a tear to a cheek.

The sun beats down on me. I feel its heat as I rise to the surface as a molecule of water. The heat intensifies. I shrink to an infinitesimal point, then explode off the surface of the sea. As I evaporate, I recognize that my transition from liquid to gas is death.

I float upward, commingling with a cloud. I drift across the delta and join other clouds. We turn dark and brooding as we huddle against the mountains waiting our turn to cross its jagged peaks.

There is a flash of light, booming thunder, and a sense of falling through air. I land as a raindrop between the eyes of my body still sitting cross-legged on the bank of the mountain stream.

I opened my eyes to the early-morning darkness and felt around the couch for the remote to turn off the TV. A furious rain pelted the windows of my apartment. A pineapple express weather system was drenching Northern California.

Still in the hinterland between wakefulness and sleep, I basked in the afterglow of my dream. I had glimpsed lifetimes within lifetimes. With a deep sense of reverence and interconnection with all life, I comprehended both my significance and my insignificance. I knew I was safely embedded in the endless tapestry of existence.

Feeling liberated and calm, I picked up my guitar, sat down at the kitchen table, and listened to the rain. I thought about the individual drops, how each had its own story to tell. A story of transformation. A ballad spilled out of me like the river in my dream. It compared living and dying to the elemental changes of water. I called the song "In a Drop of Time."*

I emerged from another songwriting-induced trance, astounded to have written a third new song. I wondered again if Lennon was watching me from some unearthly place. I laughed. A crazy thought in a field of crazy thoughts. An even heavier rain pounded the windows. An atmospheric river was hammering the Haight. It was winter in California, but spring had blossomed in my soul. I might be nuts, but I was flowering. And to quote Ian Anderson in "Aqualung": "Flowers bloom like madness in the spring."

---

* Listen to "In a Drop of Time" at JohnLennonsGlasses.net.

21   From a Pineapple Express to a Bomb Cyclone

The fishermen know that the sea is dangerous and the storm terrible, but they have never found these dangers sufficient reason for remaining ashore.

          —VINCENT VAN GOGH

A pounding on the wall interrupted my playing my third new song in less than twenty-four hours. My poor neighbors— a couple of millennials from the Midwest who came to San Francisco to join the hipster tech scene. They were sweet kids into music and the environment, but lately I was testing their limits. I checked the time. Six a.m. I must have been at it for at least two hours. I examined my scrawled lyrics. To my surprise, the song made sense even though I had written it half-asleep.

I was writing again! Nothing means more to me than writing. An overwhelming feeling of appreciation for John Lennon filled my heart. It may have only been in my head, but when he threw me off the bridge, he saved my life!

I felt solidarity with bipolar people who refuse their meds. I wanted badly to see Lennon again and hoped I was still crazy enough to do so. I was afraid regaining my sanity might put a stop to this psycho Lennon shit. It was time to put the glasses back on and find out. By his own rules I should be able to see him now. I had written three new songs! *He should be proud of me*, I hoped.

My skin prickled as I eased the temples of the glasses snugly behind my ears. Wide-eyed, I checked out the room. No Lennon. I looked toward the sofa, where I'd seen him as a teenager the first time. No Lennon. Only the crushing sight of my empty couch staring back at me. I shook my head, saying, "No, no, no. I *want* to be crazy. Sanity *sucks*. Come on, John. *Where the fuck are you?*" Nothing happened. It was just me and Chairman Meow in the dim, empty room.

Dejected, I sat down and reached to take the glasses off, when I heard a wry chuckle from the bathroom. "I had to see it for meself, James. Using a snorkel to write a song underwater in the bathtub. A bit daft, but surely original! Something Keith Moon woulda done. I used to leave the telly on at half volume while I was writing, but this takes the cake."

Out of the bathroom walked John Lennon looking twenty years older, his baby fat gone, face leaner yet more interesting, hair shorter. He was clean-shaven and wearing a fur-lined jacket with a dark sweater and his signature thick glasses. He looked like he did in the pictures taken just before he died.

He walked over and sat next to me on the sofa. "Are you surprised to see me in me middle years? Well, you shouldn't be, you loon. You kept putting the glasses on and taking them off again like we had all the time in the world. Each time I aged a little more. So—I'm afraid this is our last visit."

"*Last visit?*" My mind and tongue stumbled to keep up with his sudden reappearance and startling statement. "Last visit? I'm—I'm—I'm *sorry*, John. I forgot what you told me under the bridge, and I doubted any of this was real."

"Oh, it's *real* all right, Jimmy boy. And with a little help from your friends, you died, came back to life, and found your way back to your true self. Look at the result!" Lennon smiled and clapped me on the back, though I couldn't feel it. "You've written three good songs, man. You're on your way back!"

"You heard my new songs?"

"Well, yeah, I've been listening in."

"How were you able to do that?"

"Through your lucky Richie Havens guitar pick, James. I have to thank you because you solved a bloody riddle that's been driving me crazy."

"A riddle?"

"Yeah. Now I know who George's guardian angel is."

"George?"

"Yeah, that's right. George Harrison. Didn't I tell you? He's my guardian angel. Does that surprise you? Even on Earth he was pushing me into the bloody spiritual stuff. Now he's helping me work out my karma and get my reluctant arse to Heaven."

"How does he do that?"

"He puts me to work with clients like you. I could hear you writing songs through the Richie Havens guitar pick. It's a sound talisman with some serious mojo, so don't ever lose it."

This afterlife stuff was giving me a headache. "I'm confused! So, George Harrison is your guardian angel and Richie Havens is George Harrison's?"

"That's what I suspect. There's a ridiculous number of irritations waiting for you when you die. Since you gave your life to music, there'll be a bunch of characters from the bloody music business waiting to welcome you on the other side. They'll pester you to climb the stairway to Heaven as if it was a bloody Billboard chart."

"The stairway to Heaven? What's Led Zeppelin got to do with it?"

Lennon rolled his eyes. "Never mind. Listen, James, we're running out of time. We can chat about all this later. Eternity waits for deeper explanations. Let's stay focused on your so-called return from the dead and your new songs."

"So, you like my songs?" Being praised by my songwriting hero gave me a dopamine high.

"Well, yeah, they feel like you. They're good, but there's more stuff coming, so don't rest on your laurels, man. And, oh, like I said, you'll have to give me songwriting credit for that 'Falling' tune. I did give you that first verse after all—before I threw your fucking astral body off the bridge."

"But people will think I'm crazy saying John Lennon co-wrote the song. What if Yoko sues me?"

"That's *your* problem, James. Besides, you think you're mental anyways." Lennon smiled a sad smile, then fell silent staring out the rain-streaked window. A lit cigarette materialized between his fingers. He took a drag and blew the smoke toward the glass. It diffused through the cracked window and melded with the rain.

"What's the matter, John?"

"I need to ask a favor of you. I need to go somewhere. Somewhere only you can take me."

"Where's that?"

"I need to go back to New York City."

"New York City?"

"Yeah, I need to see Yoko one last time."

"New York? Yoko? Really?"

While my mouth was hanging open, he continued. "It's a little after 6:00 a.m. right now. If we fly this morning, we can be there in time for her evening errands. You'll have to buy two seats. Sorry. I have no material substance, but I find it very disconcerting to think of someone sitting on top of me in coach. A window seat, please. This may be my last aerial view of Earth."

"What! You want to go now, John? *Now?*"

"James, this is our last visit. You and I have a limited time together. I helped you find your way back. Now it's *my* turn. I'm the one who needs to find me way back. I've been at sea for an awfully long time. And Yoko has always been my harbor. She still is. Yoko is me in drag. Just give me one last chance to tie me ropes to her, mate!"

"Will she be able to see you?"

"I don't know. I need to go there to find out. I'm sure she'll be able to *feel* my presence, at least. I need to be with her one last time before I join the supposed *great battle* in Heaven."

"The great battle in Heaven?"

"I can't talk about that right now, James. Can you just get me back to New York? Can you please get me back to see Yoko one last time?" Lennon pleaded, looking vulnerable for the first time.

John Lennon! My imperfect hero. An icon for a whole generation. In the end, just another fallible, insecure human who tried his best to wake up the world and leave it a more peaceful place. I had to help him.

I picked up my laptop and googled "cheap flights SFO to New York City." The results included weather advisories for both airports. A pineapple express was already pounding San Francisco and something called a bomb cyclone was heading for New York City. There were lots of cancellations, so I easily found two seats on United and charged them, maxing out my credit card. "Okay. We've got a 9:00 a.m. flight reserved on United from SFO and a seven-fifteen reservation on the Super Shuttle to the airport. We better get going!"

"You did that all on that on your top-lap, then?"

"Laptop, John."

"Laptop. Laptop. Yeah, amazing! Thank you!" At the prospect of seeing Yoko, Lennon's mood lifted dramatically. He started humming the Sinatra classic "New York, New York."

I googled the satellite weather pictures and saw huge weather systems converging on both coasts. Once again, I felt myself being pulled into the danger zone by my imaginary new friend. From a pineapple express to a bomb cyclone. It would be a bumpy ride to find Yoko. Lennon stared wistfully out the living room window, softly singing, "*It's up to you, New York, New York.*" I had to admit, he did a passable Sinatra.

22 The Mocha Bomb Incident

There is always some madness in love. But there is also always some reason in madness.

—FRIEDRICH NIETZSCHE

"So, we've got just enough time to get you down to your favorite breakfast place. It's going to be a long day, and I don't want you getting low blood sugar on me. Paul could be horrible when he was low blood sugar. Besides, I want to see that girl you've got a crush on." Lennon gave me a wink.

"Wanda? How do you know about Wanda?"

"I've been given information about things that are important to my client's future. Wanda figures in."

"But I barely know her. I've said maybe three words to her in the two years she's worked there."

"Yes, I know, and you go there a lot. *Don't* you, James."

I felt myself blushing. The waitress, Juliette Serri, or Wanda the Wanderer, as she called herself, was from France's Alsace-Lorraine region. She had crisscrossed the globe, allowing whim and circumstance to guide her. I heard her say to a customer one time, "People should wander and get lost on purpose just to see where they'll end up." A professional dancer, Wanda had wound up in the Haight two years after moving to San Francisco to study theater production and choreography. She regularly performed with a few experimental theater troupes. I attended a production once. I sat way in the back, too awed by her beauty and skill to approach. She was the femme fatale of the local coffeehouse scene. Demure but enthusiastic, with curly dark hair and a body sculpted by dance and running ten miles a day as a waitress. She had the German-tinged French accent of the region. She was totally out of my league and probably ten years too young, but every time I saw her, I felt a lunar tug on my cells.

I felt Lennon's eyes on me. "So, what's your excuse? Why haven't you asked her out?"

"When I was sixteen, the first girl I ever asked out turned me down. She gave me a look like 'Are you kidding me?' That set the template for all my future contact with women. I don't hit on women. I can't take the rejection. Women have to take an interest in me first. Besides, beautiful women get hit on all the time and I never want to add to *that* fucking chorus of frogs. Wanda's never sent me any signals as far as I can tell, so I never sent any of my own. I order my mochas, smile and chitchat for a few seconds, then sit down."

"Well, I'm here on behalf of the bloody universe to help you make it happen. She's been quite friendly with you, according to my notes."

"Oh sure. She smiles and laughs with everyone. She's an equal opportunity charmer. Totally guileless, but wise and genuinely happy. Every guy in the Haight has a crush on her, even the gay ones, and many of the women too. She treats me friendly, like she treats everyone. And oh, by the way, even if she *did* like me, there's the mocha bomb incident. And I don't wanna talk about *that*."

"The mocha bomb incident? Oh, come on now, James, never leave a rock star hanging. We can't take the suspense. What the bloody hell was that?"

"Okay. Well, a couple months ago I wanted to compliment her, so I learned a phrase in Spanish."

"But she's *French*."

"I know, I know. I'm such a dork sometimes, especially around women. Anyway, I learned the phrase, 'You bring light into the world,' cause it's true, she does. So, I practiced it a bunch and while I was paying for my mocha, I said, 'Wanda, *Usted trae la luz en el mundo.*' I felt very clever and pleased with myself."

"Well? What happened?"

"She looked puzzled for a second and said, 'Oh, I am sorry. I am French. I don't speak Spanish. Something about light, *oui*?' I am such an American idiot! Of course, French, not Spanish. I just figured if she knew French, she'd know Spanish. You know, like how Americans and Canadians and even Australians can understand each other? You *know*?"

Lennon interjected. "America truly is the most language-dyslexic nation on Earth, but the French know that. She's used to it. What's the big deal?"

"While I stuttered around feeling foolish about my botched Spanish, Wanda poured my mocha with whipped cream into my plastic bike bottle. I shook the bottle to mix the chocolate in better, which I guess released the carbon dioxide in the whipped cream and *bam*! It turned into a pipe bomb and sprayed mocha all over Wanda, me, and everyone within a four-foot radius."

"Brilliant, James! I'll bet that went over like a Led Zeppelin."

"Well, to Wanda's credit, she laughed and said, '*Pas de soucis!* It is a small thing. Don't worry about it. It was actually funny, oui?' Then she handed out towels to everyone."

"She sounds great! I can see why you want to be with her. What happened next?"

"I still wanted to explain my Spanish phrase to her, but fucking *Philippe* walked in the door."

"Philippe? Who's Philippe?"

"He's half Algerian and half French, the slimy lothario of the Haight. He's got those dreamy black eyes women always fall for, plus a man bun and one of those five-day beards that you know he spends fifteen minutes a day on. Anyway, he reeks mystery and machismo that's as strong as his fancy French cologne."

"He sounds like a Latin version of bloody Eric Clapton. What did he do?"

"He walked up to Wanda, put his hands over hers on the mop, and said, 'Oh, bella Wanda. Let me help you with that.'"

Lennon rolled his eyes. "Every generation has a version of *that* arsehole. But why didn't *you* offer to help her? It was *your* bloody mocha."

"I was still in shock from the thing exploding. And let's face it, John, guys like Philippe, they *always* get the girl. You remember. Paul got most of the screams from the girls."

"I remember! Sometimes I wanted to shout at those girls, 'Hey, what am I? Tiny Tim?' It especially irritated me if they were screaming for Paul during a song *I* wrote. Well? What *did* you do when Philippe showed up?"

"I slunk out the door like a jackal when the wolf shows up. And I haven't been back since."

"That's plain cowardly, James. But hey, look! You've got your mojo back. It's time to give it another shot."

I shrugged and grabbed two umbrellas. "All right, I'll give it another shot. But I think you're mental about Wanda and me." I handed him an umbrella and said, "I'm starving. Let's go!"

"I won't be needing an umbrella, but thanks."

We walked into the downpour. Lennon seemed delighted. I half expected him to start jumping up and down. The rain poured straight through him. He was dry as a bone, while I huddled under my umbrella, getting splashed by passing cars. *Here we go again*, I thought. *Another crazy adventure with John Lennon—my mentor, my muse, my murderer.*

23 Wanda the Wanderer

All that is gold does not glitter, Not all those who wander are lost; The old that is strong does not wither, Deep roots are not reached by the frost.

—J. R. R. TOLKIEN

Sprouting Out, with its black facade, gold trim, and black-and-white checkerboard flower boxes, was a favorite eatery among locals and the perfect companion to the hipster hotel next door. It prided itself on having any kind of sprout imaginable. My favorite dish was scrambled eggs with sunflower sprouts. When we walked in the door, Wanda was at the register. She smiled when she saw me and said with her killer French accent, "James. James Drake, where have you been? I see you have new glasses. They look good! It is my pleasure to tell you that ... you are a winner! *Toutes nos félicitations.* Congratulations!"

I didn't even know she knew my name and her enthusiastic reception stirred me in places I hadn't felt for a while.

Lennon was pleased. "See, James! It's already happening, man!"

I felt myself blushing as people turned our way. "I'm a . . . a winner?"

"Oui!" Wanda replied. "You won our business card drawing two weeks ago. Where have you been? You get a complimentary breakfast!" She gave me a vivacious smile that resonated somewhere deep in my DNA.

Lennon nudged me in the ribs with several short jabs, though his elbow passed right through me. "I smell French toast in your future."

It was hard to focus with Wanda smiling at me and Lennon teasing me from the sidelines.

"James!" she repeated, trying to get my attention. "You may have anything you want this morning." She paused and flashed a coy smile. "Within reason, of course!" Her laughter bubbled over, putting a smile on the face of everyone within hearing range.

Lennon leaned toward my ear. "I like this girl, James. She's deep, but light as a feather. Reminds me of Yoko! As usual, there is a great woman behind every idiot." He nodded in approval.

Wanda continued, "I hope you don't mind, James, but I looked up the web page on your business card and listened to some of your music. You sing about universal love, oui? It's so refreshing!"

Lennon gave me a thumbs-up and said, "See? This girl's got your number—literally!"

I gazed upon Wanda. Her eyes were shining with appreciation. I felt as if I were dreaming and was suspicious of how good things were going. I tried to catch up. "So, you, you like songs about universal love?"

"Oui!" She nodded. "We need songs like yours to bring us together. The world needs it."

"I agree the world needs it, but I'm not sure the music business agrees."

Lennon rolled his eyes. "Oh, God. Not that 'woe is me' shit again."

Wanda seemed genuinely concerned. She placed her fingertips lightly on the back of my hand in a tender but electric moment and offered, "The business of art is not art. We artists must remain true to ourselves whether the business world goes along with us or not. Let the world catch up with *us*!"

Impressed, Lennon commented, "She even *sounds* like Yoko!"

"*Sí, sí!*" I lapsed into Spanish again. "I mean oui, oui. The world can catch up with us."

"Oh, that's funny. I swear you Californians have Spanish on the brain!" Wanda laughed, then noticed the growing line behind me getting restless with our banter. She got down to business. "Okay. Two scrambled eggs with sunflower sprouts, home fries, avocado and salsa, no meat, and a mocha with whipped cream. Oui? No bicycle bottle today?" she teased. My cheeks bloomed red as I relived the humiliation of the mocha bomb incident.

"Wow! You remembered my favorite breakfast. And nope, no bicycle bottle today." I studied my shoes.

"Look, James, your favorite table is available." Wanda smiled again and pointed at what I thought of as *my* table, a corner booth with custom black cushions by the window. "Seems that everything is coming your way." She winked at me, clearly in command of our encounter.

I blushed again. There was no stopping it.

She lowered her voice and said reassuringly, "I love a man that can blush. It shows vulnerability—so lacking in men these days."

I turned crimson, absolutely sunburned by her interest.

Lennon led the way to the booth. "Come on, James. Let's sit down before you faint, get a hard-on, or start speaking nonsense in Spanish again."

We sat down and I inserted my Bluetooth so I could fake-talk on my phone. Lennon viewed me over the top of his glasses and sang teasingly, "*Dear Wanda, won't you come out to play?*" in a parody of the song he had penned for Prudence Farrow to coax her out of the meditation hut in Rishikesh, India.

"Oh, come on, John. She's never been *this* friendly to me before. Are you or some of your angel friends pulling strings from the other side? Tell me the truth."

"Not a one. I think that mocha pipe bomb fiasco must have broken the ice. Maybe Wanda's right. Maybe everything *is* coming your way."

"What do you mean?"

He leaned across the table and said in a conspiratorial voice, "Your karma has changed. You're reset. Things that stymied you before will give way for a while. Take advantage of it! Who knows? Maybe someday you'll be, as the queen would say, 'cheered to the echo.'"

"Cheered to the echo?" I said.

"Cheered to the echo?" Wanda came up behind me with my mocha. "Isn't that an English phrase?"

"Oh, hi, Wanda! I'm just talking on the phone with my English friend, uh, Nigel." I pointed at the Bluetooth in my ear and said, "He's talking about *The Crown*."

"*The Crown*?"

"It's a series on Netflix."

"Oui, I've heard of it. Well, say hello to Nigel and the queen! Sorry, James, I didn't mean to interrupt, but when you're finished, I have an idea I'd like to, as you Americans say, bounce with you?"

"You mean bounce off me?"

"Oui. But it would be so much better to bounce *with* you, James!" She laughed and smiled at me with bright green eyes that said, "Very funny." Her not-so-innocent double entendre elicited images of us entangled together on a squeaky bed. The sound in my head was so loud I think Lennon heard it.

"Bloody hell. This is moving faster than the angels predicted. James, we'll have to get you back from New York as soon as possible."

Wanda returned with my free breakfast. Her dark curls sprang as she walked briskly toward us. I pretended to hang up and removed my Bluetooth. "Okay, Wanda. What's your idea?"

"Yes, *merci*! Thank you for asking! May I sit with you for a moment?" She scooted next to me. She smelled of butter and baked bread, of green things and maple syrup. I found it hard to concentrate on her words with her so close to me.

"You see, James, I am the coproducer and choreographer of a new rock ballet called *The Neural Heart*. It depicts the heart as a thinking organ. We are looking for songs that sing about the heart and I think your songs would be parfait—I mean perfect! Would you be interested?" She eyed me hopefully.

Lennon's mouth fell open. "For Christ's sake. James, this *is* your Yoko. Your soul mate is reaching out to you, man. Say yes!" Lennon tried to pound the table with his fist, but it passed right through. Still, his intention must have had serious gravitas since the sugar packets fell off their tray. I was amazed Wanda didn't notice.

Lennon looked as if he might go postal any moment. It was seriously distracting. I gaped at Wanda, hesitant and confused, blinking my eyes in astonishment like Hugh Grant when Julia Roberts hit on him in *Notting Hill*. "The h-heart as a th-thinking organ?" I stammered, blinking furiously.

Wanda continued patiently in a soft, reverent voice. "Oui, James! In evolution, before there was a brain, the heart did the thinking. That is why they say, think with your heart. What do *you* think? Do *you* think with your heart?" She smiled sweetly and put her hand on mine, waiting for an answer.

"Well, I—I—I do try to center my emotions in my body. I've studied Kriya yoga and the Chinese Five Element theory. I've taken courses in Shiatsu massage, I've participated in kirtan, I've been to therapy—"

Lennon erupted next to me. "*Stop with the bloody New Age rambling, James, and say yes to this girl or I'll throw you off the bloody bridge again!*" He rose to face me, nose-to-nose, his torso sprouting from the center of the table. His eyes bored through me in a steely stare.

I was shocked at Lennon's outburst and surprised nobody could hear or see him, but it pushed me over the edge. "Yes!

Yes! Wanda, I'd be honored to help you. Do you know which songs you want?"

Wanda clapped her hands in glee and said, "I think we should get together and talk about these in person away from these distractions. Are you free this evening?"

"Oh, no. I'm sorry. I'm flying to New York. I've, I've got some, some gigs there. But I'll be back soon."

"*Sensationnel!* New York City! Wow! Well, James, when you get back, please call or text me. Here's my number." She handed me her card. It read:

JULIETTE SERRI
Know the way you wander, but lose yourself for sure
It's not possible to always feel secure*

Then she kissed me innocently on both cheeks, gracefully slipped out of the booth, and sprang back to the kitchen smiling.

Lennon seemed relieved. "I swear, James, you're so bloody reluctant. Are you sure you're not a fifty-year-old virgin?"

"Very funny! No, I'm not a virgin. I need to be certain, that's all."

"Well, there's *sure*, but then there's *thick as a brick*. I'd say you're the latter. We've got to go. Say goodbye to your soul mate. I'm gonna have a smoke. I'll meet you outside." He effortlessly passed through the wall and emerged on the sidewalk, cigarette already lit up. I took in the surreal image of John Lennon standing on a street corner in the pouring rain with a lit cigarette glowing through the gloom.

---

* Listen to "Know the Way You Wander" at JohnLennonsGlasses.net.

Wanda came by to check on me. I asked her to save the rest of my breakfast in a takeout container for the plane. Being an ecto-morph, I always starve on long plane flights. She returned a few minutes later and handed me a brown paper sack with my leftovers.

"So, James, I'll see you when you return, oui?" She sounded hopeful and a bit wistful. Like she wanted to go with me.

I saw Lennon looking at me through the window, still smok-ing his cigarette. At first, I thought he was flashing me the peace sign, but then I saw he was mouthing the word "virgin" to taunt me.

I'll show him, I thought. "Hey, Wanda. You know that Spanish phrase I said to you a couple of weeks ago? *Usted trae la luz en el mundo?*"

"Oui. Something about light."

"It means 'you bring light into the world.' And you truly do, Wanda. You truly do! You are so"—I searched for the right word—"radiant."

It was her turn to feel the heat as her cheeks flushed apple red. She lowered her head and said shyly, "I know what it meant. I looked it up. Merci! You as well. Never doubt the mes-sage in your songs. Without universal love, all that's left is self-love that spirals into narcissism, anger, fear, war, and darkness. Have a good tour, James."

I turned to leave as she greeted new customers with her trademark smile. As I neared the door, I noticed she'd written a note on the paper bag. It read: *Like John Lennon said, "Tout ce qu'il faut, c'est l'amour, all you need is love."* I glanced up from the bag to see Wanda the Wanderer waving at me from the cash register, saying, "Bon voyage, James!"

As I stood on the sidewalk under my umbrella, I felt a flood of desire for her. I wanted to go back in there, tell her my true feelings, pull her close, and kiss her deeply on the lips. But I felt a tug on my sleeve. It was Lennon.

"Hey! I *felt* that! How did you do that?" I said.

"I can move small items like sugar packets, sleeves, and such when I really need to. Sorry to stop you, old man. But we've got to stay focused. There'll be plenty of time for hanky-panky with the French girl when you get back, but right now there's a Japanese girl waiting for me in New York, so can we please get going? We'll miss the bloody shuttle. Oh, and regarding Wanda, on behalf of myself and all the other angels, I think I can now safely say—you passed the audition!"

24 Unpacking for Heaven

We are possessed by the things we possess. When I like an object, I always give it to someone. It isn't generosity—it's only because I want others to be enslaved by objects, not me.
—JEAN-PAUL SARTRE

George Harrison drank in the paradisiacal sights of Nearer Heaven one last time. The faraway mountains framed a landscape so lovely, no mortal eyes could take it in. Harrison's friend and guardian angel Richie Havens was helping him leave a place he had thought he might never leave.

Havens was sitting on an old wooden stool in a field of daisies strumming a big Guild F-50 sunburst guitar and singing a gentle version of a song Harrison wrote and Havens covered while on Earth. "*Little darling. I see the ice is slowly melting.*"

Havens stopped playing, laid the guitar down, and offered Harrison a few words of encouragement. "Look at the bright side, George. You've never seen the inside of a star before. That's where all the spiritual mysteries you've longed to see your whole life will be revealed. Once you get unpacked, you'll see what I mean."

Harrison seemed puzzled. "Get unpacked?"

"Unpacking to leave Nearer Heaven is rather the opposite of packing for a trip on Earth. There are no material possessions to take with you. No space suit, no cell phone, no toothbrush, no luggage, no backpacks, no sushi, no wine, no marijuana, no floss. That kind of baggage only gets in the way in Heaven. Unpacking to leave Nearer Heaven has nothing to do with material reality at all. You have to *unpack* to get to Heaven."

"What gets unpacked, then?" asked Harrison.

"It's the memories and the stories that need unpacking. Entering Heaven requires a clearing of old storylines. It's not what you take with you, it's what you leave behind. Souls don't have lungs, but they remember breathing. They have no beating heart, but they remember the blood pulsing through their veins. Souls have no physical body, but they remember broken bones, broken hearts, and shuddering orgasms. Memories and stories are the final husks a soul must shed before entering Heaven."

Nearer Heaven was the most sublime of the bardos—a reward for all the souls who strove to better themselves on Earth. Harrison had been able to easily conjure his Earthly memories while living in Nearer Heaven. But of all the bardos, it was the hardest to leave. It was a tender trap for the souls who languish in the memories of who they used to be. Rock stars in Nearer Heaven are especially vulnerable to that. How do you get over a life where a good percentage of earthlings worship and adore you? That's a difficult thing to let go.

Havens sensed Harrison's distress. "Stories and memories are formidable creatures with strong instincts for survival. They die slower than the flesh. They infiltrate the souls they've lived with and slow their progress to Heaven. But, George, a greater story is coming to sweep away what we thought was important. A story so vast it has universal repercussions. Are you ready to join that story? Are you ready to clear your soul for new heavenly experiences?"

Harrison scanned a vast field of golden flowers and held out his index finger. A beautiful luminescent blue butterfly with black borders landed on it. "I'm ready, Richie."

"Okay, George. It's a small step, but you gotta start somewhere. Say goodbye to butterflies."

Harrison held the butterfly toward the sun. It left his finger and flew straight up, merging with the light high overhead, then disappeared. Harrison closed his eyes and felt a sense of emptying as he unpacked the memory of butterflies and all metaphors connected with them.

"Very good. I know butterflies are cool, but doesn't it feel kinda good to not be attached to them anymore? I mean, they start out as big green maggots anyway."

"It wasn't that hard, Richie. I mean, I never wrote a song about them. Too stereotypical. Thank God I didn't write 'Dog and Butterfly.' I preferred moths actually."

"Moths and all other beautiful, romantic flying creatures have been cleared out of your storyline by proxy. That place you just cleared of butterflies is now free to take in other realities. Like the red plasma of Proxima Centauri. Compared to that, butterflies and moths are plain boring, man."

"You know, I do feel lighter. It's a weird feeling, like I've taken off a backpack after a long climb!"

"That's right. As you unpack, you get lighter. It's what we call the 'angelic effect.'"

"Let's try something else, Richie. How about marijuana? We can't be stoned and fight the Black Chord. Let's clear that out."

"Good idea! But before we practice on that, George—and I hate to bring it up—where's John? I thought for sure he'd have my buddy Jimmy Drake all straightened out by now and I'd see both you guys here."

"I've been waiting for the right moment to tell you, but I've got some bad news. John is still on Earth. He talked Drake into flying him to New York to see Yoko. I'm not sure he'll make it back in time."

"Oh no. *No.* He's coming back all right. We *can't* do this without him. We're tied to him. Karmically."

"Well, what can we do?"

Havens stroked his beard for a time, thinking of a solution to retrieve the reluctant rock star. "We'll do an intervention."

"An intervention?"

"Yeah! We'll intercept him on the way to the airport, create a space-time bubble, and throw him and Drake a party as a diversion."

"A party held outside of the space-time continuum. Brilliant! And what about that 'Great Open Mic in the Sky' you told me about?"

"We'll bring them along! A last big party before we all join the battle."

"Maybe we shouldn't unpack cannabis yet."

"Right! Good idea! We'll wait on that. But let's try another one. Hmm . . ." He regarded Harrison, who looked as if he'd just come from 1967. "Let's get you unpacked from, say, paisley shirts."

George scowled. "It's tough to let go of paisley, man."

"I know, I know. But it's good practice for the harder stuff later. All right, George. Take off your shirt."

25 Candlestick Park

*The ground generously takes in our compost and grows
beauty. Try to be more like the ground.*

—RUMI

The rain was falling in sheets as Lennon and I prepared to board
the Super Shuttle that pulled up in front of my apartment just
as we returned from the restaurant. The driver beckoned me
out of the rain and waited patiently as I stood on the bus stairs
and shook the rain from my umbrella, folded it, and tried to
stuff it into an outside pocket of my backpack. In my haste, I
dislodged a couple of crumpled bills, which fell to my feet.
In the dark, with so few passengers, the large bus felt empty
and spooky, a ghost shuttle rolling toward the Twilight Zone.

Back at my apartment, I'd shoved the two 100-dollar bills
I made from a gig a few weeks ago into my backpack and
quipped to Lennon, "Here goes the last of my money. Spent
on a ghost."

Lennon had brushed it off. "Don't worry, James. You're
gonna be thick with the stuff soon. Yes, unfortunately for you,

you're gonna be bloody rich and famous someday." He paused, then continued, "Enjoy poverty while it lasts because, mark my words, it gets worse when the money starts rolling in."

As I fumbled about to retrieve the now wet and dirty bills from the shuttle floor, the driver surveyed me with deep-set yellow-white eyes and black pupils. He had black-on-black skin, springy gray hair, and a faraway look, as if he wasn't really on the bus but staring at a vast inner horizon. I retrieved my wet cell phone from my other pocket. The driver scanned the QR code, then said in what sounded like an African accent, "You have paid for two. Is there more than one of you?" He peered behind me in the direction of Lennon, who was standing on the curb in the rain, bone dry as usual, taking a drag on a cigarette.

"Oh. No. Sorry. Only one."

He eyeballed me disbelievingly. "Really?"

"No, really. It's just me."

"Uh-huh." The driver seemed unconvinced. Could he see Lennon, I wondered? *Shit*, I thought. *I paid to give a ghost a ride to the airport.*

I got the sense he knew what was going on. I wanted to ask if he could see Lennon too. It would ease my fear of insanity and break my lonely isolation with the rock star. Who knows, maybe he would even give me a refund for Lennon's bus fare. Instead, I pointed nervously out the windshield at the deluge and said foolishly, "Lots of rain!" The driver said nothing, just stared ahead as if listening intently to an internal voice. I said louder over the storm and street noise, "I said, lots of rain!"

He turned his solemn gaze on me and said, "Where I come from, rain is a blessing." There was that African-sounding accent again, yet somehow different.

I felt lightheaded in his presence. Like I was getting stoned talking with him. "Are you from Africa?" I asked.

"No, my brother. I am from where we all come from—Pangaea."

"Pangaea? You mean the supercontinent from millions of years ago?" I asked, feeling that the world was dissolving.

"Yes!" he said with reverence. "The motherland. Where the *first* songs were sung." Seeing my confusion, he laughed and said, "I'm pulling your chain, man. I'm from Australia. Where the *second* songs were sung. Ha!"

I looked more closely at his face, then placed it. He had the distinctive features of an Aboriginal Australian, but he looked totally incongruous in his blue bus driver uniform.

"Are you a musician?" I asked.

"On *my* bus, brother, we are all musicians." He smiled mysteriously, turning his focus to the worsening rain beyond the windshield. "The storm is here. We have places to go, brother. Take your seat." He held the steering wheel firmly in his ancient, strong hands. His expression darkened. His smile was gone. "We have a long, long way to go."

"But we're just going to the airport."

"Yes. But it takes longer to go anywhere in the rain." The driver fell silent, his eyes fixed straight ahead.

I started toward the empty seats in the back of the bus so I could talk to Lennon in peace. Looking over my shoulder as Lennon entered the bus, I saw him exchange a furtive glance with the driver. Lennon averted his eyes immediately, then quickly slipped past the driver, who watched him in the rearview mirror all the way to the back of the bus. Lennon took the window seat and stared pensively through the glass.

"What's the matter, John?"

"That driver's a strange bloke, isn't he? Gives me the shivers!"

I lowered my voice, then put in my Bluetooth to fake another phone call. "Yeah, kinda. He definitely has a mysterious air about him. It seemed like he could actually *see* you! Did you notice that?"

Lennon continued to look out the window, avoiding my eyes. "No. I don't think he saw me. He might have sensed my presence, though. They say Aborigines live mostly in the spirit world, in Dreamtime." With that, he seemed to slip into his own dreamtime as the bus slogged on through the torrential rain and morning rush-hour traffic.

Thirty minutes later, I broke the silence and pointed out the window. "Hey, John. Check it out. That's where Candlestick Park used to be."

We were passing a soaked barren plain that brought to mind a ransacked Aztec pyramid site. The stadium was gone, the ground pitted with large excavations where thieves and contractors had taken everything of value. Poor well-meaning Candlestick. It destroyed the habitat of the bird it was named for; but in the fifty-five years prior to its demolition in 2015, it brought happiness to millions of raving sports and rock 'n' roll fans, and hosted luminaries including the pope. It was now mired in mud and stuck in something even worse—redevelopment limbo land.

"That's it? That's the site of our last gig in 1966? Fuck, man. What happened?"

"I don't know, John. I guess they figured they'd make more money with high-rise condos, offices, and shopping districts. And then there's the bone-chilling weather. That didn't help."

"Yeah, I agree. The Candlestick show reminded me of gigs back home. Bloody English weather, cold and foggy, and the sound was typically horrible. Did you go to the show?"

"Come on, John. I was only nine years old. But a friend of mine, who was twelve, got in with some older kids and told me all about it."

"Did he like the show?"

"He said the feeling in the air was truly manic and labeling it 'Beatlemania' was quite accurate."

"Mania is right! It got me killed in the end! So, what happened to your friend?"

"The concert changed his life. He was just coming into puberty. After hearing all those squealing girls, he went straight home and figured out the bass line to 'Day Tripper' on his father's strung fishing pole. Then he pestered his parents into buying him an electric bass for his next birthday. Music was his life from there on out."

"Yeah, well, that's because Paul got most of the screams. Bloody bass players! Without those girls screaming for Paul, there would not be nearly as many bass players!"

"Yeah, I suppose so. Did you know he played the last show held at Candlestick in 2014?"

"Well, that's cool. Paul was always smart with business, and he liked to play live more than the rest of us. A fitting way to end the stadium. 'Live and Let Die'—I'm sure he played that one!"

"Anyway," I continued, "my friend and I both chased after those screams for decades, playing and singing in bands. We got lots of applause and standing ovations, but the only time we ever heard a woman screaming was when a tarantula got into the concert hall at this rural venue in the California foot-hills called the North Columbia Schoolhouse. It started climb-ing up her leg during one of our songs and we thought—just for a second—there it is, a screaming female fan!"

"That's funny, James! Damn venue bug stories! All musi-cians have 'em. Well, kiss the ground you didn't have actual screaming fans coming after you. Those screams can give you night terrors. I'd take a tarantula over that!"

Lennon shuddered, remembering the Beatles' Asia tour. "Beatlemania was a very scary thing to live through, mate. When you face the blade of success, it cuts your head off. Those bloody fans tore my hair out for a fucking souvenir! Some of them would jump on your back like a bloody lioness trying to take down a zebra. It was frightening! And the press. What a bunch of bloody hyenas! I will tell you this, it's a wonder I wasn't shot on that tour!"

Lennon was remembering the Beatles' final tour. Candle-stick was their last stop after he had infuriated millions of religious zealots with his sarcastic comment about the Beatles being more popular than Jesus. He also made cheeky state-ments such as "I don't know which will go first: rock 'n' roll or Christianity." During a performance in Memphis on that last tour, someone threw a lit firecracker onstage. Everyone assumed it was a gunshot meant for John. Lennon saw his three astonished bandmates simultaneously turn toward him, each thinking some crazy radical Christian had just assassinated Lennon. Fundamentalists never got Lennon's irony. He was their musical Salman Rushdie.

"Oh well, at least I made it through that tour." A wistful expression crossed his face. "It didn't matter. I got shot anyways. I guess a bullet with me name on it was waiting somewhere down the line. You know you're famous when you have a stalker.* Until then, you're nobody, man." He smiled darkly in anticipation of my reaction.

The last views of the old stadium site rolled by through a curtain of rain. It looked sad. The pineapple express was hammering it down—just as time was battering the bulwarks of my generation, melting away our heroes, places, and stories. We had gone to those big arena shows, not just to scream for the Beatles and rock 'n' roll, but also to be together in the thousands and sing for a better world. It made us feel strong, as if anything were possible.

Lennon and I stared at the ruins in silence. A high keening wind pushed against the bus, echoing the sounds of the screaming fans from the venue's halcyon days.

Lennon let out a deep sigh of resignation. "Well, James, we all get plowed under. From what I've seen in life and the afterlife, the whole fucking universe is just one big composter."

I nodded sympathetically and muttered, "All things must pass." I lamented the loss of Candlestick and everything from those years that seemed like they should have lasted forever.

---

* Listen to "I've Got My Own Stalker" at JohnLennonsGlasses.net.

"All things do indeed pass," said a pleasant voice emanating directly behind us, scaring the bejesus out of both me and Lennon.

"I knew it. I *knew* it!" said an agitated Lennon without turning around. He lit another cigarette. "It's a bloody intervention!"

PART FOUR

26 The Shuttle of Angels

*Perhaps they are not the stars, but rather openings in
Heaven where the love of our lost ones pours through and
shines down upon us to let us know they are happy.*

—INNUIT PROVERB

I turned around and was stunned to see a smiling, bearded
George Harrison. Sitting next to him was Richie Havens in a
light-blue tunic, also smiling. Before I could react, they both
said, "Surprise!" and blew red party streamers in my face.

I stood up, dumbfounded. Havens leaped from his seat
and hugged me in the aisle. "It's so good to see you again, my
friend!" He held me by the shoulders and locked eyes with me.
I felt nauseous and began to swoon.

"No, no. Now, wait a minute, Jimmy. I know this is sudden,
but don't go freaking out on me, man!"

Havens was one of the few people who knew I suffered from
panic attacks. He remembered the time I opened for him at a
venue at a high-rise hotel in Hartford, Connecticut. The back
of the stage was framed by floor-to-ceiling plate glass windows

that looked straight down to the street ten stories below. As I took the stage, the flight impulse took hold. I wanted to run for the elevator but was trapped onstage, out of my body with fear. It had taken three songs before I calmed down and settled into my set. Richie saw it all.

As my eyes began to glaze over, Havens shook me by the shoulders. "Listen, Jimmy! Look at me! It's okay. Your consciousness has been tuned to a different place. That's all. It's gonna be all right."

He motioned around the bus. Our surroundings had changed. The few sleeping businessmen had disappeared. The driver was gone, yet the bus was still moving. The rain had stopped and all I could see was a dark starry sky.

In place of bus seats there were plush dark-purple couches. Havens opened his arms in a grand and graceful gesture. "Welcome to the Shuttle of Angels, Jimmy!"

My panic eased a bit, and I surveyed the bus with astonishment. It was no longer a generic airport shuttle, but the decked-out bohemian bus of every hippie's dreams, like Ken Kesey's 1939 International Harvester school bus, Further, that carried his "Merry Band of Pranksters" cross-country to Woodstock in 1969—only *way* more comfortable. The shuttle was outfitted with rock 'n' roll memorabilia, black lights, psychedelic paintings, intricate batik curtains, lava lamps, and incense burning in gold and silver elephant heads. The retro feel was palpable.

Havens put his arm around my shoulders. "It's our way of saying thank you. This is your party, Jimmy. A party of gratitude." He shot a glance at Lennon, who was slumped in a seat.

"And a party for you too, John." Lennon wasn't convinced. He was looking at the stars through the batik-framed window, smoking yet another cigarette.

"Where are we going?" I asked Richie.

"We are on our way to a cosmic Woodstock of sorts. But way brighter."

"Brighter?" I asked, but Lennon interrupted us.

"Richie fucking Havens. *You're* George's bloody guardian angel. I should have known. I guess since the Beatles didn't play Woodstock, God has sent *you* here to annoy us. Well, as great as it is to see you again, Richie, and you too, George"— he shot an annoyed glance at Harrison—"this feels less like a party and more like an inquisition." He rose and planted his feet wide apart in the signature stance that he used while performing. He leaned forward, stiffened, and said, "I'm going back to New York City. I'm *going* to see Yoko one last time and there's *nothing* you can do to stop me!" He took a drag on his cigarette and blew the smoke at them.

Ignoring the smoke, Harrison countered, "Feeling guilty, are you, John? You *know* you're breaking the rules by having James take you to New York. You're supposed to be helping *him*, *not* the other way around."

Embarrassed, Lennon dropped his eyes. "Look, I know this is a bit—irregular. And I know there's a bloody war going on in Heaven, but I'm not going anywhere until I see Yoko one last time. That's it!"

Harrison pushed back. "John, you know you shouldn't be using a client for your own bloody purposes. You're exposing him to risk. And remember, he's the key musical linchpin on Earth. We need him alive at this end of the chain to heal the rift."

I interrupted, "I'm a linchpin? Heal the rift?" But they ignored me.

Lennon wasn't giving in. "The rift can bloody wait. We're going to New York!"

Harrison wasn't giving up either. "When we attack the Black Chord, the spiritual shock wave will reverberate all the way to Earth. James Drake will receive those effects spiritually and transmute them into new songs that will help heal and wake up the world. Just as yours and mine did when we were on Earth."

Lennon wasn't having any of it. "George, stop pushing your bloody spiritual agenda on me. As far as I can see, we're all fucked. So we might as well say goodbye to the ones we love the most."

Between speeding through the cosmos on a hippie bus, learning of my supposed coming fame, and listening in on private matters between my dead rock heroes, I was reeling.

The tension between the two was palpable. The many years of irritations and misunderstandings were coming to a head. Like when Harrison failed to mention or give credit to Lennon in his memoir *I, Me, Mine* or when the two of them got in a fist fight over who knows what during the *Let It Be* sessions.

They began shouting at each other. "You always think you're so bloody more evolved than anyone else!" Lennon accused.

Harrison countered, "Well, at least I spoke my own mind, not my wife's!" Their shouts started morphing from human speech into deafening guitar noise, Lennon's heavy distortion confronting Harrison's screaming electric feedback.

As they hurled long-held frustrations and invectives at each other, their human appearance began burning away, revealing their true nature—coiling and pulsating plasma energy. The two brilliant energy blobs collided right in front of Richie Havens. They went after each other while an energy field that looked and sounded like static electricity crackled between them.

Havens shook his head sadly as he tried to insert himself between them. His arms transformed into blue tendrils of cooling energy, not that it did much good. After several moments of trying to calm them, he abruptly pulled his arms from the fray and went into a trance of sorts. He stood motionless and serene, a solitary statue standing beside a psychedelic lightning storm.

Just as suddenly, he snapped out of it and stepped into the maelstrom, his human form disappearing like a burning photograph. Havens's blue-green energy field swirled between John's and George's, becoming ever more brilliant—calming and slowing down the fiery orange, yellow, and red tendrils that surrounded him.

"Cut it out, you two! I have a new message from the boss," Havens's voice boomed. "There's been a change of plans." The swirling kaleidoscope slowed, then reconstituted into glowing white silhouettes as Lennon and Harrison returned to their human forms. Havens continued, "John, though you did raise a few eyebrows in Heaven for this unauthorized trip of yours, you're being rewarded for a job well done with Jimmy here. Your visit to see Yoko has been approved by the highest of heavenly circles. Besides, the troops are still massing, so there's a short window of time for this little venture of yours. You may haunt Yoko for a little while. But don't dally!"

I stood there slack-jawed as three icons from my rock 'n' roll youth jousted over things incomprehensible to me. I tried again. "A war in Heaven, the Black Chord, troops are massing? Rift? What rift? Linchpin? What are you guys *talking* about?" They continued to ignore me.

Not wishing to let his old bandmate off the hook so easily, Harrison stated the obvious. "All right, so you've got permission to see Yoko, but there are two huge storms on both coasts and you're putting a mortal *musician* on a bloody airplane?"

"I know, I know. But honestly, I don't think there is much risk to Mr. Drake here. Besides, you know as well as I do, musicians only die in *small* planes."

There was a pause as we all looked at each other, then started laughing at the in-joke musicians have about getting killed while traveling in small airplanes.

With the tension broken and the vibe easing a bit, I came to Lennon's defense. "Listen, you guys! I don't mind taking John to New York. Honestly, I'm grateful for what he did. I *want* to help him. Yoko or bust, I say!" Lennon threw his cigarette on the floor, ground the butt with the heel of his boot, then threw an arm around my shoulders. We raised our chins, defiant as rugby players.

Havens and Harrison were grinning ear to ear. "Do you see that, George! Do you *see* it?"

"Yes, Richie, the final selfless act! So, events continue to unfold in our favor."

Havens noted my confusion and explained. "By voluntarily helping John with his last earthly request, you have changed the karma in our favor. This one small selfless act will trickle down the karmic chain and have huge positive personal and cosmic effects. The signs are positive." He clapped his hands. "Okay. Come on, everybody! Business is done! The intervention is over. It's party time! Let's get this party rollin'!"

Out of nowhere he produced a lit joint and handed it to me. "Try this, Jimmy. It'll remind you of that stuff we smoked after the Hartford gig. Remember?"

I did remember. I'd given Richie a ride to the airport that day and he lit a jay in the back seat. As we passed it back and forth, I'd listened as he talked about his concerns for the planet. He was a deep guy, and I was in awe of him.

I coughed out the smoke and Richie clapped a hand on my shoulder. "See? It's like that stuff we smoked in Hartford." We sat across from each other, sinking into the comfort of the soft purple couches. "Oh, it is so good to see you again! Come on now. Play us one of your new songs."

"What? You know about my new songs?"

"Yeah, we've been following you through Spacebook."

"Spacebook?"

"Yeah, it's the afterlife's version of Facebook. It allows souls to keep track of each other in the vastness of time and space. We call it 'ghost gossip.' You and John have been all over it, but let's not get distracted. Come on now, play us a song."

"But I didn't bring my guitar."

Harrison pointed to four beautiful acoustic guitars splayed out on the couches that weren't there a second ago. "Here you go! Choose one." A beautiful golden maple Taylor with iridescent abalone inlay on the neck called to me. I picked it up reverently and played an A chord. It was perfectly in tune and sounded absolutely gorgeous to my stoned ears.

The three deceased rock stars trained their eyes on me. They focused their attention the way musicians do when it's finally time to shut up and play music. There is no retreat from this gaze. I closed my eyes and tried to find the courage to play one of my new songs. New songs are fragile. They're not used to the light of day. Like sensitive plants, they find most human (and apparently posthuman) attention too bright. I wasn't sure I could do it.

Sensing my nervousness, Lennon egged me on. "Come on, James. For starters, play 'em that 'Deep Blue Sea' song you wrote yesterday." He turned to Havens and Harrison. "It'll remind you guys of 'Tomorrow Never Knows' without the crows."

Knowing that he was going to see Yoko again, Lennon's mood had lightened significantly. He seemed proud of me and boasted to the other angels, "He wrote this song underwater in his bathtub wearing a snorkel! Have you ever heard the like?"

Both Harrison and Havens smiled at the image of me writing underwater in the bathtub. Harrison quipped, "We'll have to put *that* on Spacebook. The troops could use a good laugh right now."

I started playing the guitar intro. Havens tapped his knee to the rhythm as I sang the opening line. "*There's a fire burning inside of me. That's how it begins . . ."* Like schoolboys ready to join in the fun, they picked up their own guitars, taking turns doing solos and singing harmonies on the choruses.

Harrison played a heartbreaking slide run reminiscent of "While My Guitar Gently Weeps," followed by Lennon's edgy solo, which reminded me of some of his parts on *Abbey Road.* Taking a final solo with chordal improvisations that folded into my own, Havens and I created a crunchy rhythm sandwich. The combined result satisfied like no other. We played the three-minute song for nearly fifteen minutes. At times, we transcended lyric and structure and went to that blissful place that all musicians strive for when conscious thought is gone and the song plays itself.

When the song ended, there was a curious rumbling in the floor as if the bus was traversing rough ground. I was alarmed, but Richie told me not to worry.

Havens commented, "I'm proud of you, Jimmy. You packed your soul into that one." Harrison nodded in agreement. "A new psychedelic classic, I'd say." Only Lennon offered advice. "You know, James. You do a lot of songs in A major, which is fine. But A major is better for violins and clarinets. I think you should do this one in E."

Harrison interrupted. "Oh, for Heaven's sake! I think it's fine in A major. Besides, you've written plenty of songs in A major, like 'In My Life.'" He waved Lennon off and turned to me. "Jimmy, play us another new one."

Lennon interrupted. "Yeah, James! Play the one you got after I threw you off the bridge. By the way, guys, I get songwriting credit on this one." He gave me a wink.

I addressed Harrison, who was sitting cross-legged on his couch. "So musically, this song is inspired by your song 'Apple Scruffs,' except I don't have a harmonica to do the intro."

"No problem. I've got one right here." Harrison reached behind him into the deep folds of the sofa's purple cushions and pulled out a classic Hohner blues harp in the key of C, along with a perfect neck bridge for a guitar player. Noting my astonishment, he added. "If you haven't noticed by now, this is a magic bus catering to musicians. Here you go." He handed me the sparkling silver harmonica. I put the neck bridge over my head and tightened the wing nuts into place.

I closed my eyes and shuddered, remembering my fall off the bridge only two days prior. "Come on, James! Just jump into it," Lennon teased, a smile on his face.

I cleared my mind, took a deep breath, then launched into the intro of "Falling" with the harmonica and guitar playing in unison. I watched my fingers moving madly while I matched every note with the blues harp. Wow! What was in that weed? This time my rock star angels just sat back, passed the joint, and watched me play. I closed my eyes and lost sight of time. Like Odysseus on Calypso's island, I ceased to remember where I was. I even forgot we were on our way to the airport.

When the song concluded with its big folkie flourish, they gave me a round of applause. I noticed that queer low rumbling coming through the walls and floor again. Havens distracted me with his beaming smile. "Shit, Jimmy. That's a cool start for a new album!" The rumbling stopped.

He raised a glass that hadn't been in his hands a blink before. I was astounded to see that the rest of us also held crystal glasses of ruby-red wine. He offered a toast. "Here's to new songs. May they heal the heart, stimulate the mind, and kick some ass!" We lifted our glasses and drank. The wine tasted of cherries and oak and went down like liquid utopia.

I savored the taste and leaned back into the soft cushions. All my senses felt enhanced—by the bus, the songs, the dope, the wine, and especially the company. I was acutely aware of my surroundings and felt profoundly relaxed. I didn't care anymore if I was insane, dreaming, or having an out-of-body experience. After a life of worrying about the future, I had come to a place where I was just living in the moment. It all felt perfect. A huge wave of appreciation washed through me. I turned to my mentors, my heroes, my apparitions and said, "It was great playing with you guys—really!" Without warning, the bus surged forward as if it had launched into warp. "Whoa! What was that?"

Havens ignored my question and said, "Take another sip of the wine. That's some special stuff, Jimmy. Straight from Heaven. It's not the blood of Christ, but it's damned close. By the way, you just played for a lot more angels than the three of us."

"What do you mean? We're the only ones on the bus."

Harrison nodded and said, "Yes. But there's many more listening in. You've just played for the biggest crowd of your life. All your dead heroes were eavesdropping. Didn't you feel that rumble in the bus floor?

"Yeah. What the hell *was* that?"

"That, my friend, was soul applause!"

27 Here Comes the Sun

To fly to the sun without burning a wing...
—THE MOODY BLUES, "DEPARTURE"

We come from the stars and return to the sun.
—ALYSON MARIE KING, AGE THREE

"Soul applause? From where?" I asked.

Havens rubbed his hands together. He seemed genuinely excited to tell me. "We're running a live feed from what will be the biggest show in the galaxy. It's the Great Gig in the Sky! They're waiting for us to arrive. As Ed Sullivan would say, this is gonna be a *really* big shoe."

Havens continued, "I didn't want to tell you. I figured you had enough to be nervous about just playing for us; but all your dead heroes, all your dead mentors, every dead musician who kept you up at night listening to your transistor radio under your pillow, just listened to you play. This is the last massing of souls from our generation who rocked Earth when we were alive. This is our last chance to play before we shed our memories and storylines to join the battle to save music, creativity, and light in this universe."

I had reached a point where nothing surprised me anymore. I had surrendered to the improbable and what remained was a mixture of awe and curiosity. I noted with satisfaction that my cortisol factory was not firing up.

"So, I just played for all my heroes? I'm *really* glad I didn't know that. Where exactly *are* they?"

"They are in their etheric forms waiting for us. Your love, remembrance, and respect has magnetized them to you. You more or less designated them to membership in the First Sol Brigade, and they wanted to check you out."

I paused for a stunned moment to let that sink in, then asked, "What is this great battle you keep talking about? Where are we going?"

"Where all souls go to sort things out after death—the center of the sun. And from there to the next closest star, Proxima Centauri, where the Black Chord waits for us."

My science-nerd self sprang to life. I could hear Carl Sagan in my head: "Proxima Centauri is the closest star to Earth, only 4.3 light-years away, and one of the few stars in the Milky Way that's actually moving closer to us each day."

"And what is this Black Chord?"

Havens explained the Black Chord's nefarious intentions. "The Black Chord has ripped through the fabric of space-time near Proxima Centauri, devouring music and stealing light as it spreads. All dead musicians still residing in Near and Nearer Heaven are gathering at the center of the sun for one last concert. Like I said, the First Sol Brigade—the group you played for—consists of the remaining musicians who influenced you and with whom you are karmically connected." I raised both eyebrows and opened my mouth, but Harrison cut me off and continued. "Yes, yes. You are part of all this too. They will be the lead battalion for the big push against the Black Chord. Other battalions of dead musicians—famous and not—are also forming, as are multitudes of musician regiments from other stars. But the First Sol Brigade will be the point of the spear. You'll meet them all at the center of the sun."

I had a thousand questions, but they weren't as pressing as the drama unfolding outside the window. I could see the huge yellow orb of the sun getting closer. Carl Sagan's excited voice leaped back into my head. "We must be moving at a tremendous velocity! Judging by how big the sun is getting moment to moment, I'd say we're moving at approximately a third the speed of light." I echoed his comments. "Wow! We must be goin' pretty fast!"

"Yes, about a third the speed of light. We'll be there soon," said Havens.

"Won't we burn up?" I asked, gulping down my alarm while the sun, like an enormous yellow daisy with its petals pulled off, loomed larger and larger in the bus window.

"No, don't worry about it. God is protecting us in a fortified bubble of space-time. That's why you can look at it right now without damaging your eyes. We're entering the sun through its spiritual spectrum. Light and heat don't affect us here. Carl Sagan would tell you we know very little about what light really is—like only 0.001 percent."

"Hey! Are you reading my mind?"

"A little bit. I know you well enough to know you have certain voices in your head that help you through the scary shit, and Sagan is one of them."

"Yes. That's true." I thought fondly of Sagan, the enthusiastic astronomer who did his best to get us to look to the heavens for truth. "Hey, Carl Sagan died in 1996. Will he be there to greet us?"

"Not unless he volunteered for special duty. God's only calling musicians for this battle. Dead scientists are partying away from the action. One fact that nobody knows on Earth is that musicians are soldiers in the afterlife. We may have resisted growing up and squandered our mortal lives on drugs, sex, and rock 'n' roll; but up here, we are God's shock troops for some serious cosmic duty. It's payback time. God's conscripted all of us. She's flushing the bardos of all musicians, and she's arranged this protected journey because she wants *you* to have a view of it."

"Why me?"

Lennon interrupted Havens. "Because you really will be the fucking Quasimodo of rock 'n' roll, and we're here to help you ring the bell."

Harrison agreed. "It's true. You will be the single mortal witness to the beginning of a cosmic event that we hope will heal this part of the universe and bring peace to Earth."

"But what about Sagan?" I asked. "Did he volunteer?"

"I'm not sure. I heard that after such a public life, he pretty much stayed off Spacebook, so he might not have seen the notice." Harrison snapped his fingers and a holographic smartphone appeared in his hand.

I read out loud the post asking for volunteers: "Souls wanted for hazardous journey. No wages, bitter cold, long hours fighting evil darkness. No return assured. Honor and recognition in the event of success."

Lennon chuckled. "I'm surprised Ernest Shackleton hasn't sued for copyright infringement."

Havens interrupted. "Heads up, guys! Here comes the sun. Be ready, Jimmy. The shock wave as we enter can be a bit overwhelming at first."

"Shock wave?" I said. I heard Sagan echo my question. "Shock wave?"

"Why the shock wave of love of course," Havens interjected. "What do you think makes all that light? The sun's core is pure love, where gravity and thermodynamics are passionately entangled. A titanic embrace of opposite forces that lights the universe."

From the window, the sun, which no longer resembled a globe but a giant frying egg yolk, engulfed the view in all directions. It pulsated with Texas-size globules of red-orange plasma bubbling in a great sheet of molten gold. It emitted a sound that drummed through the bus like the lowest note on a bass. The light was blinding, and the sound intensified as if an amp had been turned to eleven. The maelstrom invaded my senses and exploded inside my solar plexus. As the father of all panic attacks sang its opening chords, Carl Sagan came to my rescue, saving me from a Spinal Tap moment. "We're entering the surface zone of the sun, called the convection zone, where photons, after meandering 100,000 to 200,000 years from the core, shoot off the sun's surface and hit Earth in only eight minutes and twenty seconds."

Outside the windows, dense sulfurous clouds whipped by. I could see coronal mass ejections dissipating into the vacuum of space like hot yellow steam. It was then we pierced the skin of the sun through one of its golden globules. As we entered the body of the sun, I felt warm, sensual feelings flood my mind and body. I thought of Wanda the Wanderer enjoying the light of another day on Earth lit by these photons. Excitement spread through my body as I pictured her bathing in these very particles. I wanted to return to Earth and wrap my body around hers. I wanted to kiss her in the light of those ancient photons. I wanted to—

Havens interrupted my thought stream. "Hey, Jimmy. It's natural to get a little horny as we enter the sun. The mating instinct is strong in these upper zones. It'll pass when we reach the core."

"You really are reading my mind, aren't you?"

"Well, maybe a little. But don't be embarrassed by your thoughts. I'll leave you two alone now." He gave me a wink and averted his eyes, looking out the window.

As we penetrated the sun, the view gave way to a deeper grainy yellow that reminded me of the peel of an orange. We were shooting through what appeared to be living orange marmalade when, sensing my agitation, Carl Sagan's voice returned inside my head. "Welcome to the radiation zone of the sun, where photons from the core collide into one another for hundreds of centuries before reaching the surface." I thought of colliding with Wanda, of mixing our lives and melding our bodies, of traveling the world, and taking hot baths together. A myriad of romantic nights with Wanda flashed in my mind as we passed through the radiation zone.

Sagan continued his narration. "Each photon travels just one micron before being absorbed in an endless loop."

I envisioned an endless loop of pleasures with Wanda, the sound of her laughter and her body's release. At a certain point, I closed my eyes and felt her close to me from across the gulf of ninety-three million miles.

As we approached the sun's core, Sagan finished his star tour. "The core of the sun is one-fourth its mass, but at fifteen million degrees, it's responsible for 85 percent of its energy."

Entering the core, I felt my mind clearing of sexual thoughts about Wanda, replaced by immense love, not only for her but for everything. A pure hit of ecstasy washed through me. Outside, the marmalade texture of the sun was clearing too. A diamond whiteness lay before us as we slowed and came to a stop. We had arrived at the exact center of the sun. We sat suspended in the eye of the cosmic storm where the exquisite balance between gravity and thermonuclear dynamics creates a place of elastic reality, where anything's possible.

28 The Great Gig in the Sky

Music gives a soul to the universe, wings to the mind,
flight to the imagination, and life to everything.

—PLATO

"What happens now?" I asked.

Havens replied, "It's showtime. And we have a job to do."

"What's our job?"

"Well, for starters, we're providing the venue."

"The venue? What venue?"

"Come look here, Jimmy." He pointed out the windshield at the hood of the bus. "This will become the stage floor. And this," he said, pointing to the passenger door, "will become the door to the backstage and greenroom." He stepped down one step toward the door. "This will lead to the orchestra pit. And *this*"—sweeping his hand toward the back of the bus— "will expand into the holographic replica of the perfect auditorium for the center of the sun. The showplace of the nation. Radio City Music Hall."

"What? The hippie bus will become the Radio City Music Hall? How does that happen?" I asked.

"Dark energy, of course. God's gonna blow this bus up like a balloon. And she'll fill in every art deco detail from the seashell-curved stage to the plush red seats and, of course, the perfect acoustics. All your deceased heroes will be here. This will be our last show before we shed our stories and move on. Oh, and she's promised top-notch hospitality in the greenroom."

Havens abruptly grew silent as if someone were calling his name, then closed his eyes as if listening to an inner voice. His eyes popped open a moment later. "Heads up, guys. It's time!" He opened his arms. "Come on. It's time for a group hug."

"Oh Christ! Can't we do this without all the New Age shit?" Lennon mumbled as he reluctantly came forward. We huddled together, locking arms.

Havens admonished us to focus. "Come on! We've gotta stay together when the dark energy is unleashed. Otherwise, we'll explode into nothingness. Hold on tight, especially you, Jimmy. It'll only hurt for a second. Afterward, we can raid the greenroom." He winked at me.

A loud hissing sound rushed into the bus from all directions, and we gripped each other tight. I could feel the cells of my body quivering as if the nucleus of each one was trying to keep it together. Sensing my distress, Havens said, "Hold on, Jimmy, this won't take long."

The hissing became a roar and we gripped tighter as the bus started expanding in all directions at once. The front end got wider and deeper, and a beautiful stage began rolling out replete with gleaming backline, amps, drums, keyboards, and percussion—just waiting for the musicians to appear.

Meanwhile, an orchestra pit appeared under our feet, as did a sign pointing toward the greenroom. Down the hallway, beneath the stage, I could see tables set with food and snacks. The roaring began to diminish. My cells stopped quivering and we unlocked our embrace. I stepped up from the orchestra pit and turned around. To my wonderment, Radio City Music Hall unfurled before us with every one of its nearly 6,000 opulent, plush red velvet seats—empty. It was a perfect replica of the venerable theater in 1932, at the time the world's largest performance hall. The vacant stage with its beautiful golden backdrop gave the illusion of being inside a nautilus shell.

"Where's the audience?" I asked.

Harrison said with a wicked smile, "They're coming. Look up."

Infiltrating the theater's creamy ivory ceiling, wispy plasma streams of energy were snaking down and coiling into the empty seats. Gradually, the swirling energy fields began to consolidate into familiar forms and faces. I saw David Bowie, Prince, Aretha Franklin, Tom Petty, Glenn Frey, and many others materialize in the front row, which was apparently reserved for the recently deceased. In the second row was Nick Drake, who committed suicide in 1974, sitting with Pete Ham and his bandmate Tom Evans, who killed themselves after their band, Badfinger, broke up. *This must be suicide row*, I thought. I noticed Buddy Holly, Ritchie Valens, Ricky Nelson, Patsy Cline, John Denver, and all the other unfortunate musicians sitting in the plane crash row. The overdose section was sadly full, with Jimi Hendrix, Janis Joplin, Kurt Cobain, Gram Parsons, Dee Dee Ramone, John Entwistle, Whitney Houston, and many, many others filling the seats.

The assemblage seemed a bit dazed. They were poking at themselves since most hadn't been in a body for a while, even if it was just a holographic one. Most were smiling; but others were solemn, understanding that this was it—the last show.

Lennon, Harrison, Havens, and I took four of the empty seats in the front row on house right. (They had been reserved for any late arrivals who might gain entry by dying before the conclusion of the show.) We had backstage passes and were close to the greenroom door, which was good because I was starving. Interplanetary spiritual travel really burns up the calories.

I recognized many of the musicians sitting in the 6,000-seat auditorium at the center of the sun, but not all. I turned to Richie and asked, "Who's in the audience?"

"Career musicians mostly—some famous, many not. But check out the standing-room section." Richie motioned toward the back and sides of the theater, which glowed with scores of transparent, multicolored apparitions. "Those are the superfans, groupies, and cultural activists who answered the Spacebook ad. God comped them in as a thank-you for their service."

A loud grumbling broke out from the backstage hallway. "Okay, okay. Are we ready to fire this thing up? We've got hundreds of headliners to present. And *this time* we don't have forever!" A person obscured by shadows thumped their clipboard and shook their head impatiently.

A middle-aged man with deep lines in his cheeks and an air of unquestionable authority walked onto the stage and stepped up to the mic. His black-rimmed glasses were perched on his nose and secured around his neck by Croakies. He radiated a no-nonsense attitude that no one would dare challenge.

"Holy shit!" I said, a bit louder than I meant to. "That's Bill Graham!"

"Be quiet!" Lennon held my arm. "We have front-row seats. They can hear you over the mic! Oh shit—too late!"

Graham shielded his eyes from the lights and glared at me. "Look, Drake, you may be the next big deal on Earth, but you don't get the right to interrupt me until you've had your first hit and somebody sues your ass!"

Laughter rippled through the theater as Graham's dry humor revealed a painful truism of the music business. Yes, your first hit is usually a lawsuit.

He continued, "I know some of you are thinking, 'Hey, what's Graham doing here in rock 'n' roll Heaven? He's not a musician!' May I remind you doubters that I once played cowbell at the Fillmore!"

There were more peals of laughter as many remembered how the evil imps of acid, the Merry Pranksters, conspired to dose the ever-sober Graham with LSD and finally got their wish at a Santana show at the Fillmore West in San Francisco. The Pranksters and their coconspirators, the Grateful Dead, injected the acid into cans of soda they knew Graham would drink. Under its effects, the "designated driver of the drug generation" was seen sitting against the back of Santana's amp during the band's set, lost in the sounds of the cowbell.

Born Wolfgang Grajonca, the legendary Bay Area music promoter Bill Graham was one tough cookie. After escaping the Nazis by walking across Europe at age ten, he immigrated to America, where he washed dishes in the Jewish resorts and stand-up comedy scene of the Catskill Mountains. So, he knew plenty about comic timing. He was killed when his helicopter took off in a storm and crashed into an electric tower after a Huey Lewis and the News show at the Concord Pavilion in 1991.

Graham stopped joking and grimly took in the vast assembly of souls in the center of the sun. "We're all here tonight to celebrate the lives and music we had on Earth. Some of us burned out at an early age. Some of us had a good long ride. We each brought a piece of that life with us and now it's time to give it back. Let's show that son-of-a-bitch Black Chord how we rock! Let's shove that motherfucker back into the void where it came from. Nothing can tell us we can't make music anymore!" Applause and roars of defiance shook the auditorium.

"Before we get started, I'd like to acknowledge a special guest in the house. And unlike us, he's still breathing. Jimmy Drake, will you please stand up." Befuddled by Graham's calling me out in front of the entire gathering, I remained seated. "Yes, Drake, you. Come on. We don't have all day." My face was hot with embarrassment, but I managed to get to my feet. He continued, "Now, will all the members of the First Sol Brigade please stand up."

As I turned toward the musicians, they began clapping. My knees buckled as I gazed upon the smiling faces of the magnificent musicians who had brought me so much joy and inspiration over the course of my life. It was overwhelming to have them honor me as a peer.

"Those of you standing are linked karmically and have a special role to play. The First Sol Brigade," Graham said after the applause died down, "is our locomotive and Mr. Drake here will be the caboose back on Earth. And with the rest of us in between, this 'Runaway Train' won't stop until it meets up with the 'Peace Train' back on Earth!" Graham stood there, looking pleased with himself as the crowd went wild.

"Okay, let's get on with it. You headliners, listen up. Here's the rules. Everyone gets two songs. No exceptions, no encores. Otherwise, we'll be here forever." The groans from disappointed musicians sounded throughout the hall. Graham shrugged indifferently. "I swear, no matter what you tell a musician, they always wanna play more songs. Well, the more songs you play, the less you make per song." More laughter.

Graham glared into the crowd to see if anybody had a problem with his rules. No one uttered a peep—Graham was firmly entrenched as the mafia-style cultural boss of an entire generation.

"All right, brothers and sisters of the afterlife. We'll take this in chapters. Since we're all just souls now anyway, let's start up this show with some real soul music." The crowd applauded enthusiastically. Graham always knew how to please his audience, even when his audience was musicians, the most critical of all listeners.

"May I introduce tonight's house band. First the rhythm section. From the legendary Funk Brothers of Motown, please welcome James Jamerson and Benny Benjamin!"

My jaw dropped as I watched the legendary bassist from the Temptations, James Jamerson—otherwise known as "the Hook"—walking up the backstage hallway with his bass strapped over his shoulder. He was followed by drummer Benny Benjamin, who, after getting comfortable on the drum throne, picked up his sticks, twirled them in his fingers, then signaled he was ready to go.

"Shit! This is gonna be a hot night!" Lennon said during the applause. I turned around to see him devouring a piece of pizza and a pint of stout that he'd snuck from the greenroom. "Want a piece?" he offered. With a sudden realization I was starving, I accepted his offer. It was a vegetarian basil, onion, and mushroom pizza with fresh tomatoes, avocado, and pineapple and the best sauce I've ever tasted. Harrison and Havens must have snuck backstage too, because they were drinking sake and eating heavenly sushi and sashimi. God appeared to be pulling out all the stops on this production.

Graham waited for the applause to die down and then said, "And now, from the legendary Wrecking Crew, let's welcome Leon Russell on keyboards and our two guitarists, Glen Campbell and Tommy Tedesco!" More deafening applause.

The deceased members of the Wrecking Crew entered stage left. They had recorded backing tracks for everyone from the Beach Boys to the Association to the Monkees and Simon and Garfunkel. In those days, we all thought it was the named bands that played on the tracks of those recordings. But more often than not, it was the Wrecking Crew with hundreds of hit songs notched on their belts but no credits on the back of the albums.

With the house band in place, Graham said, "Okay, folks. Our first performer only made it to age forty-four on Earth, but his music will last forever." He abruptly walked off the stage, clipboard in hand, and disappeared. The lights dimmed and a blast of multicolored fog swept onto the stage. There was a flash of light, and then standing with his back to us was a mysterious guy wearing a gold lamé jacket, holding a wireless mic. I heard a burst of camaraderie from the backline. Then, to the thrumming of bongos, the lights came up. To my delight, with a "Hey, brothers and sisters, what's happenin'?" a smiling Marvin Gaye turned around and launched into "What's Going On." He sang, "*Mother, mother, there's too many of you crying. Brother, brother, brother, there's far too many of you dying . . .*"

Awestruck, I turned to Richie, George, and John. "Hey, guys. What *is* going on?"

Havens put a finger to his lips and whispered, "Shush! Give the band some respect. This is the last time these guys will ever get to play these songs."

The band played a soulful, definitive version of "What's Going On." Gaye took a bow and addressed the heavenly throng. "I hear we only get two songs each." He turned toward Graham, who was standing barely visible in a dark alcove just offstage and nodding sternly. Gaye winced but acquiesced. "So, for my concluding number, please welcome to the stage my very special guest, Miss Tammi Terrell!"

Out stepped a lovely young Tammi Terrell, waving at the crowd. Terrell had died of brain cancer six weeks shy of her twenty-fifth birthday after recording several hits with Gaye.

Some say Gaye never got over her death and that it contributed to his bouts of depression and drug abuse.

Gaye smiled brightly and he and Terrell embraced, reveling in being together one last time. Reluctantly, they parted and then stepped up to the mics. They sang the opening line of their number one song, which Gaye played at her memorial. "*You're all . . . I need . . . to get by . . .*" Gaye took Terrell's hand, peered into her eyes, and crooned, "*Like sweet morning dew, I took one look at you, and it was plain to see, you were my destiny.*"

They finished the song, and even stronger applause echoed through the golden venue. They took a bow and blew kisses at the crowd. Gaye and Terrell left the stage, hand in hand, rapt in the final bittersweet moments of being in each other's physical company. He departed to join his fellow murder victims and she to the cancer section, where she was seated next to a smiling Bob Marley.

Graham returned and said, "Hold tight, everybody. We're gonna do a quick set change, then we'll be back with one of my favorite performers. Oh, and a quick note from the house manager: Don't take the brown gravity. It's a real downer." Laughter erupted at Graham's reference to the brown acid that made people sick at Woodstock.

I took advantage of the set change to ask more questions. "Richie," I pleaded, "will you please tell me what's really going on?"

"Okay. But take a deep, slow breath. You're gonna have to stretch your head around this. What we're seeing is a holographically projected live show here at the center of the sun. All the deceased musical souls of our generation who still reside in Near and Nearer Heaven are soaking up the love from our home star one final time. It's a last chance to relive the days when we had bodies and sang onstage. This will be our final unpacking. A dress rehearsal to raise our energy before going into battle and leaving this realm forever."

"How many performers, Richie?"

"I don't know. Hundreds, I'd guess, so we'll be here a while."

"How long?"

"Well, time is measured differently here, but I'd guess several days if we were talking Earth time, which we aren't. But don't worry. We've got all the comforts of home, and we'll still get you to the plane on time."

The plane! I had completely forgotten about the plane. "Oh yeah, the plane! Shit!" I looked over at Lennon, who was sprawled out across several empty seats, nonchalantly eating a chocolate cookie and reading an old copy of *Rolling Stone*. "Hey, John! Are we still going to New York?"

"Bloody yes, we are! Don't worry. We're not in the same temporal zone as the airport. When this party is over we'll be back on the airport shuttle right where we left off. You'll see. No Earth time lost. Relax and enjoy the show." He pointed at Bill Graham, who was returning to the stage, and then went back to reading an article by Hunter S. Thompson.

Graham took the mic. "I'd like to introduce a guy I had to fly all the way to Georgia just to convince to play the Fillmore. Ladies, gentlemen, and spirits, please welcome to the stage the former mortal known as Otis Redding!"

There was a brilliant flash of light and Otis Redding, another musician who was killed in a small plane crash, at age twenty-six, bounded onto the stage. A blue spotlight illuminated his shining face. He smiled at his brothers-in-arms, the Funk Brothers and the Wrecking Crew. He grabbed the microphone from the stand, closed his eyes, and sang softly, "*Oh, she may be weary. Them young girls, they do get wearied. Wearing that same old shaggy dress . . .*" The band effortlessly joined in on "Try a Little Tenderness," which started slow but built to a crushing crescendo.

The applause was deafening, growing stronger song by song. You could feel it in your bones. It actually hurt my teeth! The applause subsided, and the hall went silent for a few seconds. A spotlight shone on guitarist Tommy Tedesco's fingers as he picked the familiar opening chords of "(Sittin' On) The Dock of the Bay," which Redding recorded just days before he died. The recording was released posthumously in 1968.

As a suburban middle-class white kid, that song was one of the first times I ever thought of the plight of Black people in America. A real eye-opener and heartbreaker of a song.

Drenched in sweat, Redding took a final bow, then bounded back to the plane crash section to join his Bar-Kays bandmates, who had perished with him. Graham reappeared and pointed sternly at his schedule. "Okay. It's time to switch genders for a while. Please welcome to the stage the High Priestess of Soul, Miss Nina Simone!" Simone walked onstage with a light in her eyes, looking entirely free of the demons that had plagued her on Earth. "*Oh, Lord. Please don't let me be misunderstood,*" she belted.

Jazz and soul music flowed for what seemed like days. Etta James, Ray Charles, Ella Fitzgerald, Miles Davis, Whitney

Houston, James Brown, Billie Holiday, Wilson Pickett, Dave Prater of Sam and Dave. On and on, the dead kept coming, all performing with vigor and passion. During the breaks I hung out in the greenroom with my three guardian angels, who were soon downing delicious-looking banana nut bread with Turkish coffee. Havens handed me a piece. "Here you go, Jimmy, this'll keep you going."

I devoured the banana nut bread, which was still warm. "Hey, Richie! I can't remember feeling so, so spaced out. What's in this food?"

"Just manna from Heaven. That's all. You're feeling spaced because you *are* in space! Look out the window, man."

"So, we're parked at the center of the sun, but who was driving the bus?" I asked.

Harrison responded, "That's complicated. We'll tell you later. Let's get back to our seats. Here comes Bill Graham again. Shh!"

We had learned to keep quiet during Graham's announcements. "Ladies and gentlemen, we have concluded the 'jazz and soul' part of our show." A few disappointed groans came from the house. "Now, now. You rockers gotta chill for a bit because our panel of muses has selected acoustic music as our next chapter. Please welcome to the stage Mama Cass, John Phillips, and Denny Doherty to sing a couple of Mamas and Papas songs. And standing in for the living to complete the harmonies, let's welcome Mary Travers of Peter, Paul and Mary, and for the San Francisco sound, Scott McKenzie."

The opening A minor chord of "California Dreamin'" filled the theater with melancholy and longing as the four friends from Earth's folk scene harmonized perfectly. "*All the leaves are brown, and the sky is gray . . .*" After singing "Monday, Monday," they took turns singing each other's songs, starting with McKenzie's late-1960s classic "San Francisco (Be Sure to Wear Flowers in Your Hair)," which gave many young people the idea to move west. Travers finished the set by singing "Leaving on a Jet Plane," with a cameo appearance by the song's author, John Denver, who strolled in with his trademark grin, looking youthful as always. Denver died in 1997 at age fifty-four, yet another musician killed in his prime in a small plane.

The folk dead kept coming: Pete Seeger, Glenn Yarbrough, Nick Drake, Sandy Denny, Harry Chapin, Mimi Fariña, Phil Ochs, Doc Watson, Woody Guthrie, and a host of others. Leonard Cohen finished the acoustic chapter by saying, "It's true the Black Chord is a crack in space, but the crack is where our light goes in!" Thunderous applause ensued. A fighting spirit was growing in the ranks of the souls. Each soul in the theater joined in with Cohen's heartbreaking ballad "Hallelujah," singing a requiem for all departed musical souls as their collective time neared to move on.

"Thank you, Leonard!" Bill Graham returned, holding his clipboard. "One more time, a round of applause for all our acoustic performers!" The auditorium shook madly, but I was getting used to it. Graham held up his hand and the applause died down. He continued, "Since you rockers were so patient during the acoustic set, we're going to showcase a bit of blues for you now! Please welcome to the stage Mr. B. B. King!" On and on it went. Muddy Waters, Stevie Ray Vaughan, Robert Johnson, Janis Joplin, Lightnin' Hopkins, Norton Buffalo, and many more.

The chapters continued with big band crooners, including Frank Sinatra, Nat King Cole, and Bing Crosby. All genres had their moment: rock, pop, jazz, country, metal, punk, Latin, reggae, bluegrass, grunge, rap, acid jazz, alternative, classical, and world music, to name just a few. Bill Graham rolled them in and out professionally. And if a band tried to play a third song, he'd pull the plug on the PA. He was *that* hard core.

A particularly poignant performance occurred during the glam-rock set when Freddie Mercury and David Bowie appeared together. They strolled onstage arm in arm reeking charisma. Mercury wore tight blue jeans, biker boots, and a formfitting white tank top. He raised his fist and screamed to the house, "Am I not the sexiest singer alive or dead?"

"Yes!" came the reply.

Bowie, in a sunflower-yellow sport jacket with a billowy white shirt and impeccably pressed black slacks, grabbed the mic and said in his deep baritone, "All right, you heavenly apparitions, here's a little number for any of you who might be feeling some anxiety over that Black Chord bastard. Let's show it we can handle the pressure!" He and Mercury both nodded to James Jamerson, who took the cue and began playing the signature beginning of the Queen classic "Under Pressure." *Dum-dum-dum-diddy-dah-dum.* The epic anthem shook the house, building to its crazy hard-rock crescendo, then dissolving into simple finger snaps. Queen and Bowie were both ahead of their time.

Before they left the stage, Bowie pointed his finger at the audience and said, "I know John Lennon is listening out there, and I want you to know, John, that under different circumstances, it might have been me who took that bullet." He was referring to Mark David Chapman, who had brought a concealed gun to a David Bowie concert. He thought about killing Bowie, then changed his mind last minute and went after Lennon a few months later. "I'm sorry it was you, brother." Bowie walked back to the cancer section.

Lennon looked my way for confirmation. I whispered, "It's true, John. Those details came out after you passed."

"Bloody hell!" He sat back, shook his head sadly, and said under his breath, reflecting on the song he cowrote in 1975 with Bowie and guitarist Carlos Alomar, "*Fame! What you get is no tomorrow.*"

29 Talking 'bout a Revolution

Life is in the transitions.

—WILLIAM JAMES

I continued to lose touch with my previous life. Richie said that in this compression of space-time, lengthy periods pass at an accelerated pace. I tried to remember who I was, where I was going, and what I was doing, but the salient details escaped me. Another weird effect was that I felt no fatigue or need to sleep. I didn't so much as yawn during the entire show. I figured my proximity to the dead kept me energized. Warren Zevon acknowledged his error before singing "I'll Sleep When I'm Dead." It was obvious the dead don't sleep, and I guess neither do those who party with them.

Back in the greenroom, Lennon and Harrison were eating cheese blintzes and drinking Earl Grey tea, deep in conversation. They were smiling and obviously enjoying each other's company. It seemed that any disagreements and resentments they might have had on Earth were being resolved.

I overheard Harrison say to Lennon, "Have you seen Elvis? I haven't seen him anywhere. I guess he decided not to be part of the show."

"I guess he's still sulking in some bardo somewheres, pissed that we killed the pompadour." They laughed like naughty boys enjoying a joke.

Even though Lennon once idolized Elvis, the relationship between Elvis and the Beatles was complicated. While the Beatles revered Elvis, and Elvis respected the group's raw energy, he felt threatened by their popularity. And it didn't help that Elvis warned Nixon that the Beatles were an anti-American menace.

"Hey, John, do you remember Astrid?"

"Astrid Kirchherr? Of course! Did you know she recently passed?"

"No, I hadn't heard," replied Harrison.

"When she cut Stu's hair in the mop top, I thought they were both a bit daft. Is Stu here? I haven't seen him, either."

"Richie said he's back on Earth reincarnated as a Hollywood hairdresser."

"That's perfect!" said John.

It was fascinating to hear them speak of Stuart Sutcliffe, their original bassist who died of a brain hemorrhage in 1962 at age twenty-one. At Sutcliffe's request, his German girlfriend, photographer Astrid Kirchherr, cut his hair in the first Beatles hairstyle, which he'd emulated from the trend among young German men at the time. A short time later, the band adopted the hairstyle as their signature look. It was the *German* mop top that went global.

Harrison reminisced, "It took some getting used to, didn't it? At first, I thought I looked like Moe of the Three Stooges."

Lennon laughed. "Maybe Moe was ahead of his time."

"Maybe so, but it was a brilliant stroke of luck for us. Funny how a different hairstyle can attract so much attention."

"Yeah, we stood out from the rest, that's for sure."

"I always felt bad for Elvis. I guess we did kill the pompadour."

"Yeah, we did." Harrison raised his teacup. "Here's to mop tops, pompadours, mullets, and every other kind of crazy thing we did to our hair."

"And don't forget the prellies," Lennon said, referring to the amphetamine Preludin, so popular at the time. "If Astrid's mother hadn't gotten us those from that chemist, we could never have kept up the pace at the Kaiserkeller." They clinked cups. They say on the eve of battle all men are brothers.

During the breaks, I had many conversations with Richie Havens. He said that this cosmic intervention I was experiencing was analogous to "God helping the ones who help themselves" and that my days of "living in the weeds" would soon be over.* He said that although my songs had received little attention on Earth, I got noticed in Heaven. He smiled at me with a friend's pride and said, "That's where God came in. She pulled a few strings and changed your luck."

"My luck? I haven't had much of that in this life," I said cynically. I had never felt lucky. That's why I didn't play the lotto. *I'm gonna lose anyway, so why spend a buck?* was my core belief.

"That's right. Your *luck*. Haven't you ever wondered where luck comes from? Look, Jimmy, let's say that you've been

---

* Listen to "Living in the Weeds" at JohnLennonsGlasses.net.

standing at God's deli counter all your life waiting for a sandwich, and finally through patience and persistence your number comes up, she calls out your name, and then God gives you a sandwich so fat it's hard to get your mouth around it. That's what's happening to you now."

"God's giving me a sandwich?"

"Come on, man. I'm not a metaphor hound like you. You know what I mean."

"I think I know what you mean, but do I have to eat the sandwich?"

"Listen, man, when God hands you a sandwich, you'd be crazy *not* to eat it."

"All right. Well, what happens when I eat the sandwich?"

"You'll be chewing for a long, long time.* Look, I'll tell you more later, Graham's coming back to close the show."

"The show's over? I feel like it just started."

"Time-sense makes no sense here, man. But *shh*. Don't miss the finale!"

"Okay, folks, can you believe it?" said Bill Graham. "What a show, but we've reached our big finale. This'll come as a big surprise to both of them, but let's welcome to the stage those two freeloaders who've been sitting in the front row clowning around the whole time and eating all the greenroom food. Give it up for two of the most influential songwriters of our generation, John Lennon and George Harrison!"

As the venue spotlights zeroed in on them, Harrison and Lennon had the aspect of deer caught in headlights. The crowd of souls erupted in applause.

---

* Listen to "The MetaQuizzical Café" at JohnLennonsGlasses.net.

"What's going on, Richie? You didn't tell us we had to perform," said Harrison.

"Bloody hell," muttered Lennon as he lit a cigarette and considered bolting for the greenroom.

Havens grinned and shrugged his shoulders. "It's God's request. She wanted it to be a surprise. You should feel complimented. She wants to give you one last time to work out your karma, this time onstage. She said it'll make better soldiers out of you."

Lennon bargained. "But, Richie, I barely played live *before* I died. I'm rustier than a Cornish nail." He eyed Harrison plaintively and asked, "What are we gonna play?"

Harrison winced, a little panicked himself. "Well, we get two songs, right? How about you pick one of my songs and I'll pick one of yours?"

"Sounds good."

The theater of souls was getting restless. They started clapping in unison, saying, "Lennon, Harrison, Lennon, Harrison," over and over again.

Graham glared over the top of his clipboard. He chastened the two reluctant rockers. "Guys! Come on! Never keep the audience waiting. We're ready for you. Look!"

He pointed to four guitars that had magically appeared on silver stands near the frontline. Two acoustic Gibson J-160Es, like the ones they used in the mid-1960s on *Rubber Soul*. An electric 1958 Rickenbacker 325 that Lennon nicknamed "Hamburg" for their years in Germany, and Harrison's 1957 Gretsch Duo Jet, nicknamed the "English Gentleman."

"Come on, boys! It's finale time!" Graham motioned them out of their seats and they hesitantly walked onstage. The crowd settled down as they approached the mics. Lennon talked first. "Well, when God hands you a sandwich, I guess you've just got to eat it." He looked my way and winked. He turned around and strapped on a Gibson acoustic.

Harrison did likewise and said with a smile, "That's right. I once heard a comedian say, 'You eat the audience, or they eat you!'" A wave of laughter swept through the crowd. "John, I want to hear the one you wrote for *Rubber Soul*. Shall we play 'In My Life'? I think it fits the occasion." The crowd clapped its approval.

With his eyes drifting across the vast assemblage of departed musicians in the golden theater, Lennon bowed his head and in a rare shy moment said, "I'd be glad to." Harrison began the simple but beautiful guitar intro in A major and they sang in perfect harmony, "*There are places I'll remember, all my life, though some have changed . . .*" The song evoked bittersweet last remembrances of life on Earth. By the end of the song, there wasn't a dry holographic eye in the house.

It was Lennon's turn to pick a song, and he asked, "George, have I ever told you how much I enjoyed 'Within You Without You'? Can we do that one?"

I was astonished at his pick. After all the complicated feelings he had for the Maharishi and religion in general, John Lennon liked Harrison's Eastern philosophy epic the best? Amazing!

Harrison shielded his eyes from the stage lights and said, "Well, we'll need a sitar and a tabla player." He nodded toward

John and whispered, "I guess we're about to find out whether Ravi reincarnated or not." Then, speaking into the mic, he said, "Ravi, Alla, are you out there?" He stared toward the heart disease section and, sure enough, two men stood up. John and George smiled broadly at each other as the spotlight shone on the gentle features of sitar master Ravi Shankar and his long-standing percussionist Alla Rakha. Harrison beamed in delight to be in the presence of his old friend, who after much soul-searching had decided not to reincarnate, concluding he was needed more in Heaven than on Earth.

From the sidelines, Graham snapped his fingers three times. A beautiful sitar, tabla, and harmonium with three floor cushions appeared.

While the audience applauded the special guests, a worried Lennon leaned in and whispered in Harrison's ear, "Hey, George, I don't remember the bloody chords."

"Don't worry, mate. Just keep strumming in C and you'll feel it. Follow the drone, follow Ravi." Harrison put his guitar on the stand and sat down at the harmonium.

Shankar and Rakha walked onstage, exchanging pleasantries and hugs with the former Beatles, then sat on their cushions. They picked up their instruments and began strumming and tuning. Astonished at the sound quality, Shankar said into the mic, "The sitar and tabla are perfectly in tune. I would like to thank Mr. Graham!"

Graham shouted back, "What can I say? God has the best backline. I can't take credit."

Shankar closed his eyes and began strumming the twenty-one strings of his sitar. Harrison pumped his harmonium and

Lennon played variations of the C chord, sweet but a little edgy, providing the perfect background. After the intro, the great pop raga from *Sgt. Pepper's Lonely Hearts Club Band* sprang to life as Alla Rakha hit the tablas and Harrison began singing. *"We were talking about the space between us all and the people who hide themselves behind a wall of illusion."*

I was pleased and mesmerized because it was the song that turned me and a whole generation of truth seekers on to meditation and mysticism. It pointed east to find the answers to the shallow materialism of the West and the hypocrisies of Christian dogma. How do they get past the first commandment anyway? "Within You Without You" was about taking responsibility for your thoughts and actions. For me it was the spiritual warrior's call for self-reflection.

The song reached its crescendo and Harrison pleaded to his listeners: *"Try to realize it's all within yourself, no one else can make you change. And a time will come when you see we're all one and life flows on within you and without you."* A hush fell over the crowd as we all took stock of our place in the universe. Everyone could sense the show was almost over, so they began applauding in unison and chanting, "One more song. One more song."

Graham rolled his eyes but nodded his assent from the sidelines. "Okay, guys, but please nothing too long. We're running out of time. Let's go out with a bang!"

Spontaneously Lennon took the mic and asked, "So you want a revolution?" The crowd shouted back, *"Yes!"* The more rebellious ones said, "Hell yeah!"

Harrison stood up and grabbed his electric guitar and they both turned their volume up several notches. Together they played the savage opening chords of Lennon's classic political rocker "Revolution." The stage was all Lennon's now as he rocked the house and sang full-throated into the mic, "*You say you want a revolution, well, you know, we all want to change the world.*" Holographic feet stomped the beat as everyone sang, "*And you know it's gonna be . . . all right! All right! All right!*" to finish the song.

The last chord rang out and the applause erupted. The two dead Beatles high-fived, feeling the love musicians have for each other after winning an audience over.

Lennon leaned into Harrison and said, "Hey, George, I'm sorry I didn't support you as much as I could have. You were the youngest and it must have been tough standing up to me and Paul. It was always two against one, wasn't it?"

"Yeah, well. It wasn't easy, but I appreciate your apology." Putting his arm around Lennon's shoulders, Harrison said, "I did learn from the best, didn't I?"

30 God's Last Request

The true profession of man is to find his way to himself.
—HERMANN HESSE

Bill Graham strode onstage during the applause to close the show. He had his holographic hands on the center mic and was about to speak, when the voice of his mother—a voice he had not heard since he was ten years old—sounded in his mind. Frieda Grajonca, who gave him life twice by helping him escape the Nazis, spoke lovingly inside his head.

"Please, Wolfgang. Let me have one last song." Hearing what he knew was the voice of God, Graham hung his head low and said in perfect Polish, "*Tak, mama.*" Simultaneously, inside the minds of everyone there, the voices of their own mothers spoke. "Please, John," said the voice of God inside Lennon's mind, "bring your drinking buddies up onstage and sing me one of my favorite songs." The buoyant working-class voice of Julia Lennon poured through his mind.

"What song is that?" asked Lennon telepathically.

"You know, the Pete Ham song that your friend Harry covered."

"'Without You'?" Lennon teared up and struggled to maintain his composure.

"That's the one!" said his mother's voice, full of pleasure. "I think it's an appropriate choice for a last song."

Lennon glanced over at Graham, who was leaning against the backstage wall looking pretty shook up as he reminisced about his own mother, who was killed at Auschwitz. Graham gave the nod to do one more song. Lennon stepped up to the mic and stared at the crowd, feeling overwhelmed himself. All the dead musicians were still reeling from hearing their mothers' voices speaking to them.

"Well, it seems our cosmic Mother has made a request of her own. Will Harry Nilsson, Keith Moon, Pete Ham, and Tom Evans please come up to the stage to help us with this one?"

Rising from the heart attack section, legendary singer and Lennon's infamous barroom brawler companion Harry Nilsson began winding his way to the stage. Keith Moon rose from the overdose section, waving at Nilsson from across the aisles and shouting, "I should have listened to you, Harry. Your fucking apartment was cursed!" He was referring to the warnings Nilsson had given him about staying there. Both Evans and Mama Cass died in Nilsson's London flat. Moon walked over to drummer Benny Benjamin, who handed him a tambourine. Benjamin was not willing to surrender the drums to Moon, who was notorious for destroying drum kits onstage.

Sitting next to each other in the suicide section, the two tragic members of Badfinger stood up. Pete Ham and Tom Evans had lost heart, as well as all their money, after being signed to the Beatles' Apple Records in 1968. When Apple dissolved in 1973, it took Badfinger down with it, leaving the band, in particular Pete Ham, destitute. Even after writing the megahit "Without You" that God wanted to hear, Ham received no money from the song. He hanged himself in 1975 at age thirty-five, a broken man. You'd never know it, though, as he and the others walked down the aisles to the cheers of the audience. They were all smiles as they strolled onstage, hugging Lennon and Harrison for God's last request.

Nilsson took the mic and began singing as the band backed him, "*No, I can't forget this evening or your face as you were leaving, but I guess that's just the way the story goes. You always smile but in your eyes your sorrow shows. Yes, it shows.*" Nilsson offered the mic to the song's author, Pete Ham, who sang the second verse. "*No, I can't forget tomorrow when I think of all my sorrow when I had you there but then I let you go. And now it's only fair that I should let you know what you should know.*"

The members onstage, the whole hall, even Bill Graham and Keith Moon threw their voices into the chorus, "*Can't live if living is without you. Can't give, can't give anymore. I can't live if living is without you. I can't give. I can't give anymore.*"

After the song, the theater grew silent. Then everyone heard their mothers' voices for one final time. "Thank you, my children. I have loved you all since you were stardust. Your music has inspired me and given me strength. The darkness is coming. Now we must go."

31 The Guardian

An army of sheep led by a lion can defeat an army of lions led by a sheep.

—AFRICAN PROVERB

Bill Graham took the mic, looking a bit rumpled from the arduous task of managing the huge event. "Well, it's been like juggling a bunch of wildcats, but it's been fun! I want to thank all the bands, all the songwriters, all the singers for performing tonight. You were the greatest generation for music. Thanks to the Funk Brothers and the Wrecking Crew. We really worked you guys hard tonight." The musicians stepped forward and took a bow to deafening applause. "You definitely earned your sushi," said Graham as they exited the stage for the greenroom.

"We have one last performer tonight and he's the real deal, ladies and gents." Graham looked nervously toward the backstage hallway. "I don't see him. But . . ." For the first time, Graham seemed a bit uneasy. He cast a few more anxious glances, but no one appeared. Looking embarrassed, he said,

"Ladies and gentlemen, let's take a quick break while we locate our final performer."

A deep, resonant voice came from behind him. "I am here, Mr. Graham." Graham jumped, startled by the sound, and peeked over his shoulder. And there, standing right behind him, was the driver from the airport Super Shuttle.

So, he's been driving us this whole time, I thought.

In his blue bus driver suit, he appeared strange and diminutive standing next to Bill Graham. Graham seemed cowed by the old man's presence. "Ladies, gentlemen, angels, and muses, please welcome our final performer. The first musician on Earth. And by the way, he can play as long as he wants. Please welcome *the Guardian*!" Graham hastily left the stage as a hush fell over the audience.

The Guardian cast his eyes over the heavenly throng for a few moments, then solemnly began humming as he slowly removed his uniform, stripping down to a weathered brown loincloth. The veins stood out on his black arms and legs; his springy hair stood up in the stage lights, moving like snaking creatures with lives of their own. He began chanting a deep, low rhythmic tone, "Yahh dahh hahh om," as he lifted a long beautifully painted didgeridoo that had appeared by his feet. He reverently held it out in his wrinkled hands. He took deliberate measure of all the souls in the center of the sun, who were spellbound as the tension mounted. Shaking his didgeridoo at them, he said with a voice of defiance and authority, "Do you know who you are?" He asked again, holding the didgeridoo over his head, "I said, do you know who you *are*?"

A roar of affirmation filled the hall. "*Yes!*" came the reply, and I saw that John, George, and Richie were also shouting, "Yes!"

"*Yes!* You are the warriors of *song*. You are the soldiers of *vibration*!" Eyes blazing with energy, the Guardian put the didgeridoo to his lips and loosed a sonic blast that threatened to tear the theater apart.

The Guardian never took a breath as he began shaking a rattle and making animal sounds through his didgeridoo. His eyes were rolled way back in his head; all you could see were the whites. He was lost in a deep inner place. I noticed that everyone except me had their eyes closed in a mutual trance. The walls of the old theater began to flicker as the Guardian's song called on the sun to take the souls of the musicians back. One by one at first, then in whole groups, they became translucent, swirling into pure golden plasma before they whooshed upward, out the ceiling, and back into the sun.

Sitting in the multiple organ failure section was the last soul to leave. I was stunned to see he was dead. When I left Earth, he was still alive. It was Richard Anthony Monsour, professionally known as Dick Dale, the King of the Surf Guitar, who gained his masterful and influential style from his father's Lebanese roots. Dale's passion for surfing inspired him to come up with riffs that matched the rush he felt while riding the waves. That desire combined with Eastern tonalities and the rapid-fire picking style of the oud—a lute-like Middle Eastern instrument—resulted in his signature sound, which launched the surf-rock genre in the early '60s. Most people know him for his hit single "Misirlou," a folk song that Dale adapted into a surf-rock tune and was popularized in the movie *Pulp Fiction*.

Dick Dale opened his eyes and we acknowledged each other for a moment. I had had the honor of opening for him in the '90s at the Sausalito Art and Wine Festival. He played so furiously using thick picks that you could see them disintegrating in the stage lights like falling snow. I wanted to express my appreciation, but he was morphing into a purely plasmic creature. So, I just mouthed, "Thank you." As he was turning golden, he smiled and said, "Surf's up!" then exploded off his seat and shot out the ceiling. With his departure, the theater was empty. Richie, George, John, and I stood looking at each other. Then Radio City Music Hall itself started to melt.

The Guardian's sonic blowtorch was melting the theater. I watched the walls liquefy around us like a box of molten crayons. It reduced itself in increments into the familiar shape and confines of the old hippie bus that had brought us here. The lava lamps still undulated and the string incense still burned. The Guardian stopped playing and set his didgeridoo on the seat beside him. He settled into the driver's seat and said, "We are back. Enough distraction. Now let us go!"

32 Coronal Mass Ejection

If there is a solar flare, a thousand cans of pickled turnips aren't going to save you.

—SARAH LOTZ, *THE THREE*

I eased myself onto the nearest purple couch. Havens, Harrison, and Lennon opened their eyes slowly, sized up the surroundings, and did the same.

"Wow. We made it!" said Havens with relief.

A wide-eyed Harrison said, "Yeah, Richie, it was hard not to go completely plasmic that time."

Lennon rubbed his eyes and said, "Shit! I've got a headache. Wait a minute. How can I be dead and have a bloody headache?"

"If you accept a holographic afterlife, you have to take some holographic pain." Harrison cocked his head toward Lennon. "Would you like some holographic Advil?"

"What just happened?" I asked.

Havens put a hand on my shoulder. "The show's over, Jimmy. God's let us have our fun, but now she's calling in all the troops. She's absorbed the souls of all the musicians who have passed from our generation and loaded their essence into the largest coronal mass ejection in history."

Carl Sagan returned to my head. "Some people call them solar flares, but we don't actually know what coronal mass ejections are. Perhaps the stars are pollinating space with spirits, perhaps the sun is communicating with other stars. We just don't know. CMEs are mysterious creatures. But here's the issue: a direct hit from one could wipe out civilization as we know it."

Panicked, I asked, "Will it hit Earth, Richie?"

"No. This one is aimed at a quite different part of space and for an extremely specific purpose. But get ready. It's blast-off time!"

The Guardian took the wheel, dropped the tranny into drive, and, with a wild look in his eyes, punched the accelerator. We hurtled forward, toward the surface of the sun.

As we jetted forward, a huge blob of orange plasma followed us. Traveling at a fantastic speed, we reached the surface in a matter of moments. In a spectacular eruption, we exploded into space and began warping across the solar system and past the heliosphere. A tiny hippie bus leading a dazzling, luminous comet of souls into battle.

THE ASSOCIATED PRESS BREAKING NEWS
MAUI, HAWAII (AP) At 11:26 a.m. HST, National Science
Foundation astronomers from the Daniel K. Inouye Solar
Telescope witnessed the eruption of the largest coronal mass
ejection (CME) ever recorded. It blazed forth in the general

direction of Earth's next closest star, Proxima Centauri. Had it been a direct hit, the enormous CME would have wiped out all advanced communications and wreaked havoc on the environment and the technosphere.

We hurtled toward a pulsating small red sun that was visible in the distance. Something lurked nearby. Something sinister. Something threatening. Something that resembled a huge, gaping black mouth. (I noted, with some surprise and a little pride, that this formidable sight was not triggering a panic attack.)

"There it is, Jimmy. The Black Chord." Havens pointed through the window at the enormous dark vortex. It exuded malevolence. Long black tendrils reached out from its center, swirling into space. As we got closer, it appeared less a crack in space and more of a hellish gargantuan octopus swimming toward us. It seemed to know we were here. As we neared, its tendrils reached for us.

"Is it a black hole?" I asked.

"It's the sonic cousin of a black hole. A black chord in anti–E minor. A nullifying sound of tremendous power. It thrives on silence and darkness. Its first target is Earth. Earth sings in the darkness like a mockingbird at midnight attracting unwanted attention."

"How can it steal music? Music is an etheric art form. There's nothing for it to steal."

Havens poured some peppermint tea into a cup and gave it to me. "You're still living in a body on a small rocky planet.

Beyond the grave, reality is mostly etheric. The Black Chord lives in this space. Back on Earth, nobody can see or detect it, but everyone is negatively affected by it. Think of it as a kind of dark energy, but instead of pulling on planets, it's going for the spirit, swallowing everything beautiful and creative." He paused a moment, then continued. "It wants a cacotopia, the worst kind of dystopia. The Black Chord's cacophony will consume melody and harmony in this universe. Music everywhere will start to fade, and be lost forever. And as music is squelched, so is the spirit, hope, and potential of all sentient beings."

"That sounds crazy, Richie!"

"You don't believe me? Let's try an experiment, okay? Try to remember just *one* of your favorite Beatles songs."

I closed my eyes and tried to remember "A Day in the Life," which I thought was among the greatest songs ever written. But no matter how hard I tried, I couldn't remember how it began or how it ran. I was dumbstruck.

"See? At this close distance, the Black Chord has already wiped out the memory of one of your favorite songs."

I tried to remember "Strawberry Fields Forever." Almost nothing. I tried to remember "Lucy in the Sky with Diamonds." Nothing. As we got closer, I found I couldn't even remember the titles of my *own* songs. I felt heavy and full of dread. "So how does the Guardian fit into all this?"

Havens closed his eyes and listened to the Guardian's didgeridoo, which droned on and on through the bus and out into space. It sounded soothing, like a cat purring. But a low, menacing undertone grew louder the closer we got to the rift.

He continued, "The ultralow sounds of his didgeridoo will form a sonic seal around the Black Chord and clear a space to funnel the music of Earth's departed musicians. With enough passion and conviction, we can pierce that dark rift by pouring our love into it and flooding the other side with music and light. New stars will emerge. And music will spring up from the shadows to fill that dark universe again."

As the rumble intensified, the rivets on the bus threatened to shake loose. I observed the Guardian sitting cross-legged in his loincloth with his eyes rolled back—primeval, deep in a timeless reverie. If Earth were to develop a musical weapon, this would be it.

"So musicians really *are* soldiers in the afterlife?"

"Yes! We are quite literally soldiers of vibration. We consume disharmony and make music out of it. Stars, planets, comets, almost anything can fall out of tune. We keep things tuned up."

"And I've been drafted into this army?"

"That's right! To the general public, musicians are perceived as leading rather frivolous lives, but if you average in what we do over the course of eternity, we have the hardest job of all."

Harrison, who was eavesdropping on our conversation, took a bite of a cream tangerine truffle, sipped his tea, and then leaned over from his couch. "You didn't think you were gonna get your money for nothing and your chicks for free without paying for it on the backside, did you?"

Lennon agreed. "He's right! You're being given a great gift and a great responsibility, so don't be dazzled by the lights when you get home. Let fame run off you, or you'll be embalmed by it.

You're being drafted as a field captain in the musical charge back to universal love and brotherly understanding. It'll test your limits. So, stay sober when they start handing you the drinks and adulation. And squeeze your bloody cheeks together when they start blowing smoke up your arse."

Havens squeezed my hands hard, hoping I was taking in what they were saying. He released me and said, "It's been great seeing you again, but the party's over and it's time to go." A sad, faraway expression came over his face. His gaze fixed on the ceiling as he whispered, "I'm leaving, Jimmy. We're all leaving." He sat back on the couch and closed his eyes.

The hum of the Guardian's didgeridoo magnified exponentially. It was as if the bus were a huge bass speaker that the Guardian was filling with lustrous, rhythmic waves of vibration. The sonic pounding drummed heavily in my chest, making it impossible to speak. I took stock of Harrison and Havens. They both sat erect on their purple cushions with eyes closed, in deep meditation. I stood witness as they turned translucent, then golden, then lost human form altogether. Their dancing energy whooshed out the back door of the bus turned comet and joined its tail of souls.

Lennon was awestruck as he stared out the windshield at the Black Chord, which filled the visual field and swam toward us. "Here it comes, James! Fucking shit! What a bloody monster!" A dreadful nauseous heaviness enveloped me. I didn't want to look. Instead, I curled into a fetal position on the velvet couch. The Guardian's thunderous drone continued, melting the metal of the bus. The floorboards began to dematerialize beneath me. Through the disappearing floor,

I could see a monstrous tendril of the Black Chord coming closer, almost licking the wheels of the bus. I felt my death near. My life flashed before my eyes, but was interrupted by a crazy, ironic thought. *How the hell can I die in the afterlife when I'm not dead yet on Earth?*

PART FIVE

33 Fear, Love, and Jet Flight

Do not follow where the trail leads, go where there is no path and leave a trail.

—RALPH WALDO EMERSON

"SFO, terminal 3, United terminal, domestic flights." I opened my eyes and sat up from my fetal position. A glance out the shuttle bus's window revealed rain falling in grape-size drops. The driver's African-accented voice repeated over the intercom, "SFO! Final stop for United domestic departures."

The two businessmen in gray suits gathered their bags and umbrellas and exited the shuttle. Feeling hungover and disoriented, I looked around slowly, not sure where I was or what I was doing. Lennon's voice sounded behind me. "Come on, James. Let's go or we'll miss our plane!"

My body was a heavy lump glued to the seat. Needles and pins spread through my arms and legs as I tried to stand. "Sorry. Guess I must have fallen asleep. Jesus! I just had the most bizarre dream in my life."

"That was no dream, my mate. Don't worry about how your limbs feel. It's only the aftereffects of space-time travel. Your body's getting used to the present time again."

"So all that actually happened? It feels like we've been gone for months!"

"Forty-five hours in the afterlife to be exact, but only twenty-five minutes here on Earth. No time to talk about it now. Look lively, mate! Let's get going!"

The bus started rolling forward, so I shouted from the back, "Hold on, please! This is my stop!"

The driver stopped the bus with a jerk and stared me down with his deep-black eyes, obviously annoyed.

As we edged past, I asked, "Hey, don't you play the didgeridoo?"

He gave me a sly sideways glance and considered me with one unblinking eye. "You are stereotyping me, my friend. I am just a lowly bus driver. You must be thinking of someone else."

"Oh! I'm sorry, man. You look like a didge player I used to know."

"It is no big thing, young man." He fixed his sights out the windshield, unperturbed. But as Lennon passed, he whispered sternly, "Do not stay in New York too long, rock star. You are needed elsewhere." Lennon practically leaped out the door to get away from him.

"That's the Guardian?" I asked Lennon anxiously.

"Yes, but only in his Earthly aspect. I know he's on our side, but he still gives me the willies!"

"Me too! He looks like he could shoot fire out his eyes."

"He probably can!"

We walked toward the United terminal. I was being pummeled by the rain, while Lennon strode beside me dry as toast and as unconcerned about the weather as ever. We entered the building and approached the ticket counter. The carefully groomed millennial behind the counter scrutinized my reservation. "You've reserved two seats just for yourself?" she asked quizzically.

"Yes, that's right. Is there a problem?"

"No. But if you want more legroom, why not buy one first-class ticket? You'll get free champagne, excellent food, and a movie, and you'll save a couple hundred dollars." She smiled proudly as if she was really doing me a favor.

"Thank you for the offer, but I really can't fly first class."

"Why not?" she asked, perplexed by my refusal.

My near-superhuman ability to instantly obfuscate anything came to my aid, while Lennon chuckled at my diversion. "You see"—I glimpsed her United badge—"you see, Alyson, I don't believe in first-class anything. It creates division between people; and to be honest, I'm a socialist at heart."

"What's a socialist?" she asked, starting to get annoyed.

"Someone who believes that we should be treated equally in all things."

She shook her head in exasperation. "But all you'll get in coach is pretzels and orange juice."

"Well, at least I won't get scurvy," I said, trying to lighten the conversation.

"What's scurvy?" But before I could answer, she handed me my tickets and, looking through me, muttered under her breath, "Okay, boomer."

Then she called, "Next customer, may I help you?" Later that night, she googled "socialist" and got into an argument with her boyfriend.

Lennon was quite amused by my storytelling. "People think you're a real weirdo, James. But I must admit, you're getting better at hanging out with ghosts. This is going to be a fun flight. As you living entities say now, we can 'laugh a lot.'"

"You mean 'laugh out loud,' John."

"Right, right. 'Laugh out loud,' that's better."

When we got to the gate, the airline employee also noted my double reservation and said, "Is somebody accompanying you?"

"No, I bought the two seats just for me." I leaned in and said softly, as if sharing a secret, "You see, I play with the New York Philharmonic, so I bought a seat for my cello. But I changed my mind since the weather's so bad and arranged to borrow a cello once I get to New York."

"A cellist!" she said loudly for all to hear. "How lovely! I'm a big fan of Yo-Yo Ma!"

As we squeezed onto the plane, Lennon snickered beside me. "I'm going to call you Yo-Yo Drake from now on."

We pressed our way to aisle twenty-two and Lennon slipped into the window seat, excited as a boy on his way to the circus. I took the middle seat. A minute later, a friendly, chatty woman of Indian descent in her mid-thirties sat in the aisle seat.

"Oh, you are the cellist. How wonderful! I love the cello! I'm also a big fan of Yo-Yo Ma! Hello, my name is Ritu." She offered her hand to me.

"Hello, Ritu. My name is James. Crazy weather we're having, isn't it?"

"Not to worry, we'll be flying above the storm. I see the window seat is open. Do you mind if I take it? I so enjoy looking down at the clouds."

Lennon glared at me, shaking his head vigorously in opposition. "No, no! As pretty as she is, I don't want her sitting on top of me the whole bloody flight!"

"I'm sorry, Ritu, but I bought that seat to leave it empty."

"Really? Why? You don't have your cello!"

"When I was a little boy, I saw that *Twilight Zone* episode where a passenger—a young William Shatner, by the way—was sitting in the window seat of a commercial flight. When he looks out the window from thirty thousand feet, he sees a creature on the wing pulling at the wires of the plane, trying to bring it down."

"*The Twilight Zone*? William Shatner?"

"You've never seen *The Twilight Zone* or *Star Trek*?"

"No. I grew up in India."

"Well, they're American television shows from the 1960s about the paranormal and science fiction."

"I was born in 1990, so that was well before my time. Monsters don't live on the wings of planes. You must know that logically."

"Logically, yes. But unfortunately, I suffer from panic attacks. So, I do my best to avoid situations that might stimulate one—especially when I'm flying." To show I was serious, I pulled down the window shade, much to the annoyance of both Ritu and Lennon. I feigned a sigh of relief and sat back in my seat. "Whew! The less I see the better."

Lennon was pissed. "Christ! I was looking forward to the view." He tried to raise the window shade, but his ghostly fingers kept slipping through the handle. He sat back in his seat, irritated. "Shit! My last plane ride on Earth and I don't even get to look down on the bloody planet without hanging my bloody head out of the fuselage!"

I was so agitated I turned to what Ritu thought was an empty seat and said, "Stop fidgeting, John! I'm trying to save the seat for you!" Instantly, I realized how crazy my outburst must have sounded to her. My face reddened with embarrassment.

"Who's John?" Ritu asked, perplexed.

"Oh yeah, he's uh, uh. Listen, Ritu, I know this sounds crazy. But to distract myself from panic, I imagine that someone is sitting next to me in the window seat and his job is to keep me from opening the shade. You see, I also suffer from morbid curiosity. I might lift the shade impulsively and freak myself out."

"And who do you imagine?"

"I usually visualize my favorite songwriters. For this flight, I've picked, uh, John Lennon."

Ritu paused for a moment, staring at me incredulously. Her young brow scrunched up and her pretty mouth hung open, hardly believing what she just heard. "Would you excuse me a moment?" With that, she grabbed her carry-on bag and walked hurriedly to the front of the plane, where she hailed the flight attendant. She pointed at me and shook her head, like sane people do when they seek relief from crazy people. I heard her say, "He's not a real cellist!" The flight attendant nodded sympathetically and shot me a glance as though to say, "I've got my eyes on you, buddy!" Given the several weather-related cancellations, she found Ritu a window seat in the third aisle.

With no further ado, Lennon and I were left alone, which allowed us to talk freely for the rest of the flight. I realized this would be my last chance to ask him the many questions I'd been wanting to ask. I opened the window shade to his great relief and tried to collect my thoughts.

The seat belt light came on. "Passengers and crew, prepare for takeoff," said the pilot over the intercom, his voice calm— almost bored. He seemed unflappable. It was hard to believe he could sound so casual about flying in such bad weather.

As the plane waited in line on the runway for its turn to take off, Lennon gazed out the window. There were rivers of water sweeping across the black asphalt and heading toward the sewer grates, which were backing up with dark pools of runoff. "Man, this global warming thing's no joke! It's going to be a bit of a splashy takeoff." Feeling me staring at him, pregnant with questions, he asked, "Got something on your mind, James?"

"Well, yeah. I do have a few questions I've been wanting to ask you."

He turned from the watery view of the airport and smiled at me as if he already knew the questions. "Fire away."

"Okay. Well, first off, what was it like being a Beatle?"

"Not that one again." He shook his head, then answered, "To me we weren't the Beatles. I didn't look at George and think, 'He's a Beatle.' I looked at him and thought, 'He's George, and I love George.' What other stupid fan questions you got?"

Unfazed, I asked, "What was your songwriting process?"

"*Process* is not the word I'd use. Songwriting is about getting the demons out of you. It's like being possessed. You try to go to sleep, but the song won't let you. You have to get up and make it into something and then you're allowed to sleep." He glanced over the rim of his glasses. "Next?"

"When you wrote 'All You Need Is Love,' did you really believe that to be true?"

"And I thought you were going to ask me a hard question like, 'Why does cutting onions make you cry?' or 'Are dogs *really* man's best friend?' Well, love means many things to many people, but the simple answer is yes. I believed it then and I believe it now."

"But didn't you just write the song for the BBC special *Our World*, the first international satellite broadcast in 1967?"

"Hey! It took fifty-eight bloody takes to get that song right. So don't lecture *me* on sincerity. *You* try coming up with an epic song on demand. I had to sing it live when I didn't even have the words memorized. Bloody hell. Imagine what a disaster it would have been fucking up that song in front of millions of people." Taking a gentler tone, he continued. "I will admit that my original inspiration for writing the song was fueled by that opportunity. I knew it would be big, so I wanted to write a song with a positive message. It was a brilliant production and way ahead of its time. Ten thousand technicians around the world worked on that show. It went out live to twenty-four countries on the world's first satellites. They called them the Early Birds. Something like four hundred million to seven hundred million people tuned in. It was a brilliant opportunity to reach out to the entire world. The Vietnam War was still raging, and the Middle East was falling apart. So, writing 'All You Need Is Love' was my way to counteract the craziness of the times. It was also a good therapy song for meself. The Cold War was terrifying for anyone with a good imagination." He paused, then added, "And I'll tell you something else. If anyone thinks that peace and love are just a cliché left behind from the '60s, that's a problem. Peace and love are eternal."

"You sang the word *love* III times in that song."

"Yes, that's right. Probably a Guinness record. And *you* probably counted each time, didn't you?"

"Yeah, I counted III times when I was fourteen years old. Was it a hard song to write? I mean, it affected so many people, including me."

"No, not really. In those days, flower power was everywhere. Any songwriter worth his or her salt could squeeze songs about universal love out of their arses, and people would listen. People really wanted to hear them. When there's ears to listen, we songwriters write. Don't you agree?"

"It must have been great writing songs like that when people were really listening. Nowadays people are more geared to how the world ends instead of how it can come together."

"Yes, from what I've gathered by my visits, that's true. Your brilliance, James, is that even though there were fewer ears who wanted to listen, you never stopped. You kept singing. You kept your light on, even as the room darkened. That's why I'm here with you now. Next question?"

I was so entranced by my conversation with Lennon, I forgot we were about to take off. The engines roared to life, and

I gripped the armrests as we roared down the runway. The jet ascended into the storm, a modern-day Prometheus snubbing his nose at the weather gods. The relative ease with which it rose through the clouds was tempered by my knowledge that landings are more dangerous. And we would be landing on the East Coast in a bomb cyclone in less than six hours.

"Hello! Next question?" Lennon repeated, leaning over to make sure I was okay.

Once the jet was fully airborne, its wheels retracted, thudding shut, and I recovered enough to continue asking questions. "All right. Well, if all you need is love, what *is* love?"

"Oh, bother. There's *that* ridiculous question again. It would be better to ask me what love *isn't*."

"You mean the opposite of love?"

"That's one way to look at it. So, what's the opposite of love?"

"That's easy! Hate, right?"

"No. Negative emotions like hate and anger are just symptoms of something larger and more pervasive. It's been a plague on our species since we were living in caves hiding from saber-toothed tigers. It lurks in the dark corners of our minds, always trying to make us fight or run away. Come on. You're a smart mortal. What is it?"

I was still rattled by the takeoff. Seeing my worried expression, Lennon put his weightless hand on mine and said, "The opposite of love, James—is fear."

Yes, of course. *Fear*, my lifelong nemesis. Lennon saw the look on my face and tried to reassure me. "Lucky for us, one of the laws of the universe is that opposites attract. Fear and love are in a romantic entanglement if you will. Fear has a crush on love, and she *knows* that. He's so attracted to her he'd do anything to get her. She'd be a real prize. That's when she uses her tricks to lure him in and cure him of his fearful ways."

"How does she do that?"

"She puts him to the test, makes him jump through all kinds of hoops and rakes him over the coals of his own resistance." He paused and looked out the window again. "We're almost above the clouds, James."

I ignored his comment. "What happens to fear?" I asked impatiently.

"He stops being afraid, and voilà. He morphs into courage. At that point she can't resist him. Because courage is the ultimate girl magnet."

"So, love uses fear's desire for her as a lure to transform fear into courage. And that clears the way for more love?" I asked.

Lennon nodded. "Reality leaves a lot to the imagination." He returned to contemplating the clouds.

I sat back in my seat for a moment, taking it all in. "*Courage*, then, is the fuel to make positive change in our lives and in the world. And *love* is the force that transforms fear into courage!"

"Yes! That's right. All we need is love, but we need it *all*, James—not just a little piece of it. Whether you're living on Earth or in some bardo in the afterlife, a soul must open to love and gather enough of it to shine through eternity, and the best way to do that is to transform fear."

"That explains why I've been having such a hard time these past years. I've been feeling a lot of fear and I haven't been doing much about it."

"Well, you may not have been feeling particularly courageous, but you stayed the course, and what you did in the face
of fear is what true courage is all about."

"What did *I* do?"

"You kept the faith, James! You kept writing in the face of
constant rejection. It took *courage* to play all those bloody food
court gigs. And it took *courage* when you spoke up for your
songs after taking abuse from that arsehole publisher in L.A.
That's when you got on love's radar, and she's been pulling on
you ever since. Sometimes our best intentions speak louder
than our worst fears, even when our knees are knocking or
we're pissing our pants."

"Like up on the bridge?"

"Right! Like up on the bridge. Or how you thought you
were dying when that Jolly Rancher flew out of your nose.
Powerful forces were already on their way to help you. So, what
is love? To be honest, I still don't really know, but I can tell you
this. When fear clears out, love pours in. It's the natural default
setting of this universe. The universal background energy. *Love
noise*, if you will. You're wasting your time and driving yourself
crazy by obsessing about what love is. It doesn't matter who
you love, where you love, why you love, when you love, or how
you love, it matters only *that* you love."

Lennon paused for me to acknowledge his words, then
went on. "So much human energy has been distracted by that
question. You live in a world where you have to hide to make
love, while violence is practiced in broad daylight. It's better to
clear your mind of your fears and experience love as it rushes
in. Love is an experience, not an explanation. Love's a verb,

not a noun. You'll understand more after you die, James; but for now, it's better to just do love's work." He smiled wryly, realizing how much he sounded like George Harrison admonishing him to do his own work to leave Near Heaven.

Lennon's words rang true and made sense. I had the sudden urge to write a song about fear and love, and wished I had a guitar. I voiced my thoughts. "Somebody should write a song about fear and love."

"Yeah. Somebody *should*. And since you finally coughed up that furball of fear you've been ruminating on for years, methinks it will be you. Remember to give me songwriting credit on that one, too. If I were still on Earth, I'd write it meself."

"I promise."

"Listen, James, can we please take a break from all the inquiry? I want to look down at this beast you Californians call a pineapple express. Weather is so much more dramatic now, and this is my last chance to see it."

"Okay, okay. I've got one last question and then I'll leave you alone."

"Yesss?" He peered over his glasses like a rock 'n' roll Nosferatu.

"You could have had almost any woman you wanted—at least the ones that weren't screaming for Paul. Why did you stay with Yoko?"

"Because my mate, she *saw* me. She wasn't a fan of the Beatles. When we met, she didn't know who I was. To her, I was just some bloke off the street checking out her artwork. The hardest thing is facing yourself. It's easier to shout 'revolution' or 'power to the people' than it is to look at yourself and find out what's really inside you." He paused. "I wasn't always good to women. I have a lot to answer for. I was a hitter in my earlier years. I couldn't express myself and I hit. But I sincerely believe in love and peace. I am a violent man who has learned not to be violent and regrets his violence." He stopped and looked at me until I met his gaze.

I nodded, and he continued. "You see, underneath it all, I'm really just a gardener. And every gardener knows you've got to deep water your tomatoes, or you won't get any fruit. I was an idiot when I sprinkled myself around. Every true connection I had started drying out. I'm not an easy person to be around. She put up with a lot from me. She lived in my bloody shadow. The fame, the mean fans, the racism, my moods. Yoko is my deepwater harbor and I'm sailing home to her."

With so much happening, I had forgotten that my time with Lennon was coming to an end. I felt a twinge of panic at the thought of losing him. I had gotten used to his company. He was a truly unique soul. "Thank you, John, I really appreciate your answers. I'll leave you alone now," I said to the empty seat just as Ritu walked by heading toward the bathroom.

Seeing me talking to an empty seat again and noting that my window shade was now open, she flashed her eyes fearfully. I called after her, trying to lessen her worries, "Good news, Ritu! There are no monsters on the wing." But my sarcasm only made it worse. She'd clearly had enough of me. "You're a real nowhere man," I heard her mutter.

Lennon was delighted. "I swear I haven't had this much fun hanging out with a mortal since my drinking days with Harry Nilsson. I wrote 'Nowhere Man' about myself, you know."

We were flying high above the pineapple express now. A thick layer of gray and white clouds extended below as far as I could see. It was as if they were enveloping the entire Earth. I could feel the clouds moving in on me too. A cold Northern Pacific fog was pouring into my heart the closer we got to New York. I had lost John Lennon once to murder in 1980. It was a black day for me and millions of others around the world. To lose him a second time was almost more than I could bear. Soon I would have to release my hero, my friend, this legendary apparition, and figure out how to live my life without him.

There were many more questions I wanted to ask. Answers that Google couldn't give me. Like "How did it feel being a little kid during World War II?" (I'd heard accounts that Lennon was born during a German aerial bombardment of Liverpool in 1940.) Or stupid fan questions like "What's your favorite ice cream? And is it true you loved to play Monopoly and took the game with you on the road?" But as he gazed out over the clouds, he looked like any other lovelorn guy who's been away from his lover a long time. As the miles peeled away, bringing him closer to Yoko, there was a palpable air of anticipation about him. He missed her like someone would miss a lost limb. They were inseparable until a bullet changed their realities. He started humming "Oh My Love" from the *Imagine* album. I could tell he was thinking only of Yoko, and I didn't want to interrupt.

An hour later, the pilot's voice came over the intercom. "Well, folks, as you can see, the clouds are starting to part and the skies are clear over the Midwest. That's Kansas City coming into view. We've turned off the Fasten Seat Belt sign, so you're free to wander the cabin. Thanks for holding it for so long."

"Hey, James! Look! I see it. There's Kansas City."

Lennon pointed down at the great flat heart of America with Kansas City right below us. "We played the Kansas City Municipal Stadium back in 1964. We only played for thirty-one minutes but made $150,000! Poor Charles Finley. I always felt guilty about handing him that bill. What a bloody hassle it was, though. The usual crazy female fans reaching into our car and lying in wait like lionesses in heat. A hundred cops in front of the stage. Over two hundred more out in the venue. The local police chief said instead of a British invasion he would have preferred a Martian one. Anyways," he added brightly, "we're halfway to New York!"

I was in no mood for sun. I felt sad and grew quiet, leaving John to his own reverie. The sun was indeed shining over Kansas, but a personal fog was pouring into my heart. It whispered a curse in my ear: *Of all the qualities you will miss about John Lennon, it's his sense of humor you will miss the most.* That fog spoke truth. It chilled me. No matter how serious, cynical, or raw Lennon got, his wit always saved him. He was the Joker and the Grim Reaper rolled into one, and I loved this about him. He pushed us *all* over the edge.

A little over two and a half hours later, as we neared JFK International Airport, the captain—his voice higher and speech faster—came over the intercom. "Ladies and gentlemen, I've turned on the Fasten Seat Belt sign and asked the flight attendants to be seated. We are entering an area of turbulence and I need everyone seated for safety."

Airline pilots are trained to remain calm, and they all seem to mimic the flat, folksy drawl of Chuck Yeager, the unflappable legendary pilot who broke the sound barrier in 1947. So, the obvious nervousness in the pilot's voice unsettled me. In all my years of touring, I'd never heard a nervous pilot on the intercom.

The flight attendants walked briskly through the cabin making sure everyone's seat belts were not only fastened but pulled tight. The jet lurched like it had just passed over a huge speed bump, which elicited a few startled screams and exclamations from the passengers. The flight attendants ran to their stations and buckled into their own seats. The one who had seemed most composed earlier kissed the cross on her necklace and fixed her eyes Heavenward, mouthing a silent prayer.

Lennon had his nose to the window, oblivious to the weather and the human drama as we descended through the storm. "We're almost there, James!" he said, rubbing his hands together and singing, "*It's been a long time, now I'm coming back home.*"

I felt irritated that he could be so blithe about what was going on. He was already dead, so what did he care?

"Hey, aren't you concerned that we might crash?"

"Not at all. I told you: musicians only die in small planes—mostly anyways, and besides, it's not in your karma to die that way. At least that's what the angels tell me. Lighten up, man!" He smiled and, with an elbow I could see but not feel, jostled me in the ribs. He got a crazy look in his eyes and started singing a Buddy Holly tune: "*If you knew Peggy Sue, then you know why I feel blue about Peggy, my Peggy Sue . . .*"

"Come on, man! You're jinxing the plane! I've come close to death hanging out with you once already. Please, no more Buddy Holly songs." I put my hands over my ears, praying he would stop.

"Oh, rubbish! Would you prefer a Ritchie Valens tune, then? Or Ricky Nelson, perhaps?" Lennon could see his sarcastic attempts to lighten my mood weren't working. "Hey, are you still sore about that bridge incident?"

"A little, yeah."

"But it did the trick, didn't it? You don't want to kill yourself anymore."

"Yes, I'll admit it did. Now that I'm writing again, I don't want to die." I smiled wryly. "It's hard to hold a pencil when you're dead."

"Fair enough, James. I meant no offense. I'm just so bloody excited to see Yoko again! Trust me, you really don't have anything to worry about."

The plane shot through the clouds and abruptly dropped one hundred feet, tipping wildly side to side on the tempestuous wind. I heard Ritu scream in aisle three. The Catholic flight attendant clutched her necklace and crossed herself. In the age of intensifying storms, the nor'easter that was hitting the eastern seaboard had developed into a bomb cyclone and was chewing its way across New England, daring us to land.

Lennon was impressed. "Weather really is getting worse, isn't it? A bomb cyclone, for Christ's sake! In fifty more years, they'll run out of superlatives to describe weather altogether. They'll have to invent new phrases like the ice storm that ate Chicago! Shit. You mortals are pretty fucked! Even if we defeat the Black Chord, you have a lot of work to do here on Earth."

"Shut up, John!" At this point, I didn't care who heard me. I needed anger to keep myself from panicking.

I sat with my back pressed hard against my seat, eyes squeezed shut, gripping the armrests. I could feel my adrenal glands aching to squirt fight-or-flight chemicals into my veins, but I shouted at them to *back off!* Increasingly, they obeyed me these days, but they still bared their teeth. They were tiny, fierce Chihuahuas yearning for a reason to bark.

Lennon strained to see his adopted city come into view, but not even the tallest skyscraper pierced the cloud layer. I could feel the plane descending and saw the wing flaps extend. We were closer to the runway than I thought. With a teeth-jarring *thud*, the plane performed a graceless two-stomp landing as Ritu screamed again. The reverse thrusters roared to life in defiance of nature's fury. Soon we came to a skidding stop in a blinding sleet storm. Everyone except Lennon cheered in relief.

The captain greeted us as we exited the plane, beads of sweat still visible on his forehead. Several female passengers and one gay guy hugged him. I shook his hand vigorously, quoting from *Apollo 13*, "You, sir, are a steely-eyed missile man!"

34 I Say Hello, but You Say Goodbye

Love knows not its own depths until the hour of separation.
—KAHLIL GIBRAN

Lennon couldn't get down the chute fast enough. He walked past me into the terminal. "Come on, *man*! Hail one of those Uber things, will you? Let's go or we'll miss Yoko."

"Sorry, John. I only use Lyft."

"Yeah, yeah. Whatever. Come *on*, before she's gone!"

"Okay, fine. Keep your Beatle boots on!" I grabbed my cell phone and hailed a Lyft. I still felt rattled by the rough landing. We waited under the eaves of the baggage area, watching the sleet fall at a steep angle from the low-hanging sky. It was the kind of precipitation that freezes overnight, encasing cars inside icy cocoons by daybreak. This was a reason I never settled on the East Coast. A cream-colored Chevy Volt with a Lyft sign in the window pulled up, its windshield wipers fighting valiantly against the sleet.

As we climbed into the back seat, the driver, an attractive middle-aged Latina, welcomed me with a sunny smile. "*Hola*, my name is Consuelo, but you can call me Connie. This weather is *muy* loco, sí? And where are we going today?" Her face, like mine, looked much older when she wasn't smiling; but she smiled a lot, which gave her a young woman's countenance.

I said, "Hola, Connie. Me llamo Jamie. Llévame al One West Seventy-Second Street, por favor." I loved mixing English with Spanish. It was such a fun hybrid and reminded me of Esperanto, the failed world language.

"*¡Madre de Dios!*" She crossed herself. "That's the Dakota Apartments, where John Lennon died!"

"Sí, sí. That's right. Is there a problemo?"

"No, no. It's just that I think the Dakota Apartments are haunted." If only she knew that she was presently transporting a famous ghost. "So, you are a Lennon fan, sí? Coming to pay your respects? But in a such a storm?" She shook her head, clicked her tongue, and then started driving out of the airport toward the freeway.

I glanced at Lennon, who was looking smug. I decided to tease him a bit. "No, I'm going to the Dakota to visit an old friend. I'm actually more of a Paul McCartney fan."

Consuelo's eyes lit up in the rearview mirror and she flashed a wide smile. "Oh sí, me too! Lennon was too edgy for me. I prefer romance and silly love songs."

Lennon rolled his eyes and stuck his index finger in his mouth in a vomit gesture, then returned his gaze to the window as we departed the airport.

Oh boy. I get to hassle John Lennon. The tables have turned, moth-erfucker! "I know what you mean, Connie. All that walrus stuff just leaves me cold. I mean, a song about a marine mammal. Really?"

"Sí! And why listen to songs about yellow matter, custard, and dead dog eyes? Life is already difficult without songs making it worse. Don't you think?"

Lennon shook his head. "So, James, are you practicing dime-store sar-chology on me now?"

I wanted to ask what he meant, but I kept silent as we headed west.

Once on the freeway, Consuelo kept chatting. "Growing up in Puerto Rico, I was a big Wings fan." She cleared her throat and sang in a surprisingly good voice, *"Band on the run, Band on the run . . . !"* She laughed. "So much fun! Paul McCartney seems like such a happy man. But John Lennon"— she crossed herself again—"God rest his soul, I think he was a very angry man."

Lennon rolled his eyes and muttered to himself, "Every-body either loves you or hates you when you're six feet in the ground."

Teasing Lennon was fun, some playful payback after the stress he'd put me through, but Consuelo had gone too far. I had to defend my wayward hero. "Well, Connie, he certainly was intense, I'll give you that. But writing him off as an angry man? No. That's too simple."

"How so?" she asked.

"He felt things deeply, and he thought outside the box. He saw the hypocrisies and imperfections of the world and wrote about it in his songs. Underneath it all, I think he had a sensitive, trusting nature. He lived here in New York, enjoying walking out in the open, mingling with everyday people and graciously signing autographs. Unfortunately, living in a country where crazy people can get guns as easily as a Snickers bar got him killed."

Feeling I had stirred up bitter memories, I turned toward Lennon. He remained silent, still looking out the window at the cars moving slowly and perilously through the sleet. The closer we got to the Dakota, the more remote he became. I got the sense he wasn't paying much attention to the banter between me and the Lyft driver anymore.

"I'm glad you explained that to me, Jaime. It makes me feel better about him. But what about his song 'Imagine'? Such a beautiful song! But as a Catholic, I cannot believe there is no Heaven."

Without changing his position, Lennon muttered softly, "Tell her there's actually three kinds of Heaven."

"She'd never understand, John."

The Lyft driver watched me speaking to the empty seat beside me. "What did you say?" she asked, studying me quizzically in the rearview mirror.

"Oh, I'm sorry. I was wondering what Lennon would say if he were sitting here with us."

Consuelo rolled her eyes. "*¡Siempre me tapo los ojos cuando veo!*" She crossed herself yet again. Noticing my confusion, she said, "It means 'saints preserve us.' Okay, what would he say?"

"He might say, 'Connie, there's not only one but three kinds of Heaven.'" I spoke in my best Liverpudlian accent.

Consuelo shivered. "*¡Madre de Dios!* You sounded just like him! Three kinds of Heaven? Why would God need three Heavens? You know, Jaime, you're defending an atheist. Come on, you *must* be a Lennon fan. You're, how do you say, jerking my leg?"

"You mean 'pulling my leg.' No, honestly, I am a McCartney fan." To prove it, I launched into a McCartney medley. "*Jojo was a man who thought he was a loner . . . Lady Madonna, children at your feet . . . Hey Jude—na-na-na-na-na, na-na-na-na . . . We're so sorry, Uncle Albert . . .* See?" I was hoping to amuse Lennon, but he continued to ignore us both, his stare remaining fixed beyond the window.

"But you even wear glasses like him."

"Oh, these? I only wear them to decrease my resemblance to another rock star."

"What other rock star?"

I reached up to take the glasses off and show her my Mickness, but Lennon erupted in alarm. "No, James! Stop! If you take them off now, I'll disappear forever. Soon, but not yet! Bloody hell!"

He was right! Whoa. That would have been a seriously bad move. I jerked my hand away from the frames.

Consuelo was really curious now. "Sí! Take off your glasses. Let me see!"

"No, I can't do that. It's too embarrassing."

Consuelo considered me more carefully. "I see it now . . . Mick Jagger! That's nothing to be embarrassed about. Mick Jagger is muy sexy, *much* sexier than John Lennon!"

Lennon turned and gave Consuelo a once-over. "This woman is really starting to annoy me. I haven't seen Jagger in years, but I swear he was uglier than a toad back then, and I don't think time could have possibly improved a face like that. I thought you said Lyft drivers were the cool ones, man."

I ignored both their comments and tried to change the subject. "How much further to the Dakota?"

"Not far. A few more miles." Consuelo further evaluated me in the rearview mirror. "You know, I think you should lose the glasses and get contacts." She smiled flirtatiously. "Hey, Jaime. Do you have a girlfriend?"

The surprise of having such a vivacious woman as Consuelo ask this question made me think, *Wow. Maybe things really are coming my way.* But before I could answer, Lennon interrupted my train of thought. "Tell her yes. And that her name is Wanda.'"

It felt like eons since I had last seen Wanda. Thinking of her as my girlfriend felt more fantasy than reality, but I couldn't deny the pleasure I felt as I said, "Sí, Consuelo, I have a novia. Her nombre is Wanda."

"Ah, too bad," she said as she parked the car in front of the Dakota.

I turned to Lennon and noticed a single tear falling down his cheek as he stared longingly upon his former home.

35 Bone Soup

Seduce my mind and you can have my body. Find my soul and I'm yours forever.

—ANONYMOUS

Don't cry because it's over. Smile because it happened.
—LUDWIG JACABOWSKI (ADAPTATION)

Framed by a dark sky and horizontal sleet that felt more like nails than rain, 1 West Seventy-Second Street loomed over us. With its Gothic architecture, the Dakota Apartments looked cold and empty as we waited on the sidewalk by the arch where Lennon was shot. I could see why Roman Polanski used the Dakota for his exterior shots in *Rosemary's Baby*. The place felt spooky and haunted.

"Are you sure she's going to come out?" I asked Lennon, unconvinced that Yoko would venture out in such crappy weather.

"Don't worry. She loves dramatic weather. She's due any-time. Stay poised."

Back in the early 1880s, when the Dakota was built, the area around the building was sparsely inhabited. It was so far west and north of downtown, it felt like being in the Dakota Territory—hence its name. A famous—now infamous—landmark on the Upper West Side, it borders the west side of Central Park, where Yoko Ono spread John Lennon's ashes in sight of their apartment. Many famous residents have lived there over the years, including Judy Garland, Boris Karloff, and Leonard Bernstein, but none so famous as John Lennon, Yoko Ono, and their son, Sean.

I remained doubtful that the famous widow would appear, thinking what a crazy mission I was on. But then an Uber appeared, and a youngish couple got out and ran up to the main entrance, where they huddled together against the icy rain.

Lennon shouted above the wind, "It's Sean! It's my son! Sean! Sean!" But Sean Taro Ono Lennon, who at forty-three was already three years older than his dad when he died, only heard the wind and rain. Holographic tears poured down Lennon's cheeks as he watched the couple enter the building. He quickly regained his composure, knowing that he would only get this one chance to reconnect with his family.

Lennon appeared genuinely worried for the first time since he'd contacted me. His devil-may-care facade was gone. Still, he put on a brave face. "No worries, James. He's come to get his mum. Be ready for them. They'll be out soon."

In about ten minutes, a black limo pulled up to the curb. A moment later, Yoko Ono appeared in the lobby looking composed and chic in her slim black pantsuit and trademark dark glasses. She was exchanging pleasantries with her son and his girlfriend, who embodied urban hipster culture. They waited for the limo driver to collect them. The driver emerged from the vehicle and walked toward the lobby, umbrellas in hand.

Lennon was on alert, his senses primed. "The moment they step outside, tell her I'm here! Tell her I love her and tell her I'll be sitting at my piano tonight when she returns."

Standing just outside the door to the Dakota, the chauffeur handed an umbrella to Sean Lennon and struggled against the wind to open one for Yoko. A moment later, the Ono Lennons stepped across the threshold onto the sidewalk. "Yoko! *Yoko!* I'm over *here!*" Lennon shouted for all he was worth. But she didn't react. "*Tell* her, James. *Now!*"

I felt like a total fool—as if sane behavior did not apply to me anymore—but I took a deep breath and shouted above the rain, "Yoko! John is *here*! He's *really* here! He says he loves you and he'll be sitting at his piano tonight when you return!"

The chauffeur and Lennon's family stared blankly at me for a moment. Then the driver shouted back, "Get outta here, you wacko, or I'll call the cops!" He turned to Yoko and said, "I'm sorry, ma'am, it's just another crazy. Where do they all come from, anyway? And in such weather. Let's go!"

Sean Lennon and his girlfriend got in the limo, but Yoko hesitated. She pondered me through the rain. I could sense a mixture of emotions coming from her, even through her signature sunglasses. Perhaps she sensed something.

Lennon tugged at my shoulder ineffectually, his fingers repeatedly slipping through the fabric of my coat. "James, tell her I'm sorry I died first. It wasn't supposed to happen that way. Tell her we both thought she would be the first to go. Tell her I was going to make soup out of her bones and drink her so we could be in one body. *Tell her*!"

Yuck! Where did that *come from?* I thought. But I inhaled the icy air and in one last impassioned breath repeated what he had said. "Yoko! John says he's sorry he died first. It wasn't supposed to happen that way. You were supposed to die first. John was going to make you into soup and drink you so you could be together in one body for all time!"

The driver repeated his cautions, "Ma'am, this guy could be *dangerous*. Please let's get you in the car."

"Hold on one moment, Robert." Yoko took a few steps toward me. The chauffeur held the umbrella, projecting menace should I try anything weird. He was a big guy.

Yoko's soft voice was hard to hear over the storm, but she said clearly, "I don't know who you are or how you know what you know. But it's not polite to say these things to us. Why are you out here in the cold? Are you crazy?" She seemed concerned but also detached from years of people saying all kinds of shit to her. She often said that she lived in a kind of hell, being reviled by ignorant people who blamed her for breaking up the Beatles.

"James, tell her the truth. Tell her what's happening. Make it *quick*!"

"Yoko, the glasses I'm wearing allow me to see John. He's standing right next to you. He's stroking your cheek." She put her hand on her cheek and held it there.

"He's here from the afterlife paying his karmic debts, and he's been given a brief time, a kind of shore leave, to spend with you before he goes to fight a battle in Heaven."

"A battle in Heaven?" She sounded intrigued.

"Yes, to save our universe from darkness. It turns out that musicians are soldiers in the afterlife, and John's been drafted to fight a sonic evil coming from another universe that threatens us all."

Yoko continued staring at me while the chauffeur urged her again to leave. "Ma'am, this guy is *obviously* off his rocker. We should leave. It's not *safe!*"

"John is standing next to you telling you all this?"

"Yes ma'am. As long as I wear these glasses, our souls are magnetized. He goes where I go. I brought his spirit here from California."

She held her ground, considered my deranged words, and took one more step toward me. "I like the crazy vision you have, but I think you're suffering from a delusion. We all miss John very much, but I've moved on and so should you. For Heaven's sake, get out of the rain or you'll get sick." With that, she turned away. "All right, Robert. Let's go." She got in the limo and sped off.

Lennon's shoulders slumped and he muttered sadly, "I really thought she'd be able to sense my presence, being so close."

"I think she did. That's why she came up to us. Let's try again when she comes back."

"No, James. There won't be another time."

"What do you *mean*? Of *course* we can try again. I'll drink some espresso and wait up with you all night if that's what it takes. I just need to warm up. Let's get me some hot soup."

"No, our time together is at an end."

I felt taken by surprise—panicked. "No. *Listen!* I'll help you get inside the Dakota. You'll need my help."

"Silly boy! Do you think a ghost needs to use a door to get in a building? I'm close enough now. Thank you for bringing me here. Once I'm free of you, I'll slip in through the walls. But first you must take the glasses off. I must be free of you. Yoko's right. We both need to move on. It's time to say goodbye, James."

I stood there in shock, listening to the slushy rain pelt my umbrella. "No, John. I don't think I can let you go. I need you to help me take the next steps. Whatever it takes. *Hell!* You can throw me off the bridge again. I don't think I can do this without you."

"*Rubbish!* You've put in your ten thousand hours. Your best songs lie ahead. It's time to grow up. The good news is you'll be famous. The bad news is—you'll be famous. Own up to it."

I stood there, saying nothing.

Lennon considered me then and said, "Listen to me. Everything will be okay in the end. If it's not okay, it's not the end. Take off the glasses, James. Set us both free."

"But where will you go?"

"I kind of tricked you, mate. There's something here that magnetizes me more than the glasses."

"What's that?"

He gestured toward the park. "It's me ashes across the street that Yoko spread years ago. You got me close enough to feel their sway. They'll hold me here long enough to say goodbye. So, take 'em off! Go on. *Do* it!"

With a leaden arm, I reached up to take off the glasses.

"Remember, James, all you need is love. But you need it *all*, not just a piece of it now and then when it's convenient."

I touched the frame of the glasses and then slowly took them off. Lennon began dissolving.

He snapped his fingers and sang, "*Love stays on, love stays here*," and then touching his hand to his heart, "*everything else—disappears.*" I could barely see him anymore. "Remember to give me songwriting credit for this one, too. It's okay to use your name first—Drake/Lennon. Sounds cool, doesn't it? Goodbye, James!"

I held the glasses at arm's length and squinted through the lenses to get one last glimpse of him. He was smiling and seemed at peace. The rain erased his image one drop at a time. In another instant, he washed away completely, joining the wind and rain as they blew toward the Dakota.

I felt struck, as if I'd been knifed in the side. I collapsed into a fetal position and leaned against the side of the Dakota for support. I felt utterly alone and abandoned. "*Fuck* you, Lennon! You can't just leave me here!" I shouted at the pavement. Tears sprang from my eyes, the same way they had in 1980 when I heard he'd been shot and killed. I crouched down on the sidewalk and huddled under my umbrella so no one could see me. It felt as if *I'd* been shot.

Later that night, and for three nights in a row at precisely 10:50 p.m., the time of John Lennon's death, Yoko Ono saw the ghostly image of her husband sitting at his white piano quietly playing "Imagine." After that, no mortal saw him again.

PART SIX

36 Last Stretch of Highway

I'm driving with my knees up feeling thunder through the wheel. They say we will continue, but I wonder if that's real.

—JIMMY DRAKE

I don't know how long I leaned against the side of the Dakota, but at a certain point I was spent of tears. I picked myself up and started walking in the darkness to nowhere in particular. Feeling more zombie than human and through no will of my own, I shuffled across the street and entered Central Park. The park was devoid of people and the sleet had turned to rain. My teeth chattered, and I shivered into the first stage of hypothermia. I figured if I wasn't mugged and killed, I would probably die of exposure. I was on that last stretch of highway before death steps out from the shadows, holds a gun to your head, and says, "Gimme all your money, punk. Time's up!"*

After walking an hour or so huddled under my umbrella, I popped out onto Broadway and made my way to Times

---

* Listen to "Last Stretch of Highway" at JohnLennonsGlasses.net.

Square, realizing I had miraculously made it through the park unchallenged. Compared to the relative darkness of Central Park, the lights of Times Square lit me up like a cockroach on a sidewalk. I felt vulnerable and exposed. I had devolved into that ubiquitous crazy man you see on the streets of urban America. I was ashamed by my descent. Still, if you can't come unglued in New York City, where else can you lose your mind? So, I kept moving. My shivering stopped as I entered the second stage of hypothermia. I felt as if I were walking through waist-deep mud. Still, I kept walking. When I entered Lower Manhattan an hour or so later and thought I could go no further, a familiar voice sounded over my left shoulder.

"Hey, Jimmy! What the hell are you doing in my neck of the woods? You're supposed to be dead!"

I turned around to see the sardonic gangster face of Tony Soprano illuminated by the streetlights. The rain poured through him as he pointed a finger at me. "I swear, Jimmy, you're a hard man to kill, but I've got another plan for you." Moving closer, he stepped through my umbrella and put a meaty arm around my shoulders. "Don't worry, my friend. Everything's gonna be all right. Just follow me."

I had just enough energy to ask, "Where are we going? I thought you were in San Francisco."

He smiled and nodded. "Yes, I tried to talk some sense into you there, but you and your friend Lennon botched it all up. Now look at you!" He looked me up and down, shaking his head and clicking his tongue. "I swear, Jimmy, you don't have much time left, and you keep subtractin' from it. You look terrible. Not to worry, I've got another way out for you. You'll see. It's all for the best. Let's go!"

His monster-of-Frankenstein-like frame led the way as we entered the bohemian environs of the Village. Every time I faltered or stumbled, he would say, "Come on, Jimmy. We still got a ways to go."

I followed him obediently, taking rights and lefts deeper into the neighborhoods. We walked past several shops until we came to a nondescript building. Soprano stopped and asked, "Do you recognize this place?"

We were standing at 15 West Fourth Street, at the corner of Mercer. The sign in the window read property of new york university. I stared blankly at Soprano.

"Come on! You've played here before. Don't you remember? My God, Jimmy, you really are going downhill. It's the Bottom Line!"

"The Bottom Line where I played twenty years ago?"

"Yeah! You called it your moon landing gig, and you always wanted to come back. But it's gone, Jimmy. It's gone."

I remembered walking into the Bottom Line in 1999. I had no idea what a storied and venerable place it was. Learning that everyone from Stevie Wonder to Dr. John to the Police to Joan Baez to Christine Lavin had played there had a profound effect on me. When I played that stage for two sold-out shows on a Saturday night in New York, it felt as though I had landed on the moon. I could feel the presence of those who had stood there before me. It was an honor. I had to give my *best* show. I mean, this is the club that launched Bruce Springsteen in 1975, for Christ's sake! The audience had seen it all and didn't suffer fools. My hands were so sweaty my guitar pick felt as slippery as a watermelon seed.

The backstage crew had greeted us in typical sarcastic New York fashion, saying things like, "Oh hey, aren't you guys from California? What're you gonna play? 'Puff, the Magic Dragon' or 'Kumbaya'? Nyuk nyuk!" Evidently, they had never heard of us and thought we were a wimpy West Coast folk act singing facile songs about nature and the like. They had no idea how mean we were. We were an East Coast band in a West Coast body. The way to a New Yorker's heart is to make them laugh, and that we did. Our cynical but hilarious social satire won them over. In the end we triumphed, and they begged us for our T-shirts, which we gave them. Yes, I always wanted to play there again. It was the quintessential gig by which I gauged all others. I didn't know the Bottom Line had closed. The club's signature green canopy was gone, and the windows looked sterile and unwelcoming. It had been converted to classroom space.

With dismay, I stepped back from the building and admitted to Soprano, "Yes, I always wanted to return here."

"That's right. You've said that about a lot of places, haven't you?"

"Yes, I suppose I have. What's your point?"

"My point, Jimmy, is that the places you hold dear, the places that gave you meaning, the places you used to play are disappearing. You thought they'd be there forever, just waiting for your victorious return. But instead, they've gone out of business. And with their demise, guys like you are going extinct right along with them. You're like one of those tiny butterflies nobody knows the name of that's dying off because some guy's tractor has plowed up the one plant they needed to survive. And it only gets worse from here. Watering holes like the Bottom Line are drying up everywhere. You're beating a dead horse. You're going down, Jimmy. But since you never amounted to anything anyway, you won't have far to fall. So it won't hurt a bit."

The dark truth of his words pierced my heart. The pain of getting older and becoming invisible was catching up with me. I outran it for years, but it was gaining on me. Becoming irrelevant was a greater pain than dying. I took one last look at the former home of the Bottom Line and started walking up Fourth Street.

"Hey, Jimmy! Where're you goin'?" Soprano paused. "So, you wanna go that way? Okay, we can get there from here."

"Get where?" I asked as he walked around my shuffling form and assumed the lead.

"You'll see!"

Blocks felt like miles.

"I don't think I have the energy go on. Can we please stop?" I pleaded.

"Oh, come on, Jimmy, we're almost there. I've saved the best for last!"

Somehow I managed to keep going. Fueled by cynical curiosity, I wanted to see where he was leading me.

Just as I thought I might faint, we came to a staircase. Soprano stood at the top of the stairs, encouraging me to climb. "Come on, Jimmy. You can do it. We're here!"

I started to climb, no longer able to feel my feet but managing to make it to the top anyway. "What is this place?" I asked, completely out of breath.

"Well, since you and your friend Lennon botched your suicide attempt on the Golden Gate Bridge, I've brought you to a new place to jump. Welcome to the pride of New York, the Brooklyn Bridge!" Soprano pointed proudly at the pedestrian walkway. "It's not as tall as the Golden Gate, but it'll get the job done. You'll see. Hey, splat is splat on either coast! Right?" He snickered at his own joke.

"Really? But John said that I've got more songs to write."

"Songs, schmongs! There's too many of those in the world. They're like gerbils. Better to make way for others. Look, your friend Lennon filled your head with bullshit. *You?* A latter-day rock star? *Really?* You had your shot. It's time to wrap things up and get the hell out of here. Come on, Jimmy! There's some folks out on the bridge just dying to meet you."

I followed Soprano a few hundred feet and noticed a dozen people standing around apparently waiting for us. They were dressed in the styles of the late 1800s and seemed lost and forlorn.

"Jimmy, let me introduce you to the unfortunate folks who died six days after the bridge opened in 1883."

A tall young man in a billowy white shirt approached me. He said, "Twenty thousand of us came to celebrate the new bridge when a rumor started that it was about to collapse. Everyone panicked and twelve of us were crushed to death in the stairway you just came up." He cast his gaze toward his boots and retreated back to the group.

"See, Jimmy?" Tony proselytized. "Life is too random. You work all your life and then, poof! Something stupid gets you in the end. Why bother with the effort of living when shit like this can happen? Come on. There's another person you've gotta meet."

We walked past the sad-looking group and further out onto the walkway. Standing before us was a slender middle-aged woman in a dark dress with a simple black hat.

"Jimmy, let me introduce you to Marie Rosalie Dinse. Marie, this is Jimmy Drake, failed rock star."

She took a few steps toward me. In a thick German accent she said, "I failed too. I moved here from Germany and lost all my money in a boardinghouse venture. What a waste! I had no children, so I decided to jump off the bridge. I rehearsed a few times, then one day I got in a horse car. I had no money left, so I gave the driver my beautiful moon ring. He also took my silk umbrella. Can you believe it? All for a nickel's ride. Halfway across I jumped out of the cab and leaped over the edge. People say I cartwheeled three times before hitting the water."

"So that's how you died?" I asked.

"No, but I should have. I landed feetfirst and at an angle, so my dress acted like a parachute and broke my fall. A tugboat fished me out of the water. I had no fractures or injuries. After I left the hospital, they put me in prison for attempted suicide. I should have stayed in Germany. Killing yourself there is not a crime. There, they let you do as you please."

Soprano interrupted. "That's right. She survived and went to prison, but that's not the worst part. Tell him, Marie."

"After years in prison I lost my mind, so they sent me to an insane asylum, where I spent my last days. Would you like to see what I looked like in those years?"

I stared at her plain, sad face as it weathered before my eyes and her body hunched over like the weight of the world was on her back. She cried, "If I had died here, I would never have had to go through those terrible years." With that, she let out an unearthly scream and launched herself over the bridge. I watched her cartwheel three times before hitting the water feetfirst. Then she disappeared.

"You see, Jimmy?" Soprano said. "There are worse things than dying. Sure, you can listen to your rock 'n' roll heroes and those so-called angels who've been filling your mind with false hope. But I tell you, this is your last chance to get a free ride out of this life before worse shit happens to you." Noting a glimmer of doubt in my eyes, he stopped trying to convince me and abruptly got down to business. "Okay, okay. Enough talk! This is as good a place as any. Time's up!" He pointed downward.

I looked over the edge. The 127-foot drop from the deck of the Brooklyn Bridge was daunting but less when compared to the 245-foot drop from that of the Golden Gate Bridge. Still, I knew that if the fall didn't kill me, I would surely drown in the predawn darkness, especially given my current state. I hesitated.

Soprano was losing patience. "Oh, for Christ's sake, Jimmy. Do it! I don't have time for this." I gawked as his eyes turned into dark sockets. "I've got other people to kill." His body grew larger and began turning black. "Jump! Or I'll throw you off the bridge myself."

I stood stunned and frozen as his human form morphed into a swirling black squid-like shape with tendrils reaching toward me. It looked familiar. I remembered seeing it hanging in space. "The Black Chord! Here on Earth!" I whispered to myself.

It lunged toward me and wrapped a tendril around my wrist. An intense coldness burned through my skin and ran up my arm. It began pulling me toward one of the support beams that ran up and over the opposite lanes of traffic.

"No!" I shouted back with the last ounce of energy I had left. "I know what you are!"

"Too late!" I heard its true voice hissing somewhere deep inside my head. It sounded reptilian. "Your time is up! First you, then I'll go back and obliterate all your rock 'n' roll heroes."

It dragged me, helpless as a rag doll, across the beam. A parade of cars, their headlights shining through the freezing rain, passed below. It released me at the edge of the structure, then hovered in the air above the river. Through the darkness, the water below looked like a giant, roiling black snake.

"Have some respect for yourself, human. Don't make me pull you over the edge. Jump!"

An upwelling of defiance and anger toward everyone who had ever bullied me penetrated my terror. It triggered what little strength I had left. I sat down and clung to the beam. "Fuck you and the universe you came from!" I shouted back. "I'm not going anywhere! If you want me, fucking come here and get me!"

The Black Chord thundered, "You can't stop the inevitable, human! Your race had its chance to inhabit this planet. You're too full of contradictions. When I take over, silence will bring relief to this violent, noisy universe. Your so-called God has allowed too much chaos. Her time is up, and with her, all you impotent rock 'n' rollers will be reduced to molecular ash."

I yelled back, "Oh, that's funny coming from something as ugly as you! You have no idea how powerful music can be, but you're about to find out. You made a big mistake entering this universe and underestimating us. Get ready for some real noise, Squidy. It'll make you wish you were deaf!"

"That's enough!" The Black Chord emitted a screeching metal-on-metal sound as it uncoiled a tendril to pull me over the edge and finish me off. With steely determination, I tightened my grip, locking my arms and legs around the stanchion on the beam where I sat.

The tendril was inches from my arm when the freezing rain abruptly stopped, the clouds parted, and the first rays of the morning sun broke the gloom and streamed through the breach. The fury of the sun's ancient photons hit the Black Chord like a swarm of a trillion hornets. It began to dissipate.

Just before the last of it disappeared, it roared, "I'll eat the souls of Lennon and all your frivolous heroes at Proxima Centauri. Then I'll come back for you!"

With that, the last of its stygian trails disappeared into nothingness and the morning sun asserted itself over the storm, bathing the Brooklyn Bridge in a rosy glow.

I collapsed onto the beam as the sun grew brighter. I felt profoundly sad to have lost Lennon but astonished and happy to be alive. Laying on my back as the magnificent orb bathed me in warmth and light, I took stock of all that had just happened. Tony Soprano wasn't just my death wish; it was the Black Chord trying to kill me at this end of the chain.

The events of the past few days now made sense, and for the first time since Lennon left me at the Dakota, I felt human. Sitting up, I took one last look over the edge of the bridge, thinking of all the people who had jumped and died, as well as the one who wished she had been killed. "Rest in peace, Marie Rosalie Dinse. I appreciate your advice, but I think I'm gonna stick around a while." Then I left the bridge, found a twenty-four-hour diner, and ordered a huge bowl of hot chicken soup.

37 Pop Out of the Drama

If you think you are too small to make a difference, try sleeping with a mosquito.

—THE 14TH DALAI LAMA

Revived by the chicken soup, I ordered a Lyft to the airport. The freezing rain had returned, but that wasn't going to stop me, I was ready to go home. The Lyft driver, a middle-aged man named Andriy with a sad face and red-rimmed eyes, welcomed me out of the torrent and into his silver Honda Civic. When I asked if he was okay, he said he was worried about his home country.

"Where are you from?"

He took a long, slow breath and said, "I'm from Ukraine. I left after Putin took over Crimea in 2014. My friends and family in Kyiv think I'm being dramatic, but I worry about the future."

As a globalist, I never understood why people fall for dictators. Nationalism is a political sugar high that rots the fabric of a country. It seemed evil to me. Like worshipping the puzzle piece you're on and to hell with the rest.

I wanted to comfort and reassure Andriy that a mighty confrontation between good and evil was happening in the afterlife. That if Earth's departed musical heroes could rock the Black Chord into oblivion, its negative effects would be gone. Humanity might catch its breath and find a more peaceful track. That we as a species are adolescents, only beginning to understand human consciousness, the workings of our minds and the unseen forces that permeate our existence.* We blame each other for our collective darkness just as we're handed a flashlight. I wanted to tell him all this, but he didn't deserve a weird, raving passenger spouting crazy ideas, so I kept quiet and left him alone during the ride to the airport.

We arrived at the airport minutes later and I stepped into the brightly lit terminal. I was greeted by an atmosphere of heightened tension, and soon found out why. Due to the freezing rain and treacherous conditions, all flights in and out of the Northeast had been canceled—indefinitely. Gaggles of disheveled travelers lined the walls; the lucky ones had staked out seats in the rows of uncomfortable plastic airport chairs. Many grumbled as they texted their loved ones letting them know they were stranded. A man in a blue power suit shook his head while observing the sheets of sleet and said into his cell phone, "Climate change is so fucking inconvenient!"

I walked deeper into the terminal, toward the sound of someone playing guitar and singing. There sitting cross-legged on the stained airport carpet was a young man about twenty years old with Down syndrome performing a rendition of "Sweet Home Alabama." Belting out *"Big wheels keep on turnin',"* he

---

* Listen to "Coming of Age in the Milky Way" at JohnLennonsGlasses.net.

didn't always play the right chords, but he had a strong rhythmic right hand and absolutely no inhibitions about singing.

I've known lots of people with Down syndrome. I met multitudes at a noontime concert series I ran in the Bay Area for many years. Midday was the perfect field trip time for the social service centers, and they brought the musically enraptured people with DS to the park in droves. It became the highlight of their week, a literal DS Woodstock every Wednesday at noon. Having three rather than two copies of chromosome 21 was an advantage not only for less incidence of solid tumor cancers and coronary artery disease but also for joy and music appreciation. Their enthusiasm was infectious. I took to dancing with them at the shows before the city shut it down. They chalked it up as too many "unusual" people attending. Being weird myself, I always felt fine in their company.

The young man finished the Lynyrd Skynyrd song with a joyful flourish so convincing that even though he ended with the wrong chord, I found myself applauding.

"You should set out a hat," I said, fishing for a buck to give him. He ignored my offer and waved me over.

"My name's Oliver, but you can call me Ollie. What's your name?" He studied me for a moment, then exclaimed before I could answer, "Hey! Aren't you in the Rolling Stones?"

"No. Shush, Ollie. I just look like that guy. My name's James, but you can call me Jimmy." I tried to distract him by pointing at his guitar. "Hey, that's a nice guitar you have."

He looked quizzically at me for a second, then hugged his guitar. "My guitar is my friend. You play guitar too, don't you?"

"Yeah, I've played all my life. How did you know?"

"Oh, I *know* things." He held up his guitar for me to take. "Play me a song, Jimmy."

"Here? Really?" I wasn't in the mood. I've always had an aversion to playing in places like food courts, bars, and certainly airports. I'm rather snobby that way.

"Oh, come on, Jimmy. Pop out of the drama!" Then he stood up and put the guitar in my hands. "Pop out of the drama!" he repeated more forcefully.

"What should I play?"

He leaned in and spoke like he was telling me a secret. "Play 'Honky Tonk Women.'"

I couldn't turn him down, so I took the guitar. I'd never played the Stones classic in my life, but I knew it was in the people's key of G. Ollie played air guitar as I strummed the opening chords.

We both sang, "*I met a gin-soaked bar room queen in Memphis.*" Ollie held an imaginary microphone as if he were onstage at the Oakland Coliseum. People started gathering around us. Smiles blossomed on the faces of the stranded for the first time since I'd arrived. We got a round of applause after the final chorus, and a little girl standing with her parents clapped her tiny hands, pleading, "Play another one!"

I handed the guitar back to Ollie, who immediately launched into the Stones' first hit, "(I Can't Get No) Satisfaction." He missed half the chords, but the crowd ate it up. And so it went for a couple of hours as we passed the guitar back and forth, with people putting dollars in Ollie's open guitar case. Each time my inhibitions began to rise, Ollie would say, "Pop out of the drama, Jimmy. Just keep playing!"

After several rounds of this, I asked, "What do you mean by 'pop out of the drama,' Ollie?"

He got really serious and said, "You know, pop out of your head. Think with your heart. Don't be so serious. Face piles of trials with smiles."

"Hey, isn't that from a Moody Blues song?"

"Yeah, the Moody Blues are cool!" And to prove his point he launched into "Ride My See-Saw," his rendition being mostly choruses and a lot of *ah-ah-ah-ah*s, but that didn't matter.

We finished with "Nights in White Satin" as the reality of spending the night at the airport settled in, and people drifted away. Ollie yawned. "I go to sleep now. Here, take this." He handed me his guitar. "And this." He rummaged around in his guitar case, which was strewn with dollars, and gave me a yellow notepad with a sharp pencil. "Write some stuff!" Then he curled up on the cold, hard, institutional carpet, falling instantly asleep as if he were at home in his own bed.

New songs poured out of me all through that night. I felt no need to sleep, and the melodies, rhythms, chords, and lyrics flew around in my mind like planes waiting to land. I played Ollie's guitar softly, not wanting to wake the people slumped in their chairs or sprawled on the carpet. Three new songs materialized.

The first was "The Lennon Song," which I titled in honor of the brilliant, complicated man who'd nearly killed me but inspired me to the end. It began with the words he spoke outside the Dakota as I watched him disappear in the rain: "*Love stays on, love stays here, everything else disappears.*"* He was gone, but I imagined he was still looking over my shoulder.

The second was "You Are My Window," a romantic ballad written for Wanda the Wanderer—the beautiful, effervescent Juliette Serri.* I vividly remembered the powerful, intimate feelings I'd felt while in the erogenous zone of the sun. I couldn't wait to return to her. I thought I would see the world more clearly through her if we ever got together.

The last song to appear was "Fear and Love."* It followed from the conversation I had on the plane with Lennon that likened fear and love to characters in a romantic relationship. It spoke to how the energy between the two conflicting emotions can stimulate change, transmuting fear into courage.

After penning the final lines of "Fear and Love," I noticed the sky was lighter and the clouds were beginning to break up. A hint of morning sun peeked over the parking lot, inviting the ice to melt on the runways, thus marking my second sunrise in New York as a tamer version of the first.

A few hours later, a tired but relieved voice came over the intercom. "Ladies and gentlemen, we appreciate your patience. The airport has been cleared for takeoffs and landings."

Applause and a chorus of hallelujahs ensued as people began to organize their belongings. Ollie woke, rubbed his eyes, and looked around. "Why are people leaving?" He seemed genuinely disappointed.

---

* Listen to "The Lennon Song," "You Are My Window," and "Fear and Love" at JohnLennonsGlasses.net.

"The planes are starting to fly again. Thanks for a good time, Ollie. Here's your beautiful guitar back." He hugged it, smiling at me.

"You and me. We're friends now," he said.

"Yes, we are. That was quite a show we put on in here."

His eyes grew wide as he thought back to the songs we'd sung together. "'House of Fire'! We killed 'em!" He high-fived me, then handed over half the money in his guitar case, whispering in my ear, "I know who you really are. It'll be our secret. Next time let's play 'Jumpin' Jack Flash.' Remember, Jimmy, when you feel bad, when you don't want to play, when you get stuck in your head, just pop out of the drama!"

Seeming pleased with himself, he picked up his guitar and began walking toward the gate for his flight to Omaha, which had been announced moments earlier. Without turning around, he flashed me the "rock on" hand sign, singing Steve Miller's "Jet Airliner" as he disappeared down the corridor.

The money Ollie gave me amounted to an astonishing two hundred fifty dollars. I guess stranded people are generous! He was right. I needed to play just for the fun of it. Meeting him was karmic. He was a true musical bodhisattva. With his genuine love of music, unfettered by ambition or expectation, he had reset my musical and psychological compass. To this day, I can hear him saying, "Come on, Jimmy, pop out of the drama."

I was absolutely starving, so with my ample tip money, I entered the terminal's Panda Express and ordered the largest, most expensive plate they had. As I wolfed down my food, I sensed that despite all the uncertainty, I was being supported—and it was my job to meet the moment.

Once seated on the plane, the wide-eyed wakefulness I felt at the airport left me. I had never been able to sleep on a plane. But this time, I did. Another first. It seemed I no longer had a fear of flying. There was virtually no talking on the plane as all the passengers were as exhausted as me, including my seat-mate, who gave me a look that said, "I'm in no mood to talk."

"Fine with me," I vibed back; and we both fell asleep, me against the window.

Nearly six hours later, I emerged from a dreamless sleep as the pilot announced we would be landing in San Francisco in fifteen minutes. It was 8:00 a.m. local time, with clear blue skies over the Bay.

Stepping into the crystal clarity of the storm-washed world was almost shocking. I had gotten used to dark weather, and to be truthful, I'd gotten used to it internally as well. But now sunshine lit the city where a new love and a new life beckoned. I felt excited about my prospects for the first time in many years.

I hailed a Lyft and by sheer fate, synchronicity, or who knows what, Kekoa arrived. "Howzit, mon? Aloha! Are we going back to the bridge? Ha-ha-haaa!"

There was that youthful trill and campy Hawaiian accent again. "No, Kekoa. No bridge today. Take me to the Haight."

"Yeah, mon. Are you going there to buy some weed, then? Ha-ha-haaa," he joked.

"No, that's where I live."

"I should have known. You look like a Haight Street kinda guy. So, hey, mon. That last time I took you to the bridge, what was that about, anyway?"

I felt no need to hide anymore. "Actually, I *was* going to jump off the bridge, but I changed my mind."

Startled by my off-the-cuff suicide confession, his Hawaiian accent fell away, and his East Coast roots came back. "Holy shit, man! For real?" I nodded. "Wow!"

"Come on, Kekoa, you were onto me the minute I got in your car. You knew I was up to something. You've got great instincts. You should trust 'em."

"So why didn't you go through with it? What stopped you?"

He stared at me in the rearview mirror, waiting for my reply. I thought about all I'd been through. How close I'd come to death on the Brooklyn Bridge. I shuddered as I remembered Lennon throwing my astral body off the Golden Gate Bridge, and how close I came to giving up on music and doubting my own sanity. But as I looked out the window at the mysterious golden orb rising in the sky, I just smiled and said, "I don't know, Kekoa. I guess I just had to pop out of the drama."

38   One Cat Leads to Another

Only a real risk tests the reality of a belief.

—C. S. LEWIS

Oh baby, baby, it's a wild world.

—CAT STEVENS

I had Kekoa drop me off at Sprouting Out, my favorite breakfast spot, four blocks from my apartment—and the place of my most fervent romantic hopes. He was back to his adopted Hawaiian accent. "Hey, mon, you like this place too? The omelets are onolicious!"

"Onolicious?"

"Ya, mon, onolicious. It's Hawaiian for something so good it breaks your mouth!"

We smiled and nodded, exchanged phone numbers, and with a final fist bump I sent him on his way. I watched Kekoa's car disappear down Haight Street. I knew we'd be seeing more of each other.

It felt as if I'd been gone for years, but in Earth time, I was only gone two days. I looked through the window of the café, hoping to catch sight of the lovely Juliette Serri, and sure enough, there she stood at the register, looking beautiful as always. But my idyllic reverie vanished instantly. To my horror, I saw her smiling and talking to that nasty Philippe, who handed her an envelope. The gut punch nearly folded me in half as the familiar disappointments and fearful voices rushed in. I felt sick. I turned on my heel in a maneuver that would have made the Buckingham Palace King's Guard proud. Three steps into my retreat, I straightened my spine, executed another perfect about-face, and walked through the door. "Take *that*, you ghosts of fears past," I thought.

As I approached, I heard Juliette say, "Oh! Merci, Philippe! I can't believe it!" She held a ticket in her hand. "I love Cat Stevens!"

"You mean Yusuf/Cat Stevens?" I asked.

She looked shocked. "Oh my God, James! You're back in town. Welcome home! Philippe has tickets to go see him at the Fillmore tomorrow night. You should come with us!"

Philippe's face soured at the thought of me tagging along. He shook his lion curls and feigned regret. With a smarmy smile, he said, "Sorry, mon ami. It's sold out and I only have two tickets."

"Oh, too bad." Juliette seemed genuinely disappointed. "Do you like Cat Stevens, James?"

The urge to flee had returned, but on the outside, I appeared calm. I rode the situation. "Yes, I love Cat Stevens. His songs are deep. Some of the most beautiful songs ever written. He pretty much lost me with the whole Islam–Salman Rushdie thing, but it's good to hear he's back." I marveled at how nonchalant and chatty I sounded, how I wasn't running away even though the stable of doubts inside me was stampeding.

Philippe turned to Juliette and said to the woman I wanted, the woman I felt such a strong connection with, the woman with whom I'd had imaginary sex in the center of the sun, "See you tomorrow night, Wanda!" Then, looking pleased with himself, he cocked his head toward me and said, "Yusuf/Cat Stevens, really? I just call him Cat! Meow!" Then, smiling in triumph, he walked past me and out the door.

Wanda/Juliette rolled her eyes. "He can be so rude sometimes, but he means well."

I wanted to say, "Yeah, like Hitler or Ted Bundy meant well," but instead replied, "It's good to see you. Can I get a mocha and a scone? By the way, do you prefer Wanda or Juliette?"

"Only special people get to call me Juliette. You are special, James. Your songs about universal love touch me, so you may call me Juliette. Did you just get back? How was New York?"

"I got stuck in an ice storm at the airport for two days, but I wrote a few songs while I was stranded."

"New songs? I would love to hear them! Can we still get together to discuss using your songs in my dance production?"

"Of course. What are you doing day after tomorrow?"

"I can juggle my schedule to make that work. Shall we meet at my studio? It's on Baker Street, not far from here. Say noon-ish? I'll bring lunch."

"I know the place. I'll meet you there."

As I reached into my pocket for cash, my mind played an unbidden movie trailer filled with images of her and Philippe having a grand ol' time at the Cat Stevens concert. My thin veneer of confidence began to peel. I couldn't stop the snark-tinged words that sprang from my mouth as I handed her the money. "Well, have fun at the Cat Stevens show. I'm sure Philippe will take good care of you."

Crap! I thought. *Idiot!* I turned to leave, but she put her hand on mine and said, "Hey, are you okay?"

"Oh yeah, I'm just tired, a little jet-lagged. I'll be fine in a couple of days. Wave at the Cat for me!" She looked concerned and somewhat mystified as I turned and left.

I walked toward home in a swirl of thoughts and emotions. I didn't know Juliette well enough to ask if she was interested in Philippe romantically. The fact that she was going with him to see one of the greatest songwriters of all time really chapped my ass. And why would she want to go out with *me*, anyway?

An image popped into my mind of the big round table in the *PBS NewsHour* studio. Judy Woodruff materialized with David Brooks and Mark Shields seated on either side of her. Judy started off, "So, Mark, David, what do you think of Jimmy Drake's sudden transformation?

Brooks began, "Well, Judy, I wouldn't go so far as to call it fake news, but I have my doubts. This man has a lifetime of entrenched habits and well-honed coping mechanisms that keep him living in the weeds so he doesn't have to face his profound insecurities head-on."*

Shields countered, "Yes, but transformation can happen in an instant, and topple long-held institutions. Just look at the fall of the Berlin Wall or the collapse of the Soviet Union—"

"Or the Arab Spring," Brooks interrupted. "Just look how that's turned out."

Shields smiled and continued, "Well, I don't know. I'm rooting for Jimmy. He's smart, courageous—and handsome in that ugly-sexy way. There's too much cynicism in this world. Not enough attention is given to perseverance and the power of the individual to overcome obstacles and become agents for positive change. People are full of surprises and can start anew at any time."

Brooks chuckled, shook his head and quipped, "Old dogs, new tricks—" just as Judy cut in, "We'll have to leave it there, folks."

I woke from my revery as I passed the local grocery, remembering that I needed to pick up a pint of half-and-half for Chairman Meow. Boy, was he going to be mad! I selected the organic variety, then walked the final block to my flat.

I tiptoed into my building. Even camouflaged, the Chairman knew the sound of my steps. As soon as I reached the second floor, I could hear him yowling from behind my closed door on the third floor. I stepped inside and was met with his feline laundry list of sorrows and frustrations. He yowled so loud and long, I thought my neighbors would complain.

He said clearly, as only a cat can, "Where have you been? You've never been gone this long!" (Which wasn't true, but he

---

* Listen to "Living in the Weeds" at JohnLennonsGlasses.net.

always said that.) "Other cats would have pooped on the carpets. Other cats would have thrown up on the floor, but all I did was take a tiny pee on your bed to punish you just a little bit." (I found this out later.)

I knew what I had to do to put an end to his mewling and accusations. I opened the carton of half-and-half and poured a generous amount into his bowl. The Chairman was instantly mollified. He stuck his tongue into the milk like a heroin addict sticks a needle in his arm. He lapped it up, purring as tiny droplets clung to his whiskers.

With the orange cat taken care of, I thought about the other Cat. Cat Stevens playing for my love interest, Juliette Serri, and her date Philippe at the legendary Fillmore. Was it a date? Or just a free ticket to a show? It was driving me crazy. You'd think that after all I'd been through in this life and the afterlife, simple romantic insecurities would be a cakewalk for me, but they weren't. It was unbearable to think of Juliette sitting next to that French Algerian lothario listening to Cat Stevens sing "How Can I Tell You." The image turned my stomach.

Counselors and psychologists spend a lot of time delving into our childhoods looking for the answer to our traumas. They go over and over the troubles we've had growing up, but few seem to realize how our failures in romantic relationships can truly traumatize us. After getting tossed about in the sea of love for decades and getting marginalized and mauled by sharks like Philippe, I was deeply scarred.

It all goes back to my belief that I was the last virgin of the Summer of Love. I got the latest start in my peer group. This was the last of my big insecurities. How could I get ahold of this? What should I do?

As if to answer my questions, Chairman Meow jumped up on my desk, and whether by design or accident, he stepped on my old black flip-up file, which opened to the *K* section. There in bold Sharpie was my old friend's name: Steve Kirtis, house manager for the Fillmore. Steve really liked my songs and had told me that if I ever wanted to open for someone he would try to make it happen. In a flash it all came together! I had never asked for the opportunity because so many people hate openers. I never wanted to put myself in a situation like that. The bigger the headliner, the more people revile the opener. But now I had a different reason. I dialed Steve and to my surprise he picked up.

"Hey, Jimmy. How's it going? I haven't heard from you in a while. Wuz up?"

"Hi, Steve. Remember you told me if I ever wanted to open for someone, you'd try to make it happen? Well, I'm asking you now. Have you got an opener for tomorrow night's show with Yusuf/Cat Stevens?"

"Wow! Your timing is amazing because the scheduled opener just canceled. Okay, well, let me talk with Yusuf and his manager and I'll get back to you. They're sitting right here."

A half hour later, Steve called. "Hey, Jimmy, it's all good. They checked you out and gave a thumbs-up. You passed their 'songs that are good for humanity' test. See, I told you to keep writing those. Be here around 4:00 p.m. tomorrow for a sound check. You get a twenty-minute set, no more."

"Thanks, Steve! I'll make you proud! See you at four."

I took a bath and went to bed early. It felt so good to be back in my own bed. I almost enjoyed the smell of cat piss wafting from the foot of the bed. Chairman Meow had shown me the way, and I was grateful to him. I fell asleep feeling exceedingly pleased with myself and my cat.

39 You Are My Window

You are my window; I see through your pane. I see my tomorrow inside the frame.

—JIMMY DRAKE

I dream I'm back in junior high standing in line at the annual Sadie Hawkins dance, waiting to be picked by one of the girls. The line of boys dwindles to me and the geekiest boy in school, Emmet Swearingen. We look at each other, wondering who will be the last to be picked, when the prettiest cheerleader of all, Nellie Banta, chooses me. We dance to "Shotgun" by Junior Walker and the All Stars. I'm ecstatic until I see the sour look on Nellie's face. She stares at the floor, refusing to make eye contact. The instant the song ends she runs back to her friends, who are all pointing and laughing.

I woke up vibrating to the memory. I sat on the edge of the bed, reliving the sting of that old humiliation. Eventually, I walked over to my bedroom window and pulled open the blinds. It was a picture-perfect day in San Francisco. A day without fog. The city was as bright as it ever gets. Hope filled my heart at the sight of it. I resolved to not let these old heartbreaks keep me from finding new love in my life. "Nellie Banta," I said out loud, "*you* do not get to rule over *me* anymore!"

I spent the majority of the morning practicing the songs I would play at the Fillmore, and then turned to shining up my apartment, taking plenty of breaks for generous ear-scratching sessions with the Chairman. I packed my guitar in its soft case so I could take it on the bus. I decided to dress all in white, putting on a pair of comfortable white linen slacks and a white collarless shirt that I'd found at a clothing store in Union Square but never worn. No more black stage clothes for me. I wanted to shine in the stage lights.

To finish the outfit, I laced up my handmade red leather boots with green trees etched up the sides. I bought them from a street vendor in Covent Garden in London's West End in the '90s. I loved those boots, even though they pinched my toes. They were good luck.

Before leaving my apartment, I fed Chairman Meow. I stroked his ears while he was eating and promised I'd be back that night. I don't know if he believed me, but he kept on purring.

I headed out the door around 3:00 p.m. for the first stop on the twenty-three-minute, two-bus ride that would deliver me to the Fillmore District in San Francisco's Western Addition.

The area that would house the legendary venue that became the Fillmore was largely undamaged by the 1906 earthquake and fire, so it became the City's cultural and commercial center as San Francisco was rising from the ashes. The Majestic Hall was built at the corner of Geary and Fillmore Streets in 1912. It booked ragtime, big band, and the jazz of its time.

From 1939 to 1952, it was the Ambassador Roller Skating Rink. Then, in 1954, one of the most successful African American businessmen at the time, Charles Sullivan, took over the lease and changed its name to the Fillmore Auditorium. Booking the biggest names in Black music for integrated audiences, Sullivan's venture became wildly successful. But by the mid-1960s, due to a combination of economic turmoil, struggles with urban renewal, and civil unrest, coupled with a changing musical landscape, the venue was in trouble. In 1965 Sullivan reluctantly brought in an East Coast transplant, Bill Graham, a savvy businessman who knew rock 'n' roll, in an attempt to revitalize the scene. Graham started booking acts like the San Francisco Mime Troupe and the Warlocks, who later became the Grateful Dead. When Sullivan was murdered in 1966, Graham took over the lease. He began booking and grooming all the legends of the late '60s, including Jimi Hendrix, Pink Floyd, Janis Joplin, and the Who. With the continued decline of the neighborhood, and the limited capacity of the venue, Graham closed the Fillmore in 1968 and purchased the Carousel Ballroom at 10 South Van Ness, dubbing it Fillmore West. He closed that operation in 1971 to follow the rise of arena shows. But the story of the Fillmore was not finished. In the mid-1980s, Graham's operation returned to its original location until 1989, when structural damage from the Loma Prieta earthquake forced the venue to close. When Graham died in a helicopter crash in 1991, his closest friends acted on his last wish to get the Fillmore fixed and running again. Restoration was completed in 1994 and a surprise concert by the Smashing Pumpkins marked the reopening of the storied venue. Live Nation has booked the venue since 2007, mostly to up-and-coming young bands, with the occasional inclusion of a respected headliner like Cat Stevens from the old days.

I got off the bus feeling young and mischievous. I looked at the venerable old brick building and wondered at all the stories and myths it had created over the years. Now it was my turn to use the place for my own story. I texted Steve letting him know I was outside. Five minutes later, he opened the door and greeted me warmly.

"Hey, Jimmy, you look good!" He looked me up and down. "Not bad for an old salt like you! Love the boots!" He punched me playfully in the arm, then hugged me. "Come on in. Have an apple!" He pointed to the barrel of apples in the lobby, an ongoing tradition from the Bill Graham days.

I took a bite and stepped into the large rectangular performing space, every square inch of it set up for a sellout. There was a familiar vibe in the room. It's the electricity every full house has before the audience arrives. A promise that something memorable is about to happen.

"Hey, you wanna meet Yusuf?" Steve asked.

"Really?"

"Yeah, sure, he's a friendly guy. Let's go backstage."

We headed backstage past the hundreds of posters of bands and artists that had played there over the years. Sitting in a chair looking over his notes was Yusuf/Cat Stevens, who smiled at me shyly. "So, you're the bloke who still writes songs about universal love?"

"That's me! Just trying to keep the light on for the species. I really appreciate you letting me open for you. I'm a big fan."

"Everyone says that, but I lost a lot of folks when I converted to Islam. Were you one of those?"

"Honestly? Yeah, I suppose I was. Why did you do that?"

"In 1976, I was caught in a riptide and nearly drowned off the coast of Malibu. I shouted, 'Oh, God, if you save me, I will work for you!' Just then, a wave appeared and carried me to shore. I honored my promise and have been working for Him ever since. I was fortunate that I got to know Islam before it became a headline. A lot of people would have loved for me to keep singing, but I came to a place where I felt I had sung my whole repertoire. I just wanted to get on with the job of living. My success put me in ever-bigger stadiums that made me feel isolated. It was time for me to duck out of the fast and furious life of a pop star."

"Then why are you doing music again?"

"After many years I came to the realization that music is part of God's universe, so I began singing again. I still don't like applause, though. Ultimately artists are shy creatures, aren't we?"

I agreed. "Yes, many of us are introverts, but then we get up onstage and expose our souls to everyone."

He looked thoughtful and confessed, "Yes, as much as I would like to disappear, my work won't let me. Be thankful you're not famous, James. Would you do me a favor?"

"Sure, whatever you want."

"Sometime during your set would you say, 'For those who want to remember me as Cat Stevens, you are welcome to. For those who accept me as Yusuf, I'm here!'"

"Of course, Yusuf. It would be an honor."

Just then, Steve stuck his head in the room and said, "Hey, James, get your ass—" He shot an embarrassed look at Yusuf/Cat Stevens. "I mean your behind up onstage for your sound check."

"Nice talking with you, Yusuf. I'll give it my best."

"I know you will. I can sense it. Warm them up for me, James."

"I will."

Sound checks can be a seriously stressful experience, especially when you're opening for someone famous. The mixing board is set for the headliner, and the opener must make the best of it on the fly. Luckily, my sound check went mercifully well. What a pleasure it was singing over the PA in that big, beautiful empty hall. I imagined my better angels sitting in the empty seats and wondered if, after all their efforts to guide me, I could really pull this off. As I finished sound checking, I saw an imaginary Ollie in the first row mouthing, "Pop out of the drama." I walked over to the sound booth and thanked the tattooed sound tech, Cheryl, for the great sound. She gave me a toothy smile and said, "Only *good* surprises at gigs, man. That's my mantra."

An hour later the doors opened. I watched the excited crowd filing in. I scanned the hall trying to get a glimpse of Juliette and creepy Philippe. There they were, sitting three rows back from the stage. I'll give Philippe credit. He got her good seats. Juliette looked absolutely gorgeous in a formfitting blue dress, spellbound as she beheld the room with her beautiful green eyes. Philippe was clearly staring at her cleavage from the corner of his eye, just waiting for an opportunity to make his move.

It didn't bother me. I was about to make the biggest romantic gamble of my life. It would either be a magnificent coup d'état of the heart or I would fail miserably and slink off in defeat. I put the guitar strap around my shoulders like a hangman would put a rope around a neck. Then I stood backstage waiting for the imminent curtain call.

The lights dimmed and the boisterous crowd hushed in anticipation of seeing their old hero. My buddy Steve's voice came over the PA.

"Ladies and gentlemen, we have a very special opener for you tonight."

Hearing this, many people rustled uncomfortably in their seats. A man in the fourth row said audibly, "An opener. Shit!" Someone in the wings heckled, "Okay, I'm going to the bathroom."

It's my belief based on years of experience that there's at least one asshole per two hundred people at a show. I did the math. With more than 1,300 people in attendance, I felt lucky the other six stayed silent. I chuckled to myself at the thought. *I'm gonna be all right.*

Steve's friendly introduction continued. "He's a local boy with a lot to say. From deep in the heart of the Haight, please welcome to the Fillmore stage, James—I call him Jimmy because he's a friend of mine—Drake!"

I stepped through the curtain to polite applause and looked straight into the astonished eyes of Wanda the Wanderer illuminated by the stage lights. Her mouth was hanging open in total surprise. I glanced at Philippe, who was similarly speechless, but with a scowl on his face that could peel paint. I just smiled, plugged in, and leaned into the mic. "Hello, everybody! It's a true honor to be here tonight. Yusuf wanted me to say, 'For those who are here to see Cat Stevens, you are welcome. For those who are here to see Yusuf—he is in the house!'" People laughed and applauded wildly at the mere mention of the legendary artist's names, which released the disappointment and tension of having to listen to an opener first.

Every musician who's worth their salt has an ace up their sleeve to grab the audience from the start. Mine is an open tuning acoustic instrumental where I tune the G string down to E, taking most of the tension out of the string. This gives me three open E's—a low, a middle, and a high, which makes for a rich open kind of Eastern sound.

I strummed the lush chord, which had its usual effect of, "Whoa! What's that? Maybe this won't be so bad." The other guitarists in the room were thinking, "What's *that* fucking chord?" But before they could figure it out, I launched into my version of a raga that I've played all my life, after George Harrison turned me on to Indian classical music. It sets a tone and acts as a fanfare. I must admit it's also a bit of a ruse, because it makes me sound like a better guitarist than I am. I poured all my heart and soul into it, improvising a few of the structures in ways I'd never done before. I finished with a flurry of harmonics, Michael Hedges–style, plus a last savage hit on the chord, holding the guitar up to the vocal mic rocking it back and forth to let the sound ring and disperse. Ace delivered!*

---

* Listen to "Love Is the Flame" at JohnLennonsGlasses.net.

To my surprise, the audience went crazy! No matter how good an opener is, the audience usually saves its applause for the headliner, so I was genuinely shocked at the response. I looked at Juliette, who was the last person to stop applauding. Philippe's scowl had hardened into a permanent mask of hostility.

The man who had gone to the bathroom returned to his seat. Bewildered and wondering what he had missed, he asked, "What happened?" His date, her arms folded in irritation, said, "Maybe you shouldn't drink so much beer!"

Having spent my ace, it was now up to the kings and queens in my deck of songs to keep the energy going. Anything below a jack would never win over an audience like this. Ordinarily, I would have picked a tried-and-true, road-tested song. Ordinarily, I *never* play new songs at big shows like this. But this was no ordinary moment. I decided to go out on a limb and play the songs I had just written during my time with John Lennon.

"Thank you, ladies and gentlemen. I wrote this next one imagining that John Lennon was looking over my shoulder as I was writing it. Crazy, huh? I mean, what a taskmaster! I swear! I don't recommend trying this at home." The audience laughed. "I'd like to dedicate this song to all the musical heroes we grew up with who are no longer with us. Somehow, I don't think they're so much resting in peace as they are rocking out in Heaven. This is called 'The Lennon Song.'" The audience applauded warmly. I *had* them now. What a relief!

It's said that the true test of a great new song is if it sounds like it's been around forever. Bob Dylan's and Paul Simon's songs are like this. Think of "Blowin' in the Wind" or "The

Sound of Silence." They seemed eternal upon the first listen. When I hit the opening chord of "The Lennon Song," it felt that way. Though it was only a few days old, it was as if I had played it all my life. I saw Juliette smiling and swaying to the song. She let out an enthusiastic whoop when I sang the words, *"Someone told me love is going to release all prisoners."* Philippe looked like he was going to throw up. I actually felt sorry for him. The more applause I got, the more hopelessly frustrated he became.

By the time I headed into my third song, it was a real love-fest. I had breached the opener's curse. The house was all warmed up, and as I sang my next tune, "Deep Blue Sea," the audience began singing the choruses with me. It doesn't get better than that. My short four-song set was coming to a bliss-ful conclusion. "Ladies and gentlemen, thank you for listen-ing to me. I'm as excited as you guys to see Yusuf/Cat Stevens, and I want to thank him and the folks here at the Fillmore for this amazing honor."

I looked straight out at Juliette and said, "I wrote this last song for a special person while I was stranded in New York last week in an ice storm. I believe true love is a window that allows you to see the world more clearly in all its complexity and beauty." Then I strummed the bittersweet key of a million love songs, A minor, and started singing. *"You are my window, looking at you, not many men know this beautiful view. You are my window; I see through your eyes. I see through your shadow; I see your paradise."* Juliette Serri was clearly moved. By the end of the song, she was wiping away tears. Poor Philippe looked like he might burst into tears too, but for other reasons.

It looked like I might get an encore, but I waved it away in respect to the headliner and said, "Thank you, everybody! Let's take a break and get ready to see one of the greatest singer-songwriters on the planet." Turning down the encore showed respect. This was Yusuf's night. Still, it looked like my own personal gamble had paid off. Ms. Serri was grinning ear to ear. Philippe looked angry and defeated. He gave me a look that promised retribution, but I wasn't afraid of him anymore.

Cheryl, the sound engineer, brought up Nick Drake's "River Man" during the break. I thanked her again for the great sound and complimented her on her choice for intermission music. "Hey, man, I told you. Only good surprises at gigs. Nice set!"

I floated backstage to where Yusuf/Cat Stevens stood smiling at me. I was so filled with love from the audience that I almost hugged him. He stepped back in a show of Islamic modesty and made an awkward little bow. I bowed back.

"Did you like the applause?" he asked with an impish smile.

"I'd be lying if I said no."

"You did well. Opening for a rock star, even a recycled one like me, is not easy. What kept you going?"

"It was easy. I was playing for a special person in the audience."

"You mean *that* person?" He pointed to Wanda the Wanderer, who was waiting by the backstage door, waving her hands enthusiastically for me to come over.

"I think you better get over there. She looks pretty excited to see you!"

"Thank you, Yusuf. I'm so appreciative you let me open for you."

"Songs of universal love are what God gave us lungs to sing about. Keep singing them. *Adhhab bisalam.* Go in peace."

I spun around and rushed to the backstage door. "How did you get in here?" I asked.

"I told the backstage manager we were married." Juliette giggled at the brashness of it. "Is that okay?"

"Oh! I'm complimented. Where's Philippe?"

"He said he wasn't feeling well and went home." She rolled her eyes. "Other girls to conquer, I imagine. I really don't take him seriously, but I did get a free ticket to the show, and I got to see you onstage. You were *magnifique*! I can't wait to get together and choreograph your songs. *Tu apportes la lumière dans le monde!*"

"I'm sorry. I don't speak French, only Spanglish. You'll have to translate."

"It's what you told me back at the café, remember? It means 'you bring light into the world.' It's true. Your songs will light the way!"

My heart was so filled with love for her. It was one of those rare moments in life when someone really sees you. "Juliette," I said with quiet conviction, "I believe we will shine together." My blood raced through my veins and my face flushed. Fumbling in her unwavering gaze, I asked, "What do I need to bring tomorrow? Charts, lyric sheets, muffins, dancing shoes? Anything?"

She stepped closer and rose effortlessly in her ballet slippers until her eyes were level with mine. Grinning, with a look that promised everything, she said, "Silly boy. Haven't you heard? All you need is love."

Epilogue

We all shine on. Like the moon and the stars and the sun.
—JOHN LENNON

To mortal eyes, even to the penetrating gaze of astronomers looking for secrets of the universe, there was no outward sign that a titanic confrontation between dark and light was taking place near Proxima Centauri. The Guardian successfully formed a seal around the rift, allowing all the love, creativity, and soul power of Earth's recently departed musicians to pour through.

The first to enter the rift was the angel formerly known as Aretha Franklin. She let loose a sound so pure and true that the darkness around the rift recoiled long enough for a pack of heavy metal rockers led by Erik Brann, a prominent lead guitarist from the late-1960s psychedelic era, who assumed the shape of a huge, fearsome iron butterfly. Speeding past the others, he flew straight into the blackness. As the first to sacrifice his soul to the Black Chord, his luminous multicolored wings burst into flames, punching a hole through the darkness that allowed the others to follow. After that, the entire impact of Earth's musical heroes descended upon the darkness with great ferocity. Their combined harmonic resonance in all its beauty and power pushed back the darkness to the far side of the rift.

Having milked his time haunting Yoko to the last instant, John Lennon came a bit late to the siege, but delivered the killing blow. *"You know it's gonna be!"* his soul bellowed. Lennon focused his immense vibrational energy into a powerful sonic blast that reverberated through the heavens, pounding the Black Chord until, like an immense crystal goblet, it shattered into shards of black nothingness.

Instantly, a blast of intense light—the coalesced energy of all the musicians who sacrificed the memory of their former lives, many before they were ready—pierced the dark universe. Stars formed in microseconds. Warm bright light— the essence of the newly transformed souls—emanated from nascent stars like powerful stage lights gradually coming up to reveal a changed set. A single hauntingly sweet melody line sounded from one of the stars, seeding the newly reborn universe with song, as other budding stars answered in harmony.

The Bay Area music intelligentsia was abuzz following Jimmy Drake's surprise opening gig at the Fillmore for Yusuf/Cat Stevens. He was flooded with interview requests from every minor music blogger to *Pitchfork* and *Fresh Air*. Overwhelmed and panicked, Drake called on Kekoa, who became his manager and friend for life.

Drake's album, *Pop Tunes for Mystics**, with "The Lennon Song" as its lead single, was an immediate hit when it came out a year later. Drake gave Lennon co-songwriting credit for that song as well as several others on the album. People thought it was a crazy thing to do. They asked, "How can you give songwriting credit to a dead guy?" Drake shrugged and said, "Hey, man, Lennon lives!" They thought that was crazy too. Nevertheless, the people and critics loved it, and the album went platinum.

Juliette Serri and Jimmy Drake were instantly inseparable, and *The Neural Heart* became an off-Broadway hit. Netflix commissioned a biopic of the two following the publication of an issue of *Rolling Stone* with a cover that fashioned the two as John and Yoko in a re-creation of the famous "Bed-in for Peace" photos. They married and moved to the south of France to get away from their well-meaning but rabid fans.

Mark Westhrope of Platinum Music Publishing began spamming Drake's voicemail and socials. His voice, the very heart of disingenuity, sucked up to him. "*Hey*, buddy! Where *are* you? I've been trying to get ahold of you for *days*!" He continued in an urgent voice, "Listen, Jimmy, there's a major Bollywood star; her name is Lata Chitra. Have you heard of her? What

---

* Listen to *Pop Tunes for Mystics*, the album that launched James Drake's career, at JohnLennonsGlasses.net.

a *babe*! Anyway, she heard your stuff on YouTube and wants to cover a few of your songs. *Dude.* Check it *out*! Songs about universal love are trending on the subcontinent! That's over a *billion* people! You're gonna wanna meet her, Jimmy. She's a real hottie. You know what I mean? *Dude! Call* me!"

The reincarnated soul of the Maharishi Mahesh Yogi, now known as Lata Chitra, became the first megastar to get on the universal love bandwagon. She covered Drake's "Lennon Song" and "Deep Blue Sea," both of which rose to number one on the charts and launched what would later be called the Indian Invasion.

On a business trip to L.A., Drake walked down Wilshire Boulevard to see if he could find Wilshire Annie, the street vendor. Sure enough, there she was, a beacon of color in a sea of drabness. She seemed to know he was coming because she started waving from a block away. Vibrant and friendly, she embraced Drake and whispered in his ear, "See, James, I told you you'd be back. You didn't believe me!" Drake tried to return the glasses, but Annie declined. "He's not in this universe anymore. Besides, you look good in those, handsome. Kinda like Lou Reed meets Iggy Pop."

James Drake continued to write songs aimed toward the best aspects of the human heart. He never went outside without the glasses, which became his signature look. Chairman Meow stood guard over them every night.

With the negative vibrations of the Black Chord eliminated, Earth began healing on an invisible level. Mysteriously, almost magically, people started getting along better. Internet trolls found they no longer had the desire to put people down. As conflicts and wars dissipated, humanity became engaged in more productive activities. A wellspring of compassion flooded the hearts of everyday people. Injustices large and small were transformed as historical atrocities and individual transgressions were acknowledged, worked through, and forgiven. As fear subsided, guns were turned in and recycled. No longer feeling threatened, people simply lost interest in weapons.

The world stopped burning oil and started living off the sun. Nobody was more delighted than theoretical physicist Michio Kaku, whose dream of seeing his species go from a Type 0 to a Type I civilization was realized.* He was quoted as saying, "*Finally*. Homo sapiens can live up to its Latin name."†

When the power of love overcomes the love of power, the world will know peace.

—JIMI HENDRIX

---

* According to the Kardashev scale, which measures how advanced a civilization is, a Type 0 civilization has not yet been able to harness all the energy of its home planet but is making steady progress toward that goal. Type I civilizations can manage the entire energy and material resources of their planet. Type II civilizations can harness the energy and material resources of a star and its planetary system. Type III civilizations can marshal the energy and material resources of an entire galaxy.
† The Latin meaning of *Homo sapiens* is "wise human."

Bonus materials are available! Check them out at JohnLennonsGlasses.net.

Members of the First Sol Brigade

Bill Graham (Concert producer) 1931–1991
CAUSE OF DEATH: Helicopter crash
Graham's helicopter burst into flames, crashing into a high voltage tower in severe weather near Vallejo, CA, off Highway 37 after a Huey Lewis concert at the Concord Pavilion to benefit the Oakland Hills fire victims. The helicopter hung in the tower for over a month. Three hundred thousand people attended his memorial in Golden Gate Park.

Bob Marley (Bob Marley and the Wailers) 1945–1981
CAUSE OF DEATH: Melanoma
HITS: "Get Up, Stand Up," "Redemption Song," "One Love"
Marley refused to have his toe amputated to treat a melanoma under his toenail and instead only had the nail bed removed. He collapsed jogging in New York's Central Park in 1980 and was taken to a hospital, where it was found the cancer had spread to his brain, liver, and lungs.

Buck Owens (Buck Owens and the Buckeroos) 1929–2006
CAUSE OF DEATH: Heart attack
HITS: "Tiger by the Tail," "Act Naturally"
Owens died in his sleep only hours after his last performance at his club the Crystal Palace in Bakersfield, CA.

Buddy Holly (Buddy Holly and the Crickets) 1936–1959
CAUSE OF DEATH: Plane crash
HITS: "Peggy Sue," "That'll Be the Day"
After touring in unheated tour buses that gave them frostbite, Holly rented a small plane, which crashed into a frozen cornfield in Iowa in 1959. He was twenty-two years old.

Chuck Berry (Solo artist) 1926–2017
CAUSE OF DEATH: Cardiac arrest
HITS: "Johnny B. Goode," "Maybellene"
Berry was buried with his cherry-red guitar bolted to the inside lid. "Johnny B. Goode" was included on the Voyager Golden Records that are aboard the Voyager 1 and 2 spacecrafts and predicted to outlast planet Earth.

Dan Fogelberg (Solo artist) 1951–2007
CAUSE OF DEATH: Prostate cancer
HITS: "Leader of the Band," "Illinois"
Fogelberg died peacefully at his home in Maine three years after being diagnosed with advanced prostate cancer. His ashes were spread in the Atlantic Ocean off the coast of Maine.

Dan Hicks (Dan Hicks and His Hot Licks) 1941–2016
CAUSE OF DEATH: Liver cancer
HITS: "I Scare Myself," "How Can I Miss You When You Won't
      Go Away"
Hicks died at his home in Mill Valley, CA, at the age of seventy-four. "I will always be humble to my dying day," said Hicks in an interview. "On my dying day, I will explain to the world how lucky they have been to be alive the same time as me."

David Bowie (Solo artist) 1947–2016
CAUSE OF DEATH: Liver cancer
HITS: "Fame," "Space Oddity," "Heroes"
Not wanting a funeral, David Robert Jones, a.k.a. David Bowie, was cremated, and his ashes were spread in Bali, Indonesia. He kept his illness secret and released his final album, Blackstar, including the song "Lazarus,"

shortly before his death. Scientists theorize there is a large planet orbiting past Pluto, and many want it named Planet Bowie.

Denny Doherty (The Mamas & the Papas) 1940–2007
CAUSE OF DEATH: Complications following abdominal aortic aneurysm
HITS: "California Dreamin'," "Monday, Monday"
Doherty died at his home in Mississauga, Ontario. The cause was not immediately known, but he had suffered from kidney failure following surgery for an abdominal aortic aneurysm.

Dr. John (The Night Tripper) 1941–2019
CAUSE OF DEATH: Heart attack
HITS: "Right Place, Wrong Time," "Such a Night"
Malcolm John Rebennack Jr., a.k.a. Dr. John, died at sunrise. He won six Grammys and was inducted into the Rock & Roll Hall of Fame in 2011.

Duane Allman (The Allman Brothers Band) 1946–1971
CAUSE OF DEATH: Motorcycle crash
HITS: "Ramblin' Man," "Midnight Rider"
Allman hit a flatbed truck in an intersection near Macon, Georgia, on his Harley Davidson Sportster. In 2003, he was ranked number 2 in *Rolling Stone* magazine's list of the one hundred greatest guitarists of all time, second only to Jimi Hendrix. Brothers Duane and Gregg are buried within feet of one another.

Dusty Springfield (Solo artist) 1939–1999
CAUSE OF DEATH: Breast cancer
HITS: "Wishin' and Hopin'," "I Only Want to Be with You"
Mary Isobel Bernadette O'Brien, a.k.a. Dusty Springfield, was inducted in the Rock & Roll Hall of Fame. At her memorial, Elton John called her the greatest white singer there has ever been.

Eddie Money (Solo artist) 1949–2019
CAUSE OF DEATH: Esophageal cancer
HITS: "Two Tickets to Paradise," "Baby Hold On to Me"
Money died of complications from esophageal cancer at Keck Hospital of USC in Los Angeles. A year later, his family filed a lawsuit alleging wrongful death against the hospital, with an additional allegation of medical malpractice.

Eric Woolfson (The Alan Parsons Project) 1945–2009
CAUSE OF DEATH: Kidney cancer
HITS: "Eye in the Sky," "Time," "Prime Time"
Woolfson was a partner of Alan Parsons. He cowrote and sang on some of their most popular songs. They sold fifty million albums worldwide.

Erik Brann (Iron Butterfly) 1950–2003
CAUSE OF DEATH: Cardiac arrest
HITS: "In-A-Gadda-Da-Vida," "Unconscious Power"
Brann joined Iron Butterfly as a violinist at the age of seventeen. Swapping the violin for electric guitar, he learned to play on the road and was the first to use a bow on an electric guitar, creating much of the band's psychedelic sounds. He died at age fifty-three from cardiac arrest related to a birth defect that he had struggled with for years.

Fats Domino (Fats Domino Band) 1928–2017
CAUSE OF DEATH: Natural causes
HITS: "Blueberry Hill," "Ain't That a Shame"
Antoine Domino, Jr., a.k.a. Fats Domino, had the first million-selling rock 'n' roll record, *The Fat Man*. His masters were destroyed in the 2008 Universal Studios fire.

Frank Sinatra (Solo artist) 1915–1998
CAUSE OF DEATH: Heart attack
HITS: "New York, New York," "My Way"
Sinatra was buried in a blue business suit with mementos from family members including cherry-flavored Life Savers, Tootsie Rolls, a bottle of

Jack Daniels, a pack of Camel cigarettes, a Zippo lighter, stuffed toys, a dog biscuit, and a roll of dimes that he always carried.

Frank Zappa (Mothers of Invention) 1940–1993
CAUSE OF DEATH: Prostate cancer
HITS: "G-Spot Tornado," "Bowtie Daddy," "Montana"
Zappa's cancer had been developing unnoticed for years and was considered inoperable once diagnosed. During one horrendous week in 1971, a fire at a venue in Switzerland destroyed all the band's gear; days later, in England, a jealous boyfriend pushed Zappa off the stage, where he suffered major injuries. He is buried in an unmarked grave in Los Angeles.

Freddie Mercury (Queen) 1946–1991
CAUSE OF DEATH: AIDS
HITS: "Bohemian Rhapsody," "We Are the Champions"
Farrokh Bulsara, a.k.a. Freddie Mercury, died twenty-four hours after issuing a statement that he had AIDS. His good friend Dave Clark of the Dave Clark Five was at his side.

Gene Pitney (Solo artist) 1940–2006
CAUSE OF DEATH: Heart attack
HITS: "Liberty Valence," "Town without Pity," "It Hurts to Be in Love"
Pitney was touring the UK in the spring of 2006 when his manager found him dead in his hotel room following a concert in Cardiff, Wales, on April 5.

George Harrison (The Beatles) 1943–2001
CAUSE OF DEATH: Multiple cancers exacerbated by a knife attack
HITS: "My Sweet Lord," "Something," "While My Guitar Gently Weeps"
Harrison struggled with cancer but was on the mend when he and his wife were attacked by an assailant in their home and Harrison was stabbed several times. Eric Idle described him as one of the few morally good people that rock 'n' roll has produced. Passing away at Paul McCartney's American home, his final words were: "Everything else can wait, but the search for God cannot wait, and love one another."

George Martin (The Beatles' producer) 1926–2016
CAUSE OF DEATH: Not disclosed
HITS: Considered by some to be the "Fifth Beatle"
Martin died peacefully in his sleep on March 8, 2016, in Wiltshire, England. Ringo Starr announced Martin's death on his Twitter feed. Paul McCartney considered him a "second father."

Gerry Rafferty (Stealer's Wheel) 1947–2011
CAUSE OF DEATH: Liver failure
HITS: "Baker Street," "Right Down the Line," "Stuck in the Middle with You"
Rafferty struggled with depression and alcoholism his whole life. He disdained the music business and the celebrity machine. His masters were destroyed along with hundreds of others in the 2008 Universal Studios fire.

Gil Scott-Heron (Soul and jazz poet) 1949–2011
CAUSE OF DEATH: Undisclosed illness following a trip to Europe
HITS: "The Revolution Will Not Be Televised," "Whitey on the Moon"
A music pioneer and poet, Scott-Heron, the "Godfather of Rap," was HIV positive and battled severe drug and alcohol addiction for years.

Glen Campbell (The Wrecking Crew) 1936–2017
CAUSE OF DEATH: Alzheimer's disease
HITS: "Wichita Lineman," "Gentle on My Mind"
As his Alzheimer's progressed, Campbell embarked on a final national tour with his kids and made a documentary. He used a teleprompter to remember lyrics, but his playing and singing were flawless.

Glenn Frey (The Eagles) 1948–2016
CAUSE OF DEATH: Rheumatoid arthritis, ulcerated colitis, pneumonia
HITS: "Desperado," "Hotel California"
Frey was prescribed drugs to keep his arthritis and colitis in check. These drugs lowered his immune system, and then he contracted pneumonia. His wife filed suit against the doctor and the hospital.

Greg Lake (Emerson, Lake & Palmer; King Crimson) 1947–2016
CAUSE OF DEATH: Pancreatic cancer
HITS: "The Court of the Crimson King," "From the Beginning"
Lake, one of the early innovators of progressive rock, died at age sixty-nine after what his manager called a "long and stubborn" battle with cancer.

Harry Chapin (Harry Chapin Band) 1942–1981
CAUSE OF DEATH: Car accident
HITS: "Cats in the Cradle," "Taxi"
Chapin was hit from behind by a grocery semitruck. His widow received a twelve-million-dollar settlement from the company.

Harry Nilsson (Solo artist) 1941–1994
CAUSE OF DEATH: Heart failure
HITS: "Jump into the Fire," "Everybody's Talkin'"
Four years prior to his death, Nilsson's financial advisor embezzled all the money he'd earned as a recording artist, leaving him with three hundred dollars. Born with congenital heart problems, Nilsson suffered a heart attack on February 14, 1993, and began recording a final album titled Papa's Got a Brown New Robe that the producer shelved after Nilsson's death on January 15, 1994. In 2019, this album was finally released as Losst and Founnd.

Isaac Hayes (Solo artist) 1942–2008
CAUSE OF DEATH: Stroke
HITS: Theme from the movie *Shaft*
Hayes won an Oscar, several Grammys, and a Golden Globe award for the theme from the movie *Shaft*. The Tennessee General Assembly named a section of Interstate 40 the Isaac Hayes Memorial Highway in 2010.

James Brown (The Famous Flames) 1933–2006
CAUSE OF DEATH: Congestive heart failure
HITS: "Papa's Got a Brand-New Band," "I Feel Good"
Brown, the "Godfather of Soul," died on Christmas day supposedly from congestive heart failure due to complications from pneumonia. However,

many in his circles contend he was murdered. A significant display of Brown's memorabilia can be viewed at the Augusta History Museum in Augusta, GA.

Janis Joplin (Big Brother and the Holding Company) 1943–1970
CAUSE OF DEATH: Accidental drug overdose
HITS: "Little Piece of My Heart," "Ball and Chain"
Joplin died of a heroin overdose possibly compounded by alcohol sixteen days after Jimi Hendrix. Her ashes were scattered from a plane over the Pacific Ocean.

Jerry Garcia (Grateful Dead) 1942–1995
CAUSE OF DEATH: Heart attack
HITS: "Casey Jones," "Morning Dew"
Garcia's health was in decline following long-standing struggles with drug addiction, weight problems, sleep apnea, heavy smoking, and diabetes. He died in his room at the rehabilitation clinic he'd checked himself into. Half of Garcia's ashes were spread on the Ganges River in Rishikesh, India, and the other half in the San Francisco Bay.

Jerry Lieber (Songwriter) 1933–2011
CAUSE OF DEATH: Cardiopulmonary failure
HITS: "Hound Dog," "Jailhouse Rock," "Yakety Yak," "Stand by Me,"
     "Kansas City," "On Broadway"
Leiber and Mike Stoller wrote over seventy chart hits for many artists including twenty songs for Elvis Presley. Both were entered into the Songwriters Hall of Fame in 1985.

Jesse Winchester (Solo artist) 1944–2014
CAUSE OF DEATH: Bladder cancer
HITS: "Yankee Lady," "Say What"
A tribute to Winchester titled *Quiet About It* was recorded in 2012 by many artists including James Taylor, Rosanne Cash, Jimmy Buffet, Lyle Lovett, and others.

Jim Croce (Jim Croce Band) 1943–1973
CAUSE OF DEATH: Plane crash
HITS: "Time in a Bottle," "Bad, Bad Leroy Brown"
The plane crash that claimed the life of Jim Croce and five others was deemed solely due to pilot error. Shortly before his death, Croce had written his wife saying he was going to quit music and stick to writing short stories and movie scripts and retire from public life.

Jim Morrison (The Doors) 1943–1971
CAUSE OF DEATH: Heart failure
HITS: "Light My Fire," "Touch Me"
Morrison died in his bathtub in Paris at the age of twenty-seven. He's a member of the "27 Club," joining Janis Joplin, Jimi Hendrix, Brian Jones, and Kurt Cobain, all of whom died at age twenty-seven. The official cause of death was heart failure, though there was no autopsy and questions remain unanswered.

Jimi Hendrix (The Jimi Hendrix Experience) 1942–1970
CAUSE OF DEATH: Barbiturate overdose
HITS: "Purple Haze," "Foxy Lady," "Fire"
Fatigued, in poor health, and disillusioned about the music business, Hendrix aspirated on his vomit and died of asphyxia after having taken nine sleeping pills, eighteen times the recommended dose. His death was ruled accidental.

Joe Cocker (Joe Cocker Band) 1944–2014
CAUSE OF DEATH: Lung cancer
HITS: "With a Little Help from My Friends," "You Are So Beautiful"
Cocker smoked two packs of cigarettes a day until he quit in 1991. He is buried in the town cemetery in Crawford, CO.

John Denver (Solo artist) 1943–1997
CAUSE OF DEATH: Plane crash
HITS: "Rocky Mountain High," "Take Me Home, Country Roads"
Denver, an accomplished pilot, died on impact when his experimental Rutan Long-EZ plane crashed into Monterey Bay near Pacific Grove, CA.

John Entwistle (The Who) 1944–2002
CAUSE OF DEATH: Heart attack
HITS: "Tommy," "Behind Blue Eyes"
Entwistle died in Room 658 at the Hard Rock Hotel & Casino in Paradise, Nevada, one day before the first show of their 2002 tour. The coroner concluded that the moderate amount of cocaine in his system combined with an undiagnosed heart condition brought on the fatal heart attack.

John Hartford (John Hartford Band) 1937–2001
CAUSE OF DEATH: Non-Hodgkin's lymphoma
HITS: "Gentle On My Mind," "This Eve of Parting"
Hartford was given a star on the St. Louis Walk of Fame and a posthumous President's Award by the Americana Music Association. A festival in his name is held annually near Bean Blossom, Indiana.

John Lennon (The Beatles) 1940–1980
CAUSE OF DEATH: Murder by gunshot
HITS: "I Want to Hold Your Hand," "Day in the Life," "Imagine"
Lennon was murdered in 1980 by Mark David Chapman, who remained on the scene reading *Catcher in the Rye* until he was arrested. Lennon's ashes were spread in Central Park, NYC.

John Phillips (The Mamas & the Papas) 1935–2001
CAUSE OF DEATH: Heart failure
HITS: "California Dreamin'," "Monday, Monday"
In addition to being the primary songwriter for the Mamas & the Papas, Phillips was one of the main organizers of the 1967 Monterey Pop Festival.

Johnny Cash (Johnny Cash Band) 1932–2003
CAUSE OF DEATH: Complications of diabetes
HITS: "Folsom Prison Blues," "I Walk the Line"
When Cash's health began to decline in 1997, his diagnosis was changed several times before it was finally altered to autonomic neuropathy associated with diabetes. The "Man in Black" died less than four months after his wife, June Carter Cash, who encouraged Johnny to keep working after she passed. He wrote sixty songs in the last four months of his life.

Karen Carpenter (The Carpenters) 1950–1983
CAUSE OF DEATH: Heart failure due to anorexia nervosa
HITS: "Close to You," "We've Only Just Begun"
The coroner told colleagues that Carpenter's routine use of ipecac syrup to induce vomiting had weakened her heart.

Kate Wolf (Kate Wolf Band) 1942–1986
CAUSE OF DEATH: Leukemia
HITS: "Across the Great Divide," "Give Yourself to Love"
Kate Wolf, who died at age forty-four following a long struggle with leukemia, made a significant and ongoing impact on the folk music scene. The World Folk Music Association established the annual Kate Wolf Memorial Award in 1987, and the Kate Wolf Memorial Festival in Northern California ran for twenty-five years before it ended in 2022.

Keith Emerson (The Nice; Emerson, Lake & Palmer) 1944–2016
CAUSE OF DEATH: Suicide by gunshot
HITS: "From the Beginning," "Trilogy"
Emerson became depressed after nerve damage to his hand made it difficult to play up to his own standards. He shot himself in the head at his home in Santa Monica, CA.

Keith Moon (The Who) 1946–1978
CAUSE OF DEATH: Accidental overdose
HITS: "Pinball Wizard," "Behind Blue Eyes"
Moon succumbed to an accidental overdose of clomethiazole, a drug intended to treat or prevent symptoms of alcohol withdrawal. He died in Harry Nilsson's flat, as did Mama Cass Elliott, leading some to believe the flat is haunted.

Kurt Cobain (Nirvana) 1967–1994
CAUSE OF DEATH: Suicide by gunshot
HITS: "Smells Like Teen Spirit"
After climbing a fence to leave a drug rehab center in Los Angeles, Cobain flew back to Seattle. An electrician found his body a few days later. Cobain is another member of "The 27s."

Leon Russell (Leon Russell Band) 1942–2016
CAUSE OF DEATH: Undisclosed
HITS: "Young Blood," "Tightwire"
Russell died in his sleep at his home in Mt. Juliet, TN. He had suffered a
heart attack and undergone bypass surgery three months prior.

Leonard Cohen (Solo artist) 1934–2016
CAUSE OF DEATH: Accidental fall
HITS: "Hallelujah," "Everybody Knows"
Cohen died in his sleep following a fall in the middle of the night, not long
after releasing his fourteenth album, which he considered one of his best.
As was his wish, Cohen was laid to rest with a Jewish rite, in a simple pine
casket, in a family plot.

Levon Helm (The Band) 1940–2012
CAUSE OF DEATH: Throat cancer
HITS: "Up on Cripple Creek," "The Weight"
Helm struggled with throat cancer for many years, losing and then regain-
ing his voice. He performed right up to the end.

Lonnie Donegan (Lonnie Donegan's Skiffle Group and others) 1931–2002
CAUSE OF DEATH: Heart attack
HITS: "Does Your Chewing Gum Lose Its Flavor," "Rock Island Line"
Donegan, known as the King of Skiffle, died midway through a tour that
was to include his appearance at a memorial concert for George Harrison
at the Royal Albert Hall.

Lou Rawls (Solo artist) 1933–2006
CAUSE OF DEATH: Lung cancer
HITS: "You'll Never Find Another Love Like Mine," "Dead End Street"
Rawls died following a year-long battle with lung cancer that had metas-
tasized to his brain. In a previous brush with death in 1958, Rawls was pro-
nounced dead at the scene following a car crash.

Lou Reed (Velvet Underground) 1942–2013
CAUSE OF DEATH: Liver disease
HITS: "Walk on the Wild Side," "Rock 'n' Roll Animal"
Reed died of terminal liver disease not long after having received a liver transplant. An outpouring of memorial concerts were held in his honor. A type of velvet spider discovered in Spain called Loureedia was named after him.

Louie Armstrong (The Louie Armstrong Band) 1901–1971
CAUSE OF DEATH: Heart attack
HITS: "Hello Dolly," "What a Wonderful World"
Against his doctor's advice, Armstrong kept playing and touring. He died in his sleep one month before his seventieth birthday.

Mama Cass Elliot (The Mamas & the Papas) 1941–1974
CAUSE OF DEATH: Heart attack
HITS: "California Dreamin'," "Monday, Monday"
Ellen Naomi Cohen, a.k.a. Mama Cass, died of a sudden heart attack in Harry Nilsson's flat in London. There were no drugs in her system, and the rumor of her "choking on a ham sandwich" was a fat-shaming myth. Much of her material was destroyed in the 2008 Universal Studios fire.

Marvin Gaye (The Funk Brothers) 1939–1984
CAUSE OF DEATH: Murder by gunshot
HITS: "I Heard It Through the Grapevine," "What's Going On"
Following a series of violent altercations between father and son, Gaye's father shot him in the heart with the gun Gaye had purchased for him.

Mary Travers (Peter, Paul and Mary) 1936–2009
CAUSE OF DEATH: Leukemia
HITS: "Puff the Magic Dragon," "Lemon Tree"
Folk diva Travers was diagnosed with leukemia in 2004 and received a bone marrow transplant the following year. She died four years later due to complications from the transplant and other treatments.

Mary Wells (Solo artist) 1943–1992
CAUSE OF DEATH: Laryngeal cancer
HITS: "My Guy," "You Beat Me to the Punch," "Two Lovers"
Wells, a.k.a. the Queen of Motown, is buried in the Forest Lawn Memorial Park in Glendale, CA, about 850 feet from family friend Sam Cooke. Smokey Robinson gave the eulogy at her funeral.

Maurice Gibb (The Bee Gees) 1949–2003
CAUSE OF DEATH: Bowel obstruction complications
HITS: "Massachusetts," "Saturday Night Fever"
Gibb was the fraternal twin brother of Robin Gibb. His death was caused by a volvulus, a twisted section of small intestine that causes a blockage and cuts off the blood supply.

Michael Hedges (Solo artist) 1953–1997
CAUSE OF DEATH: Car accident
HITS: "Aerial Boundaries," "Rickover's Dream"
Hedges lost control of his car on a rain-slicked S-curve on Highway 128 in Northern California, falling down a 120-foot cliff. He was thrown from his car and died instantly.

Michael Jackson (Jackson Five) 1958–2009
CAUSE OF DEATH: Drug overdose
HITS: "Beat It," "Billie Jean," "Thriller"
Jackson died from cardiac arrest caused by an overdose of propofol and benzodiazepine administered to him by his personal physician who was subsequently sentenced to four years in prison following a conviction for involuntary manslaughter.

Mimi Fariña (Duo with Richard Fariña) 1945–2001
CAUSE OF DEATH: Neuroendocrine cancer
HITS: "In the Quiet Morning," "Celebration for a Grey Day"
Fariña, Joan Baez's sister, founded and ran Bread and Roses, (now known as Bread and Roses Presents) a San Francisco Bay Area nonprofit that brings free live music to the sick, impoverished, and imprisoned. Over 1,200 people attended her funeral at Grace Cathedral.

Nat King Cole (Solo artist) 1919–1965
CAUSE OF DEATH: Lung cancer
HITS: "Unforgettable," "Mona Lisa"
Nathaniel Adams Coles, a.k.a. Nat King Cole, was a heavy smoker, diagnosed with an advanced malignancy in his left lung in 1964 after friends and family convinced him to seek medical attention for weight loss and back pain. Despite knowledge of Cole's terminal diagnosis, his publicists promoted the idea that he would soon be well and working.

Nick Drake (Solo artist) 1948–1974
CAUSE OF DEATH: Overdose
HITS: "River Man," "Pink Moon"
Drake, who reached critical acclaim only after his death, suffered from debilitating depression most of his life. He died of a self-administered overdose of the antidepressant amitriptyline. Suicide was suspected, though never confirmed. A lyric from the final song of his final album, *Pink Moon*, are inscribed on his headstone: "Now we rise, and we are everywhere."

Nicolette Larsen (Solo artist and session singer for Neil Young and others) 1952–1997
CAUSE OF DEATH: Cerebral edema and liver failure
HITS: "Lotta Love," "Rhumba Girl"
Larsen, Neil Young's half sister, was only forty-five years old when she died from complications of a cerebral hemorrhage due to liver disease, exacerbated by chronic use of Valium and Tylenol PM. She is buried at Forest Lawn Hollywood Hills Cemetery in L.A.

Norma Tanega (Solo artist) 1939–2019
CAUSE OF DEATH: Colon cancer
HITS: "Walkin' My Cat Named Dog," "No Stranger Am I"
Tanega, in addition to her hit "Walkin' My Cat Named Dog," wrote songs for her romantic partner, Dusty Springfield. She was known for her inventive chords and melodic structures.

Norton Buffalo (Steve Miller Band; Norton Buffalo and the Knock Outs; Roy Rogers & Norton Buffalo) 1951–2009
CAUSE OF DEATH: Lung cancer
HITS: "King of the Highway," "Lovin' in the Valley of the Moon"
Phillip Jackson, a.k.a. Norton Buffalo, was a singer-songwriter and master harmonica player who was a member of the Steve Miller Band for thirty-two years. Some industry insiders believe that he developed lung cancer due to a lifetime of using Chinese-made harmonicas.

Patsy Cline (Patsy Cline Band) 1932–1963
CAUSE OF DEATH: Plane crash
HITS: "Crazy," "I Fall to Pieces"
Cline was killed in a plane crash along with country performers Cowboy Copas and Hawkshaw Hawkins and manager Randy Hughes. The airfield manager at Dyersburg Municipal Airport in Tennessee, where the plane had stopped to refuel, offered the band dinner and free rooms for the night due to high winds and inclement weather, but the pilot refused.

Paul Kantner (The Jefferson Airplane) 1941–2016
CAUSE OF DEATH: Septic shock
HITS: "Somebody to Love," "White Rabbit"
Kantner died in San Francisco from multiple organ failure and septic shock after he suffered a heart attack days earlier. A notorious smoker of unfiltered Camels, Kantner once quipped, "I might as well die of something I like." He died the same day as Signe Toly Anderson, a cofounder of Jefferson Airplane.

Pete Ham (Badfinger) 1947–1975
CAUSE OF DEATH: Suicide by hanging
HITS: "No Matter What," "Day after Day"
Badfinger's manager was sued by their record label after he took off with an advance. Left penniless, Ham lost hope and hung himself. Tom Evans, colead singer and songwriter for Badfinger, also hung himself in 1983 after a dispute with a former bandmate.

Phil Everly (Everly Brothers) 1939–2014
CAUSE OF DEATH: Pulmonary heart disease
HITS: "Wake Up Little Susie," "Bye Bye Love"
Everly was one of the pallbearers at Buddy Holly's funeral. Despite the brothers' extended rifts and until his own death in 2022, Don Everly kept a small container of his brother Phil's ashes and said "Good morning" to them every day.

Prince (Prince) 1958–2016
CAUSE OF DEATH: Accidental overdose
HITS: "Purple Rain," "Little Red Corvette"
Prince Rogers Nelson, a.k.a. Prince, died in the elevator of his Paisley Park home. According to investigators, he thought he was taking Vicodin for pain, but the pills contained counterfeit opioids laced with Fentanyl. Prince died without a will, setting off a six-year battle over his estate.

Ravi Shankar (Mostly remembered in the West for his work with George Harrison) 1920–2012
CAUSE OF DEATH: Respiratory insufficiency
HITS: Many ragas
Robindro Shaunkor Chowdhury, a.k.a. Ravi Shankar, the master sitarist who influenced many musicians throughout the world, died at the age of ninety-two following heart valve replacement surgery in San Diego, CA.

Ray Charles (Ray Charles Band) 1930–2004
CAUSE OF DEATH: Complications from liver disease
HITS: "Georgia on My Mind," "Hit the Road Jack"
Ray Charles Robinson Sr., a.k.a. Ray Charles, was planning a new tour when he died age seventy-three at his home in Beverly Hills five days after Ronald Reagan. He's quoted as saying a few months prior to his death, "Until the good Lord calls my number, that's what I'm going to do."

Ray Manzarek (The Doors) 1939–2013
CAUSE OF DEATH: Bile duct cancer
HITS: "Light My Fire," "Touch Me"
Manzarek died in Germany of cholangiocarcinoma, a rare cancer of the bile ducts. He performed a private concert for his doctors and nurses and believed up to his death that Doors front man Jim Morrison may have faked his own death to escape the pressures of fame.

Ray Thomas (The Moody Blues) 1941–2018
CAUSE OF DEATH: Prostate cancer
HITS: "Legend of a Mind," "Dr. Livingston I Presume," "Eternity Road"
Thomas, the Moody Blues flutist, vocalist, and songwriter, died in his sleep six days after his seventy-sixth birthday in Surrey, England.

Ric Ocasek (The Cars) 1944–2019
CAUSE OF DEATH: Cardiovascular disease
HITS: "Let the Good Times Roll," "You're All I've Got Tonight"
Ocasek was found dead in his townhouse two weeks after surgery. He disinherited his third wife, supermodel Paulina Porizkova, and two of his six sons.

Richard Manuel (The Band) 1943–1986
CAUSE OF DEATH: Suicide by hanging
HITS: "Tears of Rage," "Orange Juice Blues (Blues for Breakfast)"
Throughout years of drug abuse and disillusioned by the promises and betrayals of the music business, the Band's pianist and singer had attempted suicide twice, once by self-immolation and once by shooting himself in the head with a BB gun, before succeeding by hanging himself just shy of his forty-third birthday.

Richie Havens (Solo artist) 1941–2013
CAUSE OF DEATH: Heart attack
HITS: "Freedom," "Here Comes the Sun"
Havens's ashes are spread over the Woodstock concert site where he rose to fame in 1967 after playing a grueling three hours and improvising a finale that later became his signature song, "Freedom." Havens performed

several times for the Dalai Lama. His music masters were destroyed in the 2008 Universal Studios fire.

Ritchie Valens (Ritchie Valens Band) 1941–1959
CAUSE OF DEATH: Plane crash
HITS: "La Bamba," "Donna"
Valens was killed in the plane crash that also killed Buddy Holly and the Big Bopper. Valens "won" a seat on the ill-fated flight in a coin toss. The flight was supposed to be a respite from riding in the freezing tour bus during the twenty-four-day Winter Dance Party tour. Don McLean, in his song "American Pie," coined the incident "the day the music died."

Rick Danko (The Band) 1943–1999
CAUSE OF DEATH: Congestive heart failure
HITS: "The Weight," "Up on Cripple Creek"
Danko, the Band's bassist, died in his sleep at his home in Marbletown, NY. He's buried next to his son Eli who died at age eighteen of asphyxiation following heavy drinking.

Ricky Nelson (Ricky Nelson Band) 1940–1985
CAUSE OF DEATH: Plane crash
HITS: "Poor Little Fool," "Hello Mary Lou"
Nelson, his band, and his girlfriend all died in the crash landing of the band's DC-3 en route from Alabama to Texas for a New Year's Eve concert. It is suspected that a fire from a faulty heater engulfed the cabin. The two pilots survived.

Roy Orbison (Solo artist) 1936–1988
CAUSE OF DEATH: Heart attack
HITS: "Pretty Woman," "Only the Lonely"
Orbison confessed to Johnny Cash that he was having chest pains, but he did nothing about it and continued a demanding schedule of appearances. A pathologist who reviewed medical records and interviewed friends and family after Orbison's death believed his heart condition was due to his addiction to yo-yo dieting.

Sam Cooke (Solo artist) 1931–1964
CAUSE OF DEATH: Gunshot wound
HITS: "You Send Me," "Cupid," "Twistin' the Night Away"
Cooke was shot by the manager of a motel where he was staying. She said
he attacked her. The court ruled it as justifiable homicide, though members of his family dispute those findings. An estimated 200,000 fans lined
up over four city blocks to view the body of the "King of Soul."

Sandy Denny (Fairport Convention) 1947–1978
CAUSE OF DEATH: Traumatic midbrain hemorrhage
HITS: "Who Knows Where the Time Goes," "Fotheringay"
Denny, preeminent British folk-rock singer, suffered from depression,
alcoholism, and self-harming behaviors that included many intentional
as well as accidental falls. She went into a coma and died following a series
of serious falls a couple of weeks prior.

Scott McKenzie (Solo artist) 1939–2012
CAUSE OF DEATH: Guillain-Barré syndrome
HITS: "San Francisco (Be Sure to Wear Flowers in Your Hair)"
McKenzie was diagnosed with GBS, a rare disorder where the immune
system attacks the peripheral nervous system, two years prior to his death.

Sonny Bono (Sonny & Cher) 1935–1998
CAUSE OF DEATH: Skiing accident
HITS: "The Beat Goes On," "I Got You Babe"
Salvatore Phillip Bono, a.k.a. Sonny Bono, singer, songwriter, actor, and
politician, died from a massive blunt trauma after hitting a tree while ski-
ing at the Heavenly Valley Resort in South Lake Tahoe.

Tammi Terrell (Solo artist) 1945–1970
CAUSE OF DEATH: Brain cancer
HITS: "You're All I Need to Get By," "Ain't No Mountain High Enough"
Thomasina Winifred Montgomery, a.k.a. Tammi Terrell, underwent eight
surgeries between 1968 and 1970, falling into a coma following the final
operation on January 21. She died on March 16, one month before her 25th

birthday. Terrell's death severely affected her singing partner, Marvin Gaye, who never got over her death.

Terry Kath (Chicago) 1946–1978
CAUSE OF DEATH: Accidental gunshot
HITS: "25 or 6 to 4," "Only the Beginning"
As a joke, gun enthusiast Kath put what he thought was an unloaded pistol to his head and blew his brains out in front of Chicago roadie Don Johnson.

Tiny Tim (Solo artist) 1932–1996
CAUSE OF DEATH: Cardiac arrest
HITS: "Tiptoe Through the Tulips"
Herbert Butros Khaury, a.k.a. Tiny Tim, suffered a heart attack on stage while singing "Tiptoe Through the Tulips" at a gala benefit hosted by the Women's Club of Minneapolis.

Tom Petty (Tom Petty and the Heartbreakers) 1950–2017
CAUSE OF DEATH: Accidental overdose
HITS: "Refugee," "Learning to Fly," "Free Fallin'"
Petty, who insisted on touring despite debilitating pain, died of multi-system organ failure due to an accidental drug overdose from a toxic mix of drugs he was taking for emphysema, knee problems, and, most significantly, a fractured hip.

Tommy Tedesco (The Wrecking Crew) 1930–1997
CAUSE OF DEATH: Lung cancer
HITS: Several Hundred Top 40 hits
The Wrecking Crew were an A-list group of studio musicians who played on hundreds of Top 40 records and TV themes in the '60s and '70s. Tedesco's guitar is on many of them, including the themes for *Bonanza* and *The Twilight Zone*.

Tony Clarke (Moody Blues Producer) 1941–2010
CAUSE OF DEATH: Emphysema
HITS: "Ride My Seesaw," "Tuesday Afternoon"
Sometimes called the "Sixth Moody," Clarke was the "George Martin" of the Moody Blues and was hugely responsible for their signature studio sound.

Walter Becker (Steely Dan) 1950–2017
CAUSE OF DEATH: Esophageal cancer
HITS: "Reelin' In the Years," "King of the World," "Do It Again"
Becker died from an aggressive and swift form of esophageal cancer while surrounded by his family, his music, and a blustery rainstorm—one of his favorite sounds. Donald Fagen, his longtime partner in Steely Dan, said he would do everything he could to keep their songs alive.

Warren Zevon (Solo artist) 1947–2003
CAUSE OF DEATH: Mesothelioma
HITS: "Werewolves of London," "Mohammed's Radio"
Zevon died of a disease most associated with exposure to asbestos. Family says he may have gotten it from playing in the attic of his father's carpet store. Given a prognosis of three months, Zevon refused treatment and instead recorded a final album, *The Wind*, which was released twelve days before he died a year later. About dying, he said, "Enjoy every sandwich."

Wilson Pickett (Wilson Pickett Band) 1914–2006
CAUSE OF DEATH: Heart attack
HITS: "Mustang Sally," "In the Midnight Hour"
Pickett, who had been in poor health and had spent much of the previous year in the hospital, died two months short of his sixty-fifth birthday. According to his sister, he died just after the midnight hour. Little Richard gave a eulogy at his funeral.

Woody Guthrie (Solo artist) 1912–1967
CAUSE OF DEATH: Huntington's disease
HITS: "This Land Is Your Land," "Tear the Fascists Down," "Deportee
        (Plane Wreck at Los Gatos)"
Huntington's disease is a rare degenerative, hereditary, and fatal disease that causes the progressive degeneration of nerve cells in the brain. Guthrie's mother and two of his eight children also died from the disease. The second of his three wives, Marjorie Mazia, became a primary caregiver and later founded Huntington's Disease Society of America, the largest nonprofit dedicated to HD support and research.

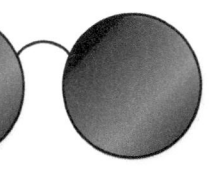

The *John Lennon's Glasses* Music Collection

To listen to the original Jim Ocean songs mentioned or alluded to in the novel, visit JohnLennonsGlasses.net.

"Coming of Age in the Milky Way" (Alluded to in Ch. 37)
An optimistic celebration of humankind's current state of evolution.

"Deep Blue Sea" (Mentioned in Ch. 18 and 39)
A song about the author's experience of terror and bliss during panic attacks.

"Falling" (Mentioned in Ch. 13 and 15)
The curious place where the pain of loss and the loss of control can lead to liberation and renewal.

"Fear and Love" (Mentioned in Ch. 33)
A fable about the power of love to transmute fear into courage.

"High on Stress" (Mentioned in Ch. 8)
A farcical tableau about addiction to the pace of contemporary American life.

"In a Drop of Time" (Mentioned in Ch. 20)
A exploration of the process of dying—a river emptying into the sea.

"I've Got My Own Stalker" (Alluded to in Ch. 25)
A tongue-in-cheek perspective on achieving fame.

"Just a Hippie Thought" (Alluded to in Ch. 17)
A glimpse into hippie wisdom including famous quotes from the era's halcyon days.

"Know the Way You Wander" (Alluded to in Ch. 23)
An invitation to break out of comfort zones and explore different shores, actual and metaphorical.

"Last Stretch of Highway" (Alluded to in Ch. 36)
An entreaty to make the most of the later stages of life.

"The Lennon Song" (Mentioned in Ch. 35, 37, and 39)
Imagined life advice from John Lennon about universal love.

"Living in the Weeds" (Alluded to in Ch. 29)
A commentary about the inequitable distribution of resources and opportunity.

"Love as Real Estate, You're My Fixer-Upper" (Mentioned in Ch. 8)
A satirical look at a common dynamic in modern romantic relationships.

"Love Is the Flame" (Mentioned in Ch. 39)
A raga-influenced song that posits Love as the background field of reality.

"The MetaQuizzical Café" (Alluded to in Ch. 29)
A song that introduces readers to the authors' signature flavor of music.

"You Are My Window" (Mentioned in Ch. 39)
A love song from the author to his wife.

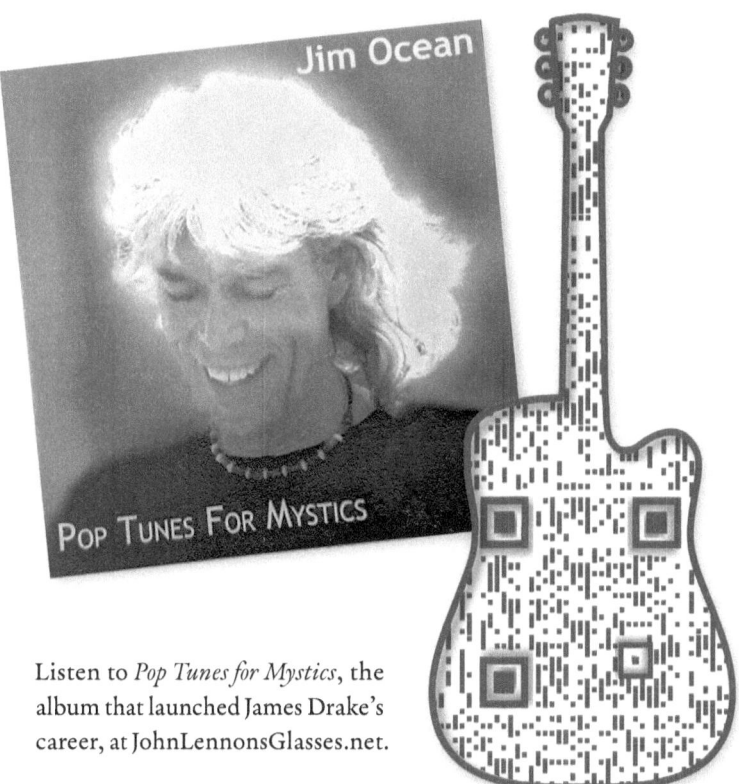

Listen to *Pop Tunes for Mystics*, the album that launched James Drake's career, at JohnLennonsGlasses.net.

A Word from the Authors
Thanks for reading and listening! Please leave a review wherever you purchased this book.

 **Acknowledgments**

It came as much of a surprise to me as it did to all my friends that after a lifetime of writing songs, I wrote this book. Many of these fine people inspired, supported, and mentored me along the way.

Over dinner one evening, my longtime friend and brilliant musician/arranger/producer Brian Whistler mused, "What if you received a pair of John Lennon glasses and something magical appeared when you put them on?" I said, "Yeah, that's fascinating; but what if Lennon himself appeared when you put them on?" Our speculations never left me nor did the feeling of Lennon hovering in the background. Thank you, Brian, for helping to spark this tale and for recording *Pop Tunes for Mystics*, the musical companion to this book and one of the best albums of my life. You have always inspired me.

This book would not be the shiny object it is without my wife, Kathy Ocean, and her writing and editing skills. She embellished the storyline, added passages, and coaxed me into expanding the ending. Her tireless efforts poring over the concepts, the structure, and each sentence many times over made my words flow and helped the story go deeper than it would have otherwise. Thank you, Kathy, for your many years of commitment to our creative process. Together we are quite a team.

Thank you, Toni Logue, Sharon Palmer, Wendy Zeigler, and Brigette Mansell, for inviting me to read chapter excerpts at the dinner parties you organized. It galvanized me to continue writing the book. Without your encouragement, I'm not sure I would have completed it. You also gave me the opportunity to practice the Liverpool "scouse" accent so characteristic of the Beatles. It's like speaking English with a cold.

Many thanks to all my beta readers for taking the time to read and comment on early versions of the manuscript. Drew Harrison—leader of the Beatles tribute band the Sun Kings and the closest thing to John Lennon still walking the Earth, kept me true to Lennon. Janet Finsilver (author of the Kelly Jackson mystery series) and her husband, E.J., gave me much valuable advice. Gregg and Gabriella McVicar read the book as a bedtime story to each other. (That was so sweet!) NASA scientist Steve Howell was my "science advisor" as the story went into outer space. Dee Murphy and Oliver Dinsmore offered tips about the scouse accent and all things British since they're from the other side of the pond. Kenny (Slomez) Spear caught a few inaccuracies, including the fact that eucalyptus trees are not native to New Zealand. Steve Sauvain helped us kill off a bunch of similes, which I used too often, probably from years of songwriting. Bodie Wagner, John Gould, Judy Sigars, Bill Meyer, George Zastrow, Georgia Rowe, David and Eileen Jones, Mark Westwind, and the Beckers—Pat, Gary, and Jason—all offered useful feedback and encouragement. A special shout-out to Mark Westwind for his decades of friendship, critique, and support of my creative endeavors. What a great group of bright, talented people. I am so lucky to know you all!

Lastly, I want to acknowledge all the musicians and songwriters who have passed away.

Your creations have inspired, fulfilled, and directed me. I hope to meet you on the other side. Maybe at the center of the sun. That's where the real parties are happening!

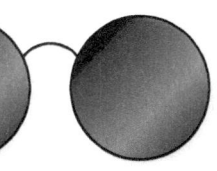

About the Authors

Music has been in **Jim Ocean's** blood since he was a young boy picking out rock 'n' roll riffs on the string of his fishing pole in his mother's kitchen. In his twenties—by then a seasoned musician and songwriter living in the burbs—Jim recognized the need for an intimate space where he and other artists could come together to perform their original music, and the Musician's Coffeehouse was born.

In the decade that followed, Jim toured the country with his darkly satirical band Celtic Elvis, founded one of the granddaddies of the civic free concert series movement—Concord, California's Music and Market Series—and started the ticketed Community Concerts Series, which was widely credited with bringing regional and national headliners to a suburban audience. Eight years after Jim's future wife joined the operation (and after they tied the knot), they renamed their joint venture OceanWorks Productions. Today, Jim and Kathy Ocean produce dozens of shows annually, including free summer concert series and benefit concerts, as well as perform-and-produce programs derived from their catalog of original music.

Jim's knack for blending the whimsical and the serious shines through in his songwriting, where he captures the complexities of the human condition with wit and wisdom. From *The Rise and Fall of Practically Everything* and *Hard to be Real* with Celtic Elvis to *Fear and Love* with his short-lived group the Dogmatics to his solo project *Pop Tunes for Mystics* to *FrankenClime* with the Jim Ocean Band, Jim's music has always pushed the boundaries, using humor and metaphor to examine scientific discoveries and societal dilemmas. Whether he's rubbing shoulders with astronauts, stage-managing music festivals, or captivating a crowd from the stage, Jim's passion for music and community-building shines through in everything he does.

Jim's dedication to the arts hasn't gone unnoticed. In 2002, he was honored with a Lifetime Achievement in Cultural Arts award by the Contra Costa County Arts and Culture Commission and the California State Assembly and Senate.

It should be no surprise to learn that John Lennon has been a significant influence on Jim's musical journey. Twelve-year-old Jim was profoundly affected when the Beatles landed in America in 1964. Jim has always admired Lennon's ability to think outside the box, his innovative approach to chord construction, and the evolution of his songwriting over

time. Lennon's messages of peace and universal love resonated deeply with Jim, as did his lyrical honesty, his efforts
to be a better person, and his continual quest to inspire positive change.

When he's not writing magical realism or orchestrating
the next musical event, Jim grows beans, greens, and broc-
coli on his little piece of paradise in the Northern California
redwoods, where he lives with his wife, Kathy.

Kathy Ocean is the spirited cofounder of OceanWorks
Productions and Jim's partner in every sense of the word. As
a young aspiring singer-songwriter and recovering clarinet
player who dabbled in the Indiana University coffeehouse
scene, Kathy left the cornfields of her adolescence for the
vibrant music culture of San Francisco. After teaming up with
Jim in 2000, she brought her energy and creativity to the concert production scene and quickly became an integral part of
Jim's business.

Kathy's expertise extends well beyond event production.
Equal parts project manager, concept shaper, and muse, she
cowrites and performs alongside Jim. Together, they create
thoughtful, lyric-driven music that explores science, philosophy, and the human experience. Their collaborative projects,
such as the immersive planetarium show Astronaut Lullabies,
the musical edutainment salon MetaQuizzical Cafe, and their
enviro-social project Party for the Planet, showcase their ability to weave educational and cultural themes into their music.

Together, **Jim and Kathy Ocean** are cultural activists who
inspire people to get out of their couches and into their communities. Whether they're producing a concert, hosting a

retreat, or performing together, the Oceans infuse their work with joy and connection. *John Lennon's Glasses* is their first novel.

Their mission is simple: to bring people together in a vibrant and engaged community through the power of music. To dip your toes further into Jim and Kathy Ocean's world, visit OceanWorksProductions.com.